SOUTH WIND

THE DEVIL IN ALABAMA

LM Lee

"Words have no power to impress the mind without the exquisite horror of their reality." ~Edgar Allan Poe

The temperature was dropping. It had been warm when Micki came out dressed in her home-made costume. The thin, gray material of her grave dress was now whipping a little in the early morning wind as she walked along the isolated rural highway. Though her skin had been numbed by the icy water of the lake, her face was throbbing now. Her costume lent itself to cuts and bruises, she thought. The few old houses that cut the edge of the gloomy horizon were dark and silent. Old, tattered roofing on the housetops reminded her of the fringe on an old tablecloth her grandmother had always used. It frayed over corners and around crumbling brick chimneys' that appeared to have burst through in the dim light. It was so quiet she could hear her heart beating just under her deep breathing. This time of night, closer to morning, always gave the southern sky a sick looking glow that Micki liked, bluish-green, like a yellowing pair of bleached-out jeans. It made her stomach stir. Her deep, steady breathing was loud and the sound reminded her of being underwater. The new stone bruises on her feet were screaming at her. Her thighs ached, every step reminded her. She had been grateful for the cool water in the lake. She felt redeemed by it. She wasn't sure where she got the adrenaline that kept her alive tonight, she wasn't yet sure it was actually over. Broken skin inside her lips cracked and bled as she began to hum a song she liked when she was younger but now she couldn't remember the words. Halloween was by far Micki's favorite holiday. It was the one night her mother would allow her to hang out on the lake all night with her friends and she didn't have to scheme, lie about it, or sneak out, (or in, for that matter.) Halloween had offered an opportunity like no other.

CHAPTER 1

That summer, Micki lived on Lake Jordan, in Alabama, with her mother Sara, her brother Brett, and her mother's boyfriend Jeff. Micki hated Jeff. He was an alcoholic, abusive, and already married to someone else. Albeit reluctantly, Jeff's wife, Jane, had become like a second mother to Micki during the first couple of years he and Sara were together. After the divorce, the only job Sara could get was as a cashier in a convenience store. She usually worked first or second shift, and it was difficult to predict her schedule. At Jeff's request, Jane had attended many of Micki's school functions over the first few years as a stand-in parent. Micki had played a tom drum in the school band the first year Sara, Jeff and Jane began their polygamist relationship and Jane had spent many days since then going to shows and parades or just showing up to support Micki if only making sure she had a ride home. Jane spent hours working elaborate hair styles for talent shows, and other school productions in which Micki would play guitar and sing songs by the Stone Ponies or perform a dance routine with a friend of hers named Shauna, wearing matching outfits that Shauna's older sister had given them. They never won, but Micki loved the attention, as well as performing. Jane loved Micki's hair, and told her so and when Micki had a part in a school play she would help Micki with her costumes, which her talented grandmother had hand sewn for countless events. Micki's grandmother had experience with period style clothing and the costumes she made were always authentic. Micki loved them, and couldn't wait for them to arrive in the mail. The dresses sometimes had hundreds of tiny buttons, most of them on the sleeves alone, as well as lace-up undergarments, corsets, bloomers and petticoats. In those instances, Micki required competent assistance, and Jane was always there with the right information. Sometimes Micki would spend the weekend at Jane's when her mother worked a double shift. Jane had a lot of old music records from her college days and Micki was fascinated with them. They were thick, heavy and a bit smaller than the records she was familiar with. There was one record, "Goodbye for the summer," that Micki loved the most and would play it and sing it over and over any time Jane would allow it. More recently, Jane had taught Micki how to make fudge from scratch as well as a few other recipes that might be impressive sometime in the future. As ironic as it seemed, Jane's family had been in Law enforcement and Jeff had been her high school sweetheart. After many years of marriage they still had no children of their own, and Micki derived a lot of confidence from her relationship with Jane. She was painfully aware of the situation between Jane and her mom, who had actually fought in the front yard once, but Micki didn't talk about it. It's just the way it was. She loved Jane. Her own mother, Sara, had been somewhat oblivious to Micki since the divorce, but Micki figured it was probably that way for a lot of kids whose parents were under constant emotional stress.

The disconnect between Sara and her daughter was born before the divorce and continued to grow at a rapid pace yet had gone unnoticed. On the lake, everyone knew about her mom, Jeff and Jane. Her mom played the beautiful tramp, the home-wrecker. She had long auburn hair and an hourglass shape that most young girls who knew her, hoped they might develop. Her big blue eyes were memorable, and men loved her. Micki was quite different, and looked like her dad. Blonde and green eyed, she had only inherited her mother's smile, even her hands and feet looked like her dads. Micki was athletic and enjoyed playing tennis, softball and swimming, so she was leaner than her mother had been. Sara would often comment that Micki, though she looked soft, was "hard like a boy." Micki didn't mind the comment; the last thing she wanted was hips like her mothers. There was a relationship between Micki and her mother, if not a good one. She tried not to blame Sara for the loss of her father, but it was always there, boiling under the surface, waiting to erupt. The fact that dampened her anger toward her mother was how quickly her dad had left and not come back. She missed him terribly, but he didn't seem to feel the same way.

Sara had been married twice before, the first time to Brett's dad Cliff. She had married him when she was just fifteen, and they'd had Brett a few years later. He was supposed to be the baby that saved that marriage, but to no avail. Cliff had been a diabetic, and didn't care for the treatment very much and he was willful about skipping it. He had been a forceful man and Sara had said that he was mean. Sara desperately wanted out of the marriage but when Brett was just two, Cliff died from diabetic shock. The problem was solved as far as Sara was concerned and she had married Micki's dad soon after that. She had met Preston when she went to work in his office. He was immediately taken with her long red hair and shapely body. He didn't mind that she had been married before, and wanted a family of his own. Until Micki, Preston believed that he was unable to father children, but in less than a year, she had been born. Her mother would tell her jokingly that neither she nor Preston really knew where she came from. A miracle baby, they named her Michelle, but everyone called her Micki.

Preston had grown up in rural Georgia on a farm, and he wanted more out of life than peaches and tomatoes. His own mother had been somewhat detached and his father had been a hard-working farmer. One day, for no reason at all, when Preston was still very young, his dad didn't go out to work the field. Instead he spent the days reading the bible to Preston and his sisters. Too many days went by until eventually; Preston's mother had his dad committed for evaluation. They were losing everything, and she was afraid. "Back then, it was a different time," Preston told her before explaining that her grandfather was treated to several rounds of shock therapy. Micki was horrified by that story and wondered why her dad would tell her such things. Pop had never been the same after that according to Preston, but he did go back to the field. Micki loved him dearly, he taught her how to roll cigarettes and he was always interested in what she had to say, He died when Micki was still very young.

When Preston was nine he began to spend afternoons with a man learning to build radios and eventually became an electronics engineer. He built his business in Montgomery, two shops and a store where he sold TVs and radio equipment. After Marrying Sara, he added another store, and called it the "Curiosity Shoppe," just for Sara to sell handmade jewelry and other "curiosities" she had made or discovered. When Micki was a small girl, she enjoyed being at the TV shop with her dad. She would tune every TV in the store to the same channel to watch Sesame Street. She would lay in the floor coloring until it was time to go home. Micki loved her dad, and tried to go everywhere with him. At home, she would sit with him in the recliner watching nightly news, and informational programs on the weekends. Once he had been out of town and was late for her birthday. When he got home, her mother had gotten her out of bed and told her to go out to the patio where her dad was sitting on a chaise lounge with presents for her. She remembered fondly opening the package that contained the Treasure chest jewelry box he had given her that year. It had held quarters, beach glass and a box containing a thin gold chain with an ever so small diamond pendant. She had been genuinely surprised and thrilled and felt like a pirate. She thought her dad was the best dad in the world. Every evening she would wait for him to come home. As he sat in his recliner, Micki would help him remove his shoes and socks. Get him a glass of iced tea and walk on his back until it cracked. She would fall asleep in his lap and he would put her to bed. She would awaken many times, but would play along anyway. Micki loved music and would sometimes sing when she couldn't sleep, and it could be heard all over the house. Her dad would ask Sara, "Do you think she'll do that all night?" and Sara, frustrated after many unheeded requests, would say through her door, "Michelle, will you please shut up?" Micki loved it, it was a game. She and her brother performed for both parents and their friends, skits like "Washington crossing the Delaware" or scenes from the continental congress. They used Brett's Boy Scout flag as a prop and made their own hats, as well as any other props they wanted to use. It was good family time.

Brett had an old spoke-wheeled car that Preston was "helping him fix," which was really just a learning tool. Preston was like that. He had his own club house in the back yard with a basketball goal attached to it. In actuality it was a modified garage. In 1975, Preston had a new attached garage built onto the kitchen entrance, so Sara could park her Mercedes, and easily get inside out of the rain. It was the old garage he had turned into a wonderland for his stepson. It had working lights, plugs, a kitchenette with working sinks and a fridge, a console stereo and a huge Zenith TV. Brett slept out there a lot of nights, with his friends, who Micki thought were jerks. Micki thought Brett was a jerk, and he was for the most part. Preston had been disappointed that Brett was behind in school, and in frustration had whipped him with a belt until he could recite his multiplication tables. That was the darkest week in Micki's life at that point. She had never seen her dad so angry. She felt bad for her brother. He hated Preston, before and after the whippings, and would constantly point out that Preston was not his dad.

Brett wrecked his motorcycle not long after that. The kick stand had gone through his ankle and it wouldn't get well. Sara kept taking him back to the Doctor, and specialists and so forth. In the end it was realized, just in time to save his foot that Brett always wore real leather boots, and when the kick stand punctured his foot, a small round piece of leather was pushed inside as well. It was explained that because leather is an organic substance, it wouldn't have shown on the X-Rays. Sara agreed to let them try to find it. Dr Odom did the surgery and sure enough, removed the small, round piece of leather. In no time Brett was back up and around.

Preston left Sara and moved to Florida before Micki was even thirteen. The year before that, Preston's business partner and best friend Richard, had been murdered in Montgomery. Preston and Richard were both from Georgia, and Preston had known him "All my life," he would say. Preston, Richard and Brad, another partner, worked together on a number of projects. Richard was a business man, and had a side job dealing in whatever was profitable. At that time, it was cocaine and guns. Preston and Richard had been notorious for high stakes' poker as well. Every night they were out playing cards for big money. They had met many people at these poker games, very wealthy, well-placed people. One of those people was Wendell Jacks. Jacks had been indicted for selling illegal weapons, and Richard, having been present at the transaction, had been subpoenaed to testify in court. One night for no reason at all, Preston came home early and stayed home with Sara and the kids while Richard went out gambling alone. Sometime during that night, Richard had been on Day Street with two unknown gentlemen. The next morning, Richard's body was found. He had been shot, which killed him. His body had been thrown off the Day

Street Bridge onto the rail road tracks below. He was wearing his robe, and looked as if he were sleeping. The house slippers he always wore were placed neatly next to his body. The coroner said he did not die immediately. That whoever placed his slippers was the last person to talk to him. The rumors were rampant, "he'd been killed by some paranoid drug king pin," or "he'd been caught cheating at cards" or "someone thought he was cheating." Sara always believed it was Wendell Jacks, whose weapons indictment went away after the murder. The police initially suspected Preston, as he appeared to be a co-owner with Richard on some high-end investments. They picked up Preston for questioning, but Sara told the detectives that he had been home all night, giving him an alibi, although others had testified that Preston was with Richard every night. As it turned out, Preston stood to lose greatly from Richard's death, and was no longer a suspect. Still, Preston's world was spiraling out of control. He threw himself into his work.

Preston and Sara had been very close to Richard and his live-in girlfriend Linda. When Richard was murdered, he left Linda with a toddler, and no legal rights to anything. She had to move back in with her parents until she could win the rights to a settlement in order to support her child. Sara didn't see Linda much after that. Perhaps believing they were immortal, Preston and Richard had not been prepared for a death. Financial disasters ensued as the ownership of everything came into question. Richard, who had been previously married to a woman who devoured his assets as a hobby, had put everything he owned in his sisters name. When he was killed, she sold his property, as well as his interest in everything else. She even sold the family home that Richard and Linda had shared. After a lengthy court battle, Linda was finally able to provide for their child. Preston had lost an undisclosed amount in assets and had no legal rights to claim anything. He'd made a deal with Richard's sister and called on another friend, Pierce James, to purchase Richard's interests where he could, and Pierce was happy to do so. He had always disliked Richard, and wanted to be Preston's partner. In the end, Preston still had his business but he was terribly affected by the ordeal and shouldering a lot of debt. He and Brad worked long hours innovating and trying new things. They were in such close contact; Preston rigged a phone he could use on a radio frequency, so he and Brad could talk at any given moment.

Arguments ensued at home, Sara was certain that Brad and Preston were gay lovers. Preston was hardly home, he and Brad were constant companions, and now this radio phone rang at all hours, if Preston did happen to be home. Preston bought her a Chrysler New Yorker. She was happy to have it but still loved her Mercedes she said, "But the Chrysler will be better for taking the kids where they need to go." One night when Preston told Sara he was going away with Brad on a bass fishing tournament for the weekend, she didn't believe it for a moment. She went nuts and called him a "faggot" before going out and getting into the Chrysler. She pulled out into the street and then held the brake while she floored the gas. White smoke from melting tires filled the road in front of their house. Micki and Brett watched separately from their bedroom windows. Neither Preston nor Sara seemed to notice them much anymore. The Chrysler was gone the next week. Preston and Pierce scraped and borrowed to try and survive the financial devastation. Pierce had not been as good with business dealings as Richard was and too soon, Preston's business went bankrupt from the fall out.

Preston, Richard and Brad had designed and built a house on Lake Martin. It was one of Preston's proudest moments. They called it the "Round house." In truth, it was more octagonal. It had a sunken fireplace in the middle, and the entire two-story house was designed around it. Later on, new owners would fill the center hole, and the fireplace would be gone. Some of Micki's earliest memories had been on Lake Martin. She thought it was all amazing like a fairy tale. The families would go there and stay forever it seemed to her. She loved the house and all the modern electric gadgets in it as well as the iron work that adorned it, the smell of the lake, the redwood deck and the brand-new pier. The lake house was sold along with the other assets Richard had left behind. Preston always resented losing it, and never spoke to Richard's family again. He told Micki that "Even good people are inherently selfish, if you know that up front, you can act accordingly."

Preston began to spend many days out of town, making deals, collecting information and connecting with others in his field. He and Sara fought all the time at that point. Preston became increasingly suspicious of Sara's behavior while he was out of town. Friends had told him that she was being unfaithful. Unsure what to believe, and insecure from the accusations, he asked Brett if his mother had company over when he was gone, if they were men? Brett, who was angry with Sara at the time, hated Preston anyway and was too naive to understand the consequences of his answer, said "Yes." he didn't really know the answer but he didn't care either. Eventually, Preston left Sara because he was certain she had cheated on him with one of his employees, maybe more. Pierce seemed to be the author of this information, but no one knew for sure. Brett had told Micki the whole dirty rumor, as if it was true, and Micki had been mortified. She accused him of making things up.

The divorce had been financially devastating as well as an emotional nightmare for the whole family, and coupled with the losses that were the result of Richard's death, they had been unable to sustain their standard of living. Preston moved to a small house in Daytona. Sara, who had been used to a life of luxury, had to leave her beautiful home and her maid, and move her children into a smaller house in a modest neighborhood outside the city limits. As the months went by, she had been unable to afford even that. She met Jeff one night in a bar where she was working part-time for extra money, and he helped her find a place she could afford. So they moved to the country.

Micki never knew if the story about her mother was true or not, she hoped it hadn't been, but her dad believed it, and that had been the determining factor in the end. She got letters from her dad on her birthday, along with some trinket designed for someone younger than herself, but she wasn't bitter. She just day dreamed of his return. The day he moved out, Micki had stood at the door crying softly as he fought with her mother. When he headed out the door, he had gotten down on one knee to console her. He said that she shouldn't cry, he was just going away for a few days and then he would come back. Micki, who didn't care about the complications surrounding his departure, knew he was lying. It was the first time she had ever felt any real sense of dread. He never did come back, and early in the summer of 1981, he landed a contract to build satellites in the Middle East. For eleven years after that, he wouldn't return for more than a visit. Micki internalized most of her emotions, it became a habit.

It had only been a little more than two years since the "Jeff Incident," as Micki liked to call it now in the name of civil discourse. Jeff was a spoiled man who was used to getting his way. He spent most of his time womanizing, drinking Jim Beam, and listening to country music. He was a gifted mechanic, and all the hotrod enthusiasts in that area looked to him as their mentor. Soon after they moved to the lake area, he taught Micki to drive a stick when she was still thirteen, telling her, "a straight shift is the way to go, get five gears," holding up his outstretched hand to demonstrate the number. When Jeff was home, he was always outside working on someone's car. A loud engine roaring until midnight (sometimes even later) was a common thing in Micki's life. In Sara's defense, Jeff was attractive and well-built if you like the brawny type. He was also ready to help her most of the time and Sara was vulnerable to an extreme. Most women, who spoke about it, sympathized with Sara. She was clearly obsessed with a man who needed constant validation that he was still "the cutest boy in class." He had real problems, and while he was married to Jane and keeping a home with Sara, he had countless other relationships that didn't surprise anyone. Micki could hear the women at church talking in hushed tones about Sara, "I wouldn't want a man that good looking. Why would you want someone that everybody else wanted?" To which some version of the reply, "nobody wants to work that hard to keep a man," would follow. It was scandalous, and small towns do love a scandal.

Sara, insecure and lonely, had begun dating Jeff within months of the divorce. They did a pretty good job of hiding Jeff's marriage until they moved to the lake town. There, in the same community with Jeff's family and his wife, it wasn't long before Micki, Brett and everyone else, knew what was going on. Jeff swore to Sara that his relationship with Jane was only a legal one, and Sara wanted to believe him, so she did.

When Micki was still thirteen and for lack of a better model, she had developed a semi-paternal attachment to Jeff, "Semi" because she had always been her father's daughter, and it would have been impossible for her to be anything less. Jeff had treated her well until then, they had fun like a father and daughter and she had no reason to be apprehensive around him. In the beginning, Sara and Jeff didn't fight and they seemed to want to be a family. Jeff had, however, always been a drunk, and that was the main problem in their relationship. When Jeff drank, anything could happen. If he didn't come home for a few days, Sara would be certain he was with Jane even though he was usually just off on an alcohol adventure. She once went into the kitchen and declared she was going to commit suicide, because Jeff was spending so much time with "her." Sara had taken a kitchen knife and threatened to cut her wrists. A friend of Sara's had been there that day, and was trying to talk her off the ledge. She said to her. "Sara, you can't kill yourself, Micki still needs you." And Sara had replied, "No, she doesn't, Micki doesn't need anyone," she had laughed maniacally. That stuck with Micki for years. It was another of those things she didn't talk about, to anyone. It was too real, too painful.

There were better days, and sometimes there were good ones. Micki would sit with Jeff in the recliner and watch TV with Brett in the living room while her mother made dinner. Sara had gotten quite good at cooking some foods. Her own mother had always said she "couldn't keep her in the kitchen long enough to teach her anything." Her culinary skills, although limited, had become "tasty," Micki told her once. One such afternoon, Brett had been at football practice. Micki and Jeff were watching the "Dukes of Hazard" while Sara made spaghetti. Jeff suddenly put one hand between Micki's legs. It was clear sexual intent, and to confirm this, he rubbed his hand back and forth on her shorts. Looking at her with a half-grin, he leaned over and kissed her cheek, lingering a bit too long. It was a weird feeling that both startled and scared Micki. She knew Jeff had been drinking, so she just got off his lap and went to her room. She didn't sit with him after that, and hoped that would be the end of it, but of course, it wasn't. Micki started avoiding Jeff. Embarrassed by her body, she hated what was happening to it. He teased her about it relentlessly in ways that made her increasingly uncomfortable. Her mother didn't seem to notice how inappropriate his behavior had become and was unavailable for the most part, especially for any real conversations.

One night, Brett had skipped school and didn't come home until late. Jeff, drunk, had beaten him with a garden hose until Sara tried to intervene, at which point Jeff turned his anger on her and that was the first time Jeff kicked Sara's ass. Micki slipped out the back door, to a clearing nearby. She lay down and watched the stars above her, trying to mentally provoke God to kill her. Sara and Jeff had begun to fight a lot and Micki was in constant fear of what Jeff might do to her. She did her best to stay out of his way. Of course, these precautions were in vain. It was just a matter of opportunity.

When Micki was four months from fourteen, he'd just come home drunk at daybreak, and lay down next to her in her bed when he was supposed to be getting her up for school. Micki had been up late reading "The Exorcist" by streetlight shining in her window, and had overslept. She liked to read at school but her teacher, Ms Steele, had taken this particular book from her the day before, and said the book was "too mature" for her. Micki thought she was too mature for Ms Steele. No matter what Micki said, she was unmoved or intimidated and had kept the book till the end of the school day saying she would throw it in the trash if she saw it again. Micki was forced to read it at home. Brett had already gone to school that day and Sara was leaving for work by then. Micki awoke to the smell of whiskey and was instantly apprehensive. He was behind her, under her blanket, breathing on the back of her neck just touching her shoulder with his lips and squeezing her hip underneath her t-shirt while he pushed his erection firmly against her butt. He whispered in her ear, "Come on Micki let me put it in." Sheer terror coursed through her, she knew exactly what was happening. She bravely said "No!" as she jumped out of bed, quickly pulling on her jeans from the floor and readying for school as she headed to the door.

Without brushing her hair, she bolted out the door putting on a hat, walking fast down the dirt road that led to the back of the school. She heard Jeff come to the screen door and he was just standing there in the doorway, holding the screen open with one hand and the bottle in the other, laughing at her. Walking backward, she gave him the finger. He laughed again and called out to her, "I'll see you after school." But he wouldn't. He wouldn't see her again for months. Micki never went home that day, or the next. She had gone to her English teacher, but even after she told her, Ms Steele said she should just go home. That Jeff was "probably sober by now," and not likely to do anything. Ms Steele obviously didn't understand. Micki was a bright girl, she'd had a good dad and she wasn't acclimating to the dysfunction. Going home was no longer an option.

At first she had stayed with a friend, who had wanted her to spend the night. Another friend happened to live next door, and another friend next to her. She started over again after the third house, and went back to the first. The next day she went to her friend Tanya's house next door. Her friends were all privy to her situation and had been helping her hide. They went to school and acted like they hadn't seen her, but would act like she came home from school with them when they got there. After two weeks of this, borrowing clothes all the while, Tanya's mother became suspicious and asked her why she hadn't been home. Micki told her about Jeff's advances flatly, in her best grown-up voice. The look on Ms Millers face had been grave, and the next thing Micki knew, she was at children's social services telling a social worker the same story. After that, Micki had gone to stay with Libby, a foster mother, until she could be reconciled with her own mother. She had fun with Libby's family. Libby, her daughter, who was a freshman in college, as well as a foreign exchange high school student from Mexico, amounted to an all-female family where even the dog was a girl. These were interesting, nice and educated people unlike anyone Micki normally interacted with as of late. Micki, most importantly, felt safe there. After a couple of months, Micki's mom promised children's services that Jeff was gone and would not be coming back. The social worker asked Micki if she would want to go home under those conditions. Micki said she would, and the gradual reunion began. Micki loved her mother. No matter what her grandparents said, her brother or anyone else, Micki thought her mom was great, a tragic heroine, a princess in a tower.

It wasn't the homecoming Micki had wanted. The social worker took Micki to the small country convenience store where her mom worked and Micki, though happy to see her mother, could sense instantly that all was not well. As soon as the social worker left the store her mother turned to her and said, "I don't want to speak to you, you have hurt everyone. Sit down and read something till I get off work and when we get home, you can clean up the kitchen." Micki was resilient, used to surprise endings, and mostly unaffected by the coolness in her mother's demeanor. She sat on a stool behind the counter with a comic book called, "The Punisher" and losing herself in the story, didn't say another word. There was a lot of yelling and crying over the next few weeks. Sara told Micki she was selfish, and how could she say those things about Jeff? Micki began spending even more time alone and out of the way. Her brother Brett had unbelievably taken Jeff's side, and thought Micki was just "trying to ruin everything." Slowly, Jeff started coming around again. He wouldn't get out of his car, but would offer to take Brett, for fast food, or some other outing Micki pegged as a completely phony attempt to isolate her. Micki had always been a loner anyway, and would rather be alone than with anyone else in the world. When she was alone, she could read whatever she wanted, she could write songs no one would ever hear, dream and talk to God. With Jeff coming around again, Micki spent many nights away from the fighting, sitting in the clearing nearby where there was nothing but white sand and weed grass. She loved the way the moonlight bathed the sand in a silvery glow. It was comforting, and she would sit there and smoke the cigarettes she had taken from Brett's room the day before, not quite far enough away to drown the sound of it.

Micki had a friend named Sam who lived nearby, and Micki had been fond of staying at her house on the weekends. Sam's older brother, Cameron, drove an old Ford Pinto with an 8-track tape player and sold weed as a side project. He was eighteen and already had a construction job with his father and Micki had been secretly daydreaming of him since they met. Just after her fourteenth birthday, Micki spent the night with Sam, as she often did when school was out. After talking about boys all night, pretending to have a séance and sneaking a pack of cigarettes from her dad, they sat in the dark of Sam's room and talked about everything. It was the first time Micki had a friend like that and the first time she really had someone she could talk to. It was about one in the morning when Sam finally stopped responding. Micki tossed and turned but was unable to sleep. She got up to sit in the chair looking out the window. The full moon, she thought, it always kept her up. That was something her grandmother had been telling her since she was a child and first showed signs of insomnia. The house was so quiet she could hear the creaking and settling as if the house was alive. She remembered the pizza they'd had for dinner and decided that she might be able to sleep if she ate or had some milk. She just happened to be lurking around the kitchen for food when Cameron was sneaking home, trying not to wake his parents. He was drunk, nauseous and looking for something to help him sober up. He put his head in the sink and started drinking water from the faucet. Cameron had quit school a few years before and everyone said he was a "stoner," but Micki had always thought he was cool. He wasn't an A student, or even a C student, but he was a nice guy and very attractive in her opinion. He had been suspended for skipping school once too often and his parents, exasperated with him, had made him get a job. Micki had liked him since the first time she met him at Sam's house, but she had also seen him on the lake with his friends, always looking for a reason to get in his way. He loved to swim and dive and she loved to watch him do it. A bonafide secret crush had developed. Cameron had blonde shoulder length hair. The blonde was exaggerated by sun exposure, a lot like Micki's. He was of average proportion, but very lean and strong. "Built" or "fine" as the girls would say. He had thoughtful green eyes and a kind heart. When he finally pulled his head out of the sink and took off his wet shirt, he leaned against the counter, drying his face with a kitchen towel. He looked at her and slurred through a wet smile, "Don't I know you?" She said yes, and reminded him that she was Micki. He sniffled and wiped his mouth again before he smiled at her again shyly and said "oh yeah. Micki. So, what are you doing up, where's Sam?" She told him she couldn't sleep but Sam was sleeping like the dead except for the snoring. She told him she was looking for a snack or something and trying to be quiet. She said it with just a hint of playful bitchiness and Cameron chuckled quietly as he rolled his eyes toward the ceiling. He said he'd been out playing quarters with some guys from work and it had gotten late fast. Although he had a job, he still had a curfew and he told her, "Don't tell Sam . . . she'll tell my parents and they're on my ass plenty already." Micki didn't speak because she was transfixed and a little blown away by the fact that she was actually alone with Cameron Jones. She had never told anyone how much she liked him, and now it was taking a moment to process. She had watched him work in his parent's yard with no shirt on so many times but had never been this close to his naked abs. She had started to wonder what his skin really felt like. He interrupted her train of thought saying, "Promise and I'll let you get high with me," He was staring at her expectantly as he pulled a joint out of his cigarette pack on the counter and pulled it under his nose as if he were smelling a fine cigar. She finally found her voice to say she wouldn't tell, and she wouldn't. She had wanted to smoke weed since she'd overheard Jeff and his brother Jim getting high together the year before when Jim had said he'd gotten the weed for free from some dealer they both knew. He'd said "it was easy cause I've been grinding his old lady" and laughed as he choked on the smoke. For some inexplicable reason, Jim became one of her favorite "anti-relatives" (As she referred to Jeff's family) that night. She was now trying to hide her excitement because she didn't want Cameron to know she'd never been high before. Cameron then casually asked her if she wanted to watch TV. She said she did. She would have said yes to anything. When they got to the living room, Cameron turned on the TV and turned the volume down low. He was smiling at her again and it made her stomach flutter as he went to the front door and opened it. He told her that she had to turn off the TV before she went back to bed; he lit the joint, took a deep drag before blowing the smoke out the door and gestured for her to come and smoke. Every time he moved his arms would flex and it was very distracting, he had a barbed wire tattoo on one arm and something about it kept drawing her attention. She walked slowly across the shag carpet and took the joint from him and hit it just like it was a cigarette and tried to hold the smoke the way she had seen people do it, which made her lungs expand and something resembling a sneeze escaped her as the smoke blew painfully out her nose. Cameron looked instinctively down the hallway but no one seemed to be stirring. He put a hand on her shoulder and leaning into the huddle, told her not to try to hold it, that she would still get high. Her heart raced when he touched her. He was so casual and refreshingly jovial with no obvious intentions. She liked him so much right then she was bubbling over and probably never would be or could possibly be more blown away by a guy than she was by Cameron Jones right then. She was a little better prepared for the next turn at the joint and before she knew it she was giggling madly and feeling light on her feet. She was conscious of and afraid he might be able to see her leg shaking so she went over to the floor in front of the television and drank from a jar of ice water he had sat on the table there. He smiled after her knowing full well she'd never been high. Amused, he watched her for a few moments more as he finished the joint and thumped the roach off his thumb into the front yard like a paper football. Then he sat on the couch, laying his head back with his eyes closed, to "stop the room from spinning," he said. She watched him now, laying there with a damp cloth over his eyes. She really liked the way his skin looked in the faint lights flickering in the room. It was golden and somewhat shiny, almost glowing. Unlike most men she had seen, Cameron didn't have any hair on his chest, just a thin silvery hint of a mustache on his lip. He worked hard, and the muscle in his stomach reflected it. Right then, she thought he was the definition of beautiful and then wondered if she had said it out loud. His faded jeans provided just the right contrast to keep drawing her attention to his lean stomach. The button was undone and she couldn't stop looking at it. Stoned from the weed, out of the blue she had the urge to kiss him. She just knew what she was going to do. She crawled into his lap, and moved the cloth from his face, placing it on the armrest of the sofa. She put her hands in his tussled hair and kissed him right on the mouth. She'd never kissed anyone before. He responded eagerly and put his hands up the back of her T-Shirt to caress her lower back, sliding one hand down to her butt, and she got chills. She was drinking him in, kissing him the way she had always imagined she would kiss the boy she loved someday. His lips were soft and he tasted like water and weed. When he found her breast his touch electrified her and she kissed him more urgently. His hands were strong and sure, knowing just how to hold her without holding her back. She wanted to touch his shoulders, his arms and his stomach, his back. He let her explore his body freely, responding to her every touch. She wanted to stay there like that forever. She felt tingly everywhere, even in places where their bodies weren't touching and she thought she finally understood what all the fuss was about. It was divine. They made out for all of five, maybe ten minutes with his erection groaning between them before he passed out. Micki was surprised, unaware that a man could pass out with an erection. She didn't know what to do, but she knew his skin smelled like sunshine, and though he had appeared to be hard like chiseled stone, was actually soft and warm. She caressed his chest as he slept, and kissed the corners of his mouth gently. She wasn't ready for it to be over yet, she missed his attentive lively hands that now lay useless, one on her hip and the other had come to rest on her thigh just above the knee where her leg was tucked neatly between his. So she laid her head on his chest trying to imagine what it might be like to be married to someone and sleep with that someone every single night. She wondered if she might have sex with Cameron sometime and what that might be like. She wanted to touch it, just on the outside of his jeans to see if it would wake him, but she was afraid. She resisted the urge. Feeling warm and content she lay there in his arms listening to him breathing over the sound of his heartbeat. His stomach rose and fell and she traced her finger to his belly button and then laid her hand flat on his abdomen, feeling him breathe. Sometime later, she turned off the TV, took his shoes off his feet and covered him with a small blanket before going back to bed. She never did sleep. She wasn't sure why she did it, but she didn't regret it. Micki never got tired of his friendship and nearly drove him crazy.

She began getting weed from him to sell to get the extra money she needed for school. Her mom had signed her up for free lunches but Micki had never turned in the form. She was too proud and instead ate white rice from home every day. Suddenly she was selling weed to all Brett's friends and enemies too. Word travelled and soon enough she had been introduced to people who liked to buy ounces and would pay top dollar for the convenience. Cameron told her how to price it and within weeks she was a dealer selling to the guy at the gas station who still talked about lids and the seventies. She sold to girls from school that scored it for their boyfriends or just wanted to try it. She even sold it to the librarian and the post office lady. The money she made from the weed solved her food problem the next school term and her mom was mostly clueless. She never even asked about the people coming by to see her, even though Micki was ready with imagined explanations she never had to use. Sara was happier to not hear about her day. Eventually she had enough money to buy new clothes. That had changed Micki, she felt stronger somehow, capable and she thought she suddenly had it all figured out.

Cameron became more and more attached to her but Micki would only make out with him if no one could see them. She was so hurt by the rumors about her that she didn't want anyone to see her kissing anyone. She knew she was fucked up, but she couldn't help it, she had not escaped the Jeff Incident unscathed. When she spent the night with Sam, which was more often around that time, she would go to his room where she knew he would be waiting and straddle him on his bed in a t-shirt and a pair of panties just like that first night but they never talked about it. She loved how strong and firm he was. He picked her up often upon her arrival and pulled her legs around his waist and held her like she was weightless while they couldn't seem to get enough of each other. It was a good feeling, she was so happy when she was with him. They shared a playfulness that would prove to be rare in relationships for both of them in the future. Lately, an insufferable tease, she'd been taking off her shirt so she could press her breasts against his chest. She was fascinated with how sensitive his nipples were and she would lick one and laugh. She was making him insane and finally one night he told her she needed to go back to Sam's room, but she ignored him and kept playing until he told her in a serious voice she needed to go. He'd decided that she was too young to understand what she was doing to him and that sex with her was probably not going to be an option for a long time. As much as he liked her, and knowing he would never turn her away, he wasn't sure how long he could play with her before his need to make her became stronger than his need to make her happy. He was all ready to set some ground rules with her when she got up off the bed and stood beside him with her t-shirt in her hand and asked him point blank, "Are you going to masturbate now?" Stunned, he flushed and said, "You're not supposed to ask me that," but she was undeterred, "but are you?" He lay down and put his pillow over his face so he could growl into it before he gave up. "Yeah, I'm going to masturbate." She smiled; she was so beautiful standing there in the moonlight drifting through the billowing sheer curtains hanging on his open window, her nipples reacting to the breeze. His mother had those same sheers on every window in the house. "I want to watch, I can help," she said quickly, and he gave a surprised laugh, sure she really would make him crazy. At first he protested saying he didn't think he could do it in front of her but when she dropped her shirt, got on the bed behind him with her knees apart, and leaning against his back, put her hands on his shoulders and started kissing his neck again while sliding her hands across his chest, occasionally letting her nails drag lightly across his skin, he finally stood up and removed his sweats. When she touched him again, it wasn't long before she saw what she had wanted to see. Twice since then, she had come to him only in a t-shirt so when she removed it he was looking at her completely naked body. He asked her once if she was trying to get him to rape her, and she laughed and asked if she should be worried. He said "no," but he wasn't smiling anymore and he told her that he had real feelings for her. She didn't know what to say so she didn't say anything. She let him pose her body on the bed, she would dance naked for him and twice she had let him go down on her, once briefly because the feeling scared her and she left quickly, but she still couldn't leave him alone. The second time, he'd been so warm and his hands were so firm and knew just where to touch her, he said she'd been unbelievably warm and wet inside, she'd had a powerful orgasm and it freaked her out. There was only one thing left to do, and she began putting him off, not because he was pressuring her, she knew he would never do that, but because she was afraid of herself. She had to fight the urge but she had amazing will power and fear is a powerful motivator. She began to cut back on Cameron time.

Cameron eventually became upset and one afternoon on the dirt road between their houses where they had been parked getting high, he accused her of being ashamed to be seen with him in public, but it had been okay, that when she needed weed or needed to kill some time, he was the first guy she called but now even that was becoming rare, "Do you think I do that for you because you're making me rich? Hell no sunshine, I give that shit to you at cost and you know why, don't fucking play with me." He turned his back on her and looked up at the sky bleeding through the trees. "What the fuck are we doing here? I need to know right now." He looked back at her, mentally exhausted, standing beside his old pinto in torn jeans, a jacket and no shoes. She thought he might be the most beautiful man she would ever see, but she just couldn't be serious about a boy at that point. She just wasn't ready; she hated herself for being such a pussy. She felt like a fraud. She hugged him and kissed him letting him hold her body close before saying "thank you" and "I'm sorry" softly, in his ear. She really enjoyed the things they did together, but it was always on her terms. He'd stopped trying to predict her weeks before. She kissed him and made him forget. There was something desperate about her, but he couldn't put his finger on it, it was contagious. He'd stopped sleeping with other girls, even though you couldn't really call what he did with Micki sex. In reality, it was more "like driving fast to the edge of a cliff every other day and then slamming on the brakes at the last minute hoping you don't slide off the very soft ledge." That's what he'd told the guys at work. She was going to be fifteen the coming summer. "Still a baby" he would tell himself sometimes but he loved her, there was no doubt. He put up with all sorts of shit from her family, his family, his sister, his friends, assholes she'd already jilted, and lived the life she was allowed to live, forgoing his own legal right to exist as an adult and sneaking around with her as if he were still in high school and even then only when she could get away with it. It was fun, he had to admit, and had already decided it was worth it. It was all he really wanted to do anyway. He worked his ass off, he knew he'd be working his ass off the rest of his life, she was a daydream, her body was warm and he craved her heat. She tasted like sugar. She wanted him, his arms, his kiss, his soul. He was powerless to demand anything from her. He'd wait, and hope because that's all he could do.

She and Sam were getting high every day after that, and Micki, nearly every night and even some mornings. Cameron would come by some afternoons just to hang out and smoke. Micki was not allowed to leave with him because Jeff, jealous as far as Micki was concerned, told her mother he was a "dog, always sniffing around for pussy down at Shad's bar, he'll have her pregnant! You know she's fucking him!" So they just smoked pot and made out in his car. Her mother was unable to prevent Micki for the most part, she was headstrong, and would do whatever she wanted anyway. So Sara had learned to supervise as best she could instead. Micki liked that Cameron didn't get scared and stop coming around just because her mom didn't like it. That one fact alone made him delicious to her and she spent many days anticipating his arrival. When school started he drove her and Sam every morning. Every day that he could, he would go home after work, shower and go straight to her house. It was always exciting and she couldn't wait to be with him. The days she didn't see him were the worst days of her life at that time. She'd begun to despise her family and her situation. She spent most of those days disgusted with Brett, Jeff and her oblivious mother. She felt like she might drown in the misery and disappear as if she was never there at all. Cameron made her forget, offered an alternate reality and she couldn't imagine not having him around. Some nights he would come and meet her at her little spot in the clearing and sit on the white sand and smoke and talk. He was her best friend; he would say they were "making love without having intercourse." She felt safer just knowing he was in the world looking her way every day, watching and waiting for her. Someone was paying attention.

Right around then, Jeff was having a "war" with some cousins of his over some family property. One afternoon they wanted to send him a message. Micki never knew exactly what it was about but that afternoon she and Brett were home alone, fighting over the radio in the kitchen. She was cleaning up and liked to listen to the rock station while she worked. Brett had come in and changed the station about three times already and she snapped. She had just thrown two knives at him as he ran from the kitchen, the second of which stuck in the door frame just inches from his head. He had turned to run anticipating another wondering why she hated him so much, and she was indeed coming after him when he noticed the three trucks outside. Brett watched through the huge living room window as six men got out of the trucks with guns. "Micki…" He yelled at her, "Get down!" and then the glass from the window was flying through the room. Micki was instantly crawling on her stomach back toward the hallway while Brett crawled over to lock the door before the same door was cut in two with bullets. For more than ten minutes they were assailed with shotguns and a couple of 3006 that left their signature holes in the walls. Glass and splintered wood was flying everywhere. Micki finally made it to the back door and lunged out to crouch behind the stone steps that led down to the ground, ready to bolt if she heard them coming around the house. Once outside she became afraid to move so she crouched there and cried as quietly as she could. Brett made it to the back-door and stopped there on his belly with the screen open to offer her a lit cigarette. Brett was breathing heavily and smoking his own, "It's Ray and his brothers." he told her "Looking for Jeff and Jim" He smiled as she took the lit cigarette from him and revealed some blood on his teeth and in his mouth where glass had sprayed his face. It seemed like forever before the trucks drove away and it was still a few hours before Jeff and Sara came home. Micki had swept up most of the glass by then but it never occurred to her to call the police. The police were Jeff's relatives too. Sara freaked out and started cursing at Jeff but he just laughed and said, "They weren't trying to kill anyone, they didn't know the kids were here." and unbelievably to Micki, Sara calmed right down and seemed to feel better about it. Micki never told anyone, not Sam or

Cameron, no one. Micki wanted to tell Cameron, but what would he think? It was too hard, she couldn't bring it up, her humiliation was already too heavy.

Jeff had the house fixed the very next day and life seemed to get back to normal for a few weeks. Then one night Jeff had taken Brett to hang out with his Klan buddies for lessons on "How to be an asshole," Micki had said to Brett before they left. Sara wasn't raised to be a racist, and neither were her children, Jeff came from an entirely different world where hating people was a local hobby. That entire area had been known for some time as a white's only location. It was common knowledge among the locals but it had taken Micki a little while to understand what was going on. She found out Shauna's dad had hosted the meetings one night when she thought they were just visiting. Shauna and Micki had played in the barn while they'd had their gathering. Micki thought they were a lot like the satanic churches she'd read about and was always afraid they might need to sacrifice a virgin in some twisted black mass. It was all very scary and she'd stopped going to Shauna's some time before.

That night, Micki was in her walk-in closet pretending to be a rock star in the mirror when she smelled the smoke. Two hours later their house was engulfed in flames and various furniture and dishes as well as other things precious to Sara were in the yard. Micki had saved her treasure chest, a guitar and some random trinkets of her own and then had ran all the way down that long dirt road, cut through the school yard and another quarter mile to get to the center of town to tell someone at the only gas station there to call 911. The volunteer fire department finally showed up but it was far too late. Micki was exhausted. Her feet were cut and bruised but they were so numb from the cold she couldn't feel them anymore. Underneath the panic, Micki realized she was happy that the house was burning and all the shitty memories with it. Her prayers had been answered, now they would have to move.

They went to Jane's that night, it was awkward but Micki was happy to see her because their relationship had been strained since the Jeff incident. Jane was accommodating, but her affection toward Micki had cooled. Sara told her that very night that Jeff's cousin had a house on the lake road, and they were going to move there and start over. Micki slept on the couch and cried herself to sleep. Jeff was back in, permanently. He did have a new found respect for her position, he understood that she would tell, or worse. Once he had gotten drunk and in a violent rage told her mother he would kill Micki if she ever said anything like that about him again. Micki knew he was bluffing, defensively, for the sake of her mother, who was still pretending that Jeff was the victim of her "too smart, jealous, rejected kid." Pick an adjective. In his eyes though, Micki could see that Jeff was afraid of her, and that he knew she was not afraid of him. She had begun to imagine what it would be like to point a .38 at his head and make him beg for his life. She imagined him tied to a tree deep in the woods, rotting away.

When they moved to the lake road, Sam had been very upset, as well as Shauna. Micki would be another ten miles away from both of them. Although Cameron didn't show it, everyone knew that he was bummed out about Micki moving. Even his parents knew that Cameron had a serious thing for Micki, and ten miles wouldn't change it much. Nobody ever talked about it, it's just another of those things that fell through a crack. Brett had told Micki that she was "stupid" to hang out with Cameron, that he had 'lots' of girlfriends. As if he was giddy about telling Micki something that would hurt her but Micki knew she was the girl people had seen with Cameron. She loved the suspense of it all. She liked to make people wonder, especially Brett who was becoming more and more of an asshole. She was sure he had been stealing her weed but she hadn't caught him yet. Fortunately for her she wasn't holding any when the house burned so she didn't lose anything. As she went back into the house that night to drag furniture, she made sure to get all the money she had saved and had tucked it safely in the pocket of the cut-offs she had intended to sleep in. She wanted to give it to Sara after the fire, but she didn't know how she would explain having it. Jeff had nearly convinced her that Micki was a prostitute, telling her how she was always talking to boys in town and lingering behind walls and bushes. Micki couldn't tell her she was selling weed so she just kept the money to herself. She spent it on clothes and a new pair of boots that she had wanted. She was careful to remove the tags before she got home so when Sara asked about them Micki would just say that her friends had given them to her. Micki had changed. She no longer wanted to play in the school band or participate in clubs. After spending her elementary years winning medals and awards, she consciously let them burn that night. She never even tried to take one off the wall. It wasn't because she wasn't proud, but those medals and awards never meant anything to anyone in her opinion. They never made her life any better. She had to be the one to do what no piece of paper could ever do. She wanted to be free from all of it.

The more Brett gave her a hard time about Cameron, the more fun it was to sit in his car. He had all the best music, and he could talk about rock and roll with her for hours. She thought he was gorgeous, he grew weed and taught her all the basics of cultivation. She never embarked on that project, however, because she was afraid of being caught, but she did slip away and ride along with him a few times to see what he was talking about. She loved having the knowledge. It made her feel something profound and she started to think she might have deep feelings for him after all. She also began to realize that Brett was jealous. He had been acting so weird and then one day when Cameron couldn't come over, he was being a particular pain in the ass anyway and then he grabbed her breast from behind while she was cooking dinner for Sara. It was totally inappropriate between a brother and sister she pointed out but he wrapped his arms around her waist laughing and said she was only his "half-sister" and he just wanted "to touch the other half." She stomped his foot hard and he let her go to turn around and show him a kitchen knife. He had to be drunk or something she thought, when he said seriously in an attempt to be persuasive, "Come on Micki, show me that ass, I know you've been showing it to everyone else." She put down the knife and slapped him hard and told him if he touched her that way again she would fucking kill him. He sat down in a chair and smiled a sick smile that faded into an uncomfortable silence dripping with sadness and disappointment. He was actually expecting something different. That was how their relationship had been redefined after the move. As a new level of disgust washed over her, she went to her room and locked the door. She was so angry, and she cried angry tears, she felt isolated, alone, disgraced, she wished Cameron had come that day. School was almost out, she would miss Cameron she knew, but she wanted her grandparents and she left on her birthday.

Micki's grandfather was a WWII veteran and a career soldier. He had given 29 years to Uncle Sam. Micki had an uncle, her mother's brother, who had disappeared in Laos, after his helicopter crashed during the Vietnam War when Micki was not yet two. She'd been his favorite niece and he had been trying to teach her to count change and eat chocolate the last time he was home. That was the story of his last moments with his family, and one Micki heard often. His flag and Purple Heart had been especially precious plunder when she played at her grandparents' house as a child. Her grandfather had given Micki a gold Bulova watch that belonged to him. The watch still worked, and Micki kept it like treasure in a box she'd gotten from her own dad. Another uncle, the youngest brother of her mothers, had been brutally beaten and left to die with a punctured lung in a Chicago alley when he was just 18 years old. He'd cashed out his bank accounts and left with the woman he said he loved. Just a few weeks later, his body was shipped home on a train shortly before Micki was born. That didn't even begin to tell the stories of how her other four aunts and uncles died. No one ever saw the woman he'd left with again; His cause of death was listed simply as "pneumonia."

As a child, Micki and her cousin Selena would play in the woods behind their farm. They played chicken with knives and married trees with flowers and vines in their hair. They wore snakes for pets that of course had to live in the trees of their betrothals. When Micki was nine years old, by formal invitation, her grandmother had walked up that hill in those woods to reach a clearing at the top where she sat in a chair beside stuffed animals and dolls to hear Micki talk about God while a ten year old Selena burned incense and kissed the occasional tree. Her grandmother had said it was all very silly, but she had smiled the whole time.

Sara was the youngest living child and the youngest daughter among her siblings. Her mother was in her thirties when Sara had been born. After suffering the loss of twins, and a two-year old angel to yellow fever, Sara had been born. Although she, like Micki, was close to her own grandmother, her relationship with her mother had always been strained. When Micki fought with Sara she wondered if it was some old family curse, and prayed to end it. Due to her mother's constant instability, Micki had spent a lot of time with her grandparents even before the divorce, and as a result, she had grown-up in the shadow of the harsh reality of war, hard sacrifice and extreme loss. Sara didn't get along with her parents and Micki was always between them. Her grandparents had a library on the other end of a huge hall they used to age wines, brandies and store vegetables. There was a fireplace on that end and Micki spent hours beside it reading dusty old books long forgotten. They also had an upright saloon style piano Micki played too often. Though her grandfather had been an adept musician, he had been blown up on a land mine in Korea, and couldn't take the ringing in his head. He smoked a pipe, and Pall Mall cigarettes that Micki would pretend to smoke as a child. He taught her to shave him with a straight razor, and Micki always loved to do it. To her delight, he told her impossible stories of giants in Germany, Black Forest witches and South Pacific cannibals. She loved the darkest tales. She could recite stories that would make the hair stand up on the stiffest red necks in Alabama. Micki realized that most people were afraid of things they couldn't see, things that weren't there. Her mother had always asked her why she wanted to be "so morbid," but Micki didn't really understand why her mother was so averse to darker subjects. For Micki, it was as natural as cookies and milk. She loved the night, the rain and the storms. She was taken with graveyards and mourning. Micki read her grandmothers books on The Eastern Star, and loved the rituals. She would play them out in some old costume her grandmother had made. She loved the ceremony of it all. She'd already read most college level dark-literature, as well as less respected texts like the "Necronomicon", and the "Sixth and Seventh Book of Moses." She was a big fan of all supposed magic, including the bible and the book of Enoch. Modern horror was also a favorite of hers, as well as psychological horror and couldn't get enough of Stephen King, reading "The Stand" several times by then. In a dark intellectual romance with all literary tragedy, she was respectfully sober on the point and known to laugh hysterically on certain occasions when she would be surprised at her own depravity. Her grandmother had told her that snakes had been looking for her since she was born and she should be careful not to step on a poisonous one. She'd spent hours catching them in the woods just to show her grandmother she was right, they really did like her. Brett was certain she was demented. He was mortally afraid of snakes, and that worked for her. After a few months Micki returned to her mother's house, the lake, Jeff and Brett.

Although Micki's mother was poor and Micki was in a consistently challenging situation, the lake was an equalizer. No matter who they were, or what they came from, they were all stuck on that lake together, and it could have been worse. Lake life is generally a good life, although isolated from contemporary society. A few small stores dot the lake for weekenders renting cabins and those who visit their vacation homes. A few full service country-stores are spaced every few miles on the main highway through that area, but for the most part, they were on their own. 10 miles or so down the highway would lead you to town. Town consisted of a strip mall where they could shop for clothes and other personal goods. A fast food restaurant that kept changing owners and names at the intersection and there was a gas station on one corner and a bait shop across from it called "The Boys Store". The Boys Store sold propane and other household supplies, groceries and keys to the gate of a private lake club that people in the cities liked to visit on the weekends. A left at that intersection, led toward Wetumpka, and eventually, Montgomery. Taking a right would lead you to the high school Micki attended. Town was called "Slap-Out," technically, but it was just "town" to everyone around there. The kids who lived on the water threw parties. Everyone from thirteen to twenty-five would attend. They behaved like they had their own little country. Some of the parties would take place further up the lake, past "town", at Bobby's house. Bobby was a boy in Micki's class who lived on that side of the lake. He and his brother, who was a senior, would throw parties there whenever their parents were away. They had a deck on the water with lights and electricity and redwood walkways leading to the house, and one to the second floor bedrooms. There was an island like atmosphere at Bobby's. The ground here was made up of mostly sand, unlike where Micki lived, where grass grew everywhere and the bare earth is always clay or rock. Micki would play an acoustic guitar that belonged to Bobby's parents around a patio fire, near the house. Micki would discretely sell weed and they would get high and swim in the warm lake water. Micki had written many songs, and she would play them for interested listeners. Someone would always get too drunk and stories that would follow the next day, about girls being taken advantage of, were common. Bobby liked Micki, but she thought he was a clown. The fact that he was a friend of Brett's didn't help. Cameron would attend the parties but Micki wouldn't even let him hold her hand there. He just sat next to her or joined in some party game momentarily before he found her again. Couples sat around making out, some clearly having sex, and others just holding each other by the fire and that's what he wanted with Micki but she wouldn't have it. He began to think it was because of Bobby, he'd begun to hate him for the way he flirted with her and desperately wanted to explain the situation to him but Micki was unyielding. Something in Cameron had changed. She told him that she didn't want other boys to think that she was interested in fooling around, and that they might think they can hit on her too when Cameron wasn't there. He never believed that, but she really meant it. Micki was already damaged in that way, she didn't know how to express it, and just wanted him to understand. He had become more suspicious of her intentions, and it irritated her. One night after a party at Bobby's, Cameron told her she should find another ride home. She was shocked, wounded but said okay. Before she even turned around he had grabbed her arm and pulled her into his embrace and kissed her passionately on the pier. She didn't run or pull away and when he backed off he said, "See? The world didn't end, nobody's lining up to rape you, I would never let anything happen to you," and he pulled her close into his arms, swaying back and forth to the music that was still wafting from the speakers on the deck. She was angry, but she choked it back. He'd said he would never play with her feelings, but now that's what he was doing. She knew she deserved it, that he'd needed to see something in her eyes resembling emotion. She always had to be so tough, he just didn't understand. In a perfect world, she could have fallen for him completely, gotten pregnant and had a shotgun wedding, but no matter how much fun she had with him, she couldn't relax. He would go to his house at the end of the night and everything would be fine, but she would have to go home to Jeff and Brett, and she never knew what that might entail. She couldn't afford to let down her guard, and he couldn't grasp the gravity of it.

Lately, the parties had been at Cal's house, a senior who lived with his dad on the lakeside near Micki. Cal was cool, everyone thought so. He was the ideal candidate to host, as his dad didn't care if he had the parties, and there was no need to wait for him to be out of town. These parties had been more about dancing, drinking and getting stoned. That was fine with Micki, she loved to dance. It made her feel alive and she had started trying to relax with Cameron, dancing with him and even finding quiet places to sit together, yet she still would not let him announce to the world that they were in a relationship. She would dance with almost any boy who asked her, and told Cameron it was just dancing and that she would save the slow ones for him. Their relationship became tense and the new had worn off the partying. By that time they only partied because there was nothing else to do. Micki was getting older, but so was Cameron.

Cal was also the local coke dealer, and after one party he and Micki exchanged some weed for coke. She tried it, approved, and before long she was selling that as well as the weed. Unlike Cal, who sold grams and half-grams to anyone with money, she only sold eight-balls, exactly the way she got it from Cal, but for twenty-dollars more than she paid. She hardly ever did the coke, only as a gesture for a new buyer. She was more interested in the money. Soon enough, she nearly had enough money saved to buy a used car and even though she wouldn't buy one, just knowing she could gave her peace of mind. She dreamed of escape and wondered if Cameron would just leave with her, but knowing how close he was to his family, she doubted he would and never brought it up mostly because if he said no it would have destroyed her. She began to cling to him in a way that surprised even her, but Micki wanted out.

That year in October, Alabama was unseasonably warm, and the Indian summer weather was very popular with the young people who lived on and around the lake. The lake road where Micki lived was off the highway a few miles. About a half mile down lived Sophia, one of Micki's new friends. She had just turned sixteen and had been using her mom's car a lot. She lived with her mother and sister Delores.   Another friend of theirs named Toni, who had not yet turned fifteen, lived just next door to Sophia. Her father had just died, and she was injured in an accident right after the funeral. She went everywhere on crutches now. Another mile past Toni's house was a small bridge that crossed a creek that flowed behind Micki's house and fed into the lake. After the bridge, it continued around the lake, or a right turn, would trace the lake in the other direction. About two miles down that road, just past a pasture where horses could be seen grazing year round, is where Micki lived. Another half mile past Micki's house, lived Jenny. They had gotten very close since Micki moved there and spent most everyday doing something together but Micki kept her business to herself. She never sold coke or weed to her close friends.

Only about five families lived on that end year round. There were more houses and cabins down on the water there, but they were rentals that were mostly used on the weekends. Some were vacation homes, but the owners hardly ever used them. It was a quiet place to live, everyone was very casual, and laid back. They left their doors unlocked and slept with the windows open. Even the county sheriff had a cabin on that part of the lake, although he didn't stay in it very often. During the summer months the kids spent their time swimming, boating and diving, and they tried to push those activities as far into the fall as the temperatures would allow. Some of the boys, including Brett, Cameron and Cal liked to shallow dive, as a sort of contest. The guy who completes a successful dive in the shallowest water wins. It was dangerous. Brett had many accidents already, and seventeen times he had to get stitches. He was famous for it on the lake. As for Micki, creepy tales of underwater pockets of air where swarms of water moccasins lived, and bodies, floating, bitten thousands of times, didn't deter too many kids from the red clay and rock walls that were perfect for deep diving. Though, like shallow diving, it was forbidden by most of the parents. Still, it was the ultimate adrenaline rush for a fifteen-year-old thrill seeker. That's how Micki spent a lot of days on the lake. The cool air came and went, time passed casually. Micki was somewhat desensitized by the violence at her home. She missed the clearing in the woods, she missed who she used to be, but she chalked it up to growing pains. Everything was changing. She spent less time with Sam and she knew something was different between her and Cameron, mostly because he was too far away for her to run to. School let out in May, Micki turned sixteen in June and the summer games began again.

CHAPTER 2

"I am above the weakness of seeking to establish a sequence of cause and effect, between the disaster and the atrocity." ~Edgar Allan Poe

Billy was making his horse run when Sophia showed up. The chestnut quarter horse was about fifteen hands high bolting away from Billy and then running back quickly to beg for quartered apples. The horse was more of a pet than most dogs and cats and he had a special relationship with Billy who had been living in a small groom's house by the horse pasture on the lake road for a few months when he met Micki. She was a friend of his cousin Sophia. Billy had come to Alabama from New Orleans where his mother lived to spend some time with his father before going back to the university. His dad, known as Uncle Freddie to all the other kids on the lake owned the big house attached to the pasture. Billy had been staying in the small house about halfway down the drive since he got there because he couldn't stand living with his dad in the big house higher on the hill. He helped Freddie train and feed the horses he kept there. In the weeks before, on Billy's twenty-first birthday, he finally had enough hours to earn a pilot's license. Since then, he'd been taking Sophia and her friends, two at a time, out to the airfield to ride in a Cessna. It was a lot of fun to fly over the lake, and look at the little houses, and boats, and cars. The girls all liked Billy and he tried to be like an older brother to all of them, patient and accommodating. He humored them and enjoyed their attention. Sophia's uncle Freddie, was divorced and had kept horses there for years. He had an amusing reputation as a "dirty old man." They called themselves "coon-ass," and Sophia, born in New Orleans, but raised in Alabama, considered herself to be a "coon-ass" too. She even had a t-shirt that said so. Billy's younger brother Danny had been visiting this summer as well. Danny was a senior, or would be when he went back to start school. He had been an all-American athlete the year before and was looking forward to a stellar senior year. Most of the girls on the lake thought Danny was the "finest guy" they had ever seen, dark, Italian and a perfect athlete. He got a lot of attention wherever he went.

Jenny had been in love with Danny since he had visited the summer before. Micki had been at her grandparents' house her first official summer on the lake and had not met him. Although Jenny rarely went into details about it, it was clear that she carried a very hot torch for this boy. As school had let out before the summer, it was all she talked about. Her cocoa brown eyes were all sparkles when she was asking Sophia daily about Danny's trip, and "how long before he gets here?" Sophia was thrilled at the prospect that Jenny might date her cousin. She loved Jenny, and Danny could have done a ton worse. Jenny and Micki had lain in the sun every day in search of the perfect tan before he arrived. Micki told Jenny she was beautiful trying to reassure her, and she really was. She had an Egyptian look that Micki actually envied. The anticipation about her summer romance took on a fantasy life. The human factor, however, is unpredictable. When Danny arrived at Freddie's house, all the girls were there waiting to see his reaction to Jenny. In truth, they were all the same, different shades of hair; blonde, brown and black. Different body types; thin, athletic and voluptuous, but they all had the same thick black, water-proof mascara, healthy skin of varying shades of tan, and lips of pale pink that bordered, straight, white teeth, shining gold necklaces, dangling earrings and French manicures. Billy really liked having them around, and he had told Danny before that he could have his pick of girls there if he wanted to. Billy never really thought Danny would take that seriously, it was just a comment, something to say. He drove up with him in the car the day he arrived and anyone could see the excitement on Jenny's face. When they walked through the door, her eyes lit up. He greeted his dad first, then a hug to Sophia's sister Delores. And finally he turned to the girls. He offered a big hug to his cousin Sophia, but only said "hello" to Jenny, as if he had just met her. He was clearly interested in Micki. Micki had stayed home this summer, and suddenly Danny couldn't see anyone else. Jenny, who was clearly upset, left Billy's house hurriedly with Micki following after her. When they were gone, Sophia told Danny he was an asshole, and she and Delores went home. As soon as they were gone Danny said to Billy, "Oh my god where did that blonde come from? She is so fine, why didn't you tell me about her?" Billy just got himself a beer out of the refrigerator without looking at him. He opened it as he stared out the window. His mind was racing. He told Billy he wanted to go out with Micki while he was in Alabama. Freddie laughed and commented that she looked "like a fire cracker," saying "if she was eighteen," Danny "wouldn't have a chance with her." Laughing at his father, he half-asked what Billy thought of her and his plans. Billy was still looking out the window and put down his beer before he said "I think you should do what you want. You want me to help you take your shit up to the house?" He sounded a little impatient, edgy, which was totally unlike him. Danny was caught up in his thoughts and didn't even notice. He grabbed a bag and his dad took another one and said "Nah, we got it," as they walked out the door heading to Freddie's. Billy loved his brother, and promised him a good time this summer. He went into his bedroom and slammed the door behind him.

Danny had been trying to get Micki's attention ever since. He spent a lot of time trying to flatter her, and make her feel special, but Micki already felt special. She had a big out of town family, and most of them thought highly of her. She had been an exceptionally curious child, and had a legendary intellect at the family reunions. She was always thinking about something else and only half noticed his efforts. She knew he was attracted to her blonde hair and filled out body, and like a lot of boys, wanted to play with both, but she didn't think he really was interested in her as a friend or anything more than a good time. The way he had dissed Jenny, really pissed her off. That was not what Micki wanted out of life. For her, everything had to mean something. Danny had recently asked her to be his date at a party at Cal's house. She originally said no, but Danny had gone to Billy, and asked him to try to convince Micki to go out with him, "just once, before the summer's over." Billy had looked at him strangely for a moment, but quickly said, "Okay Danny." and went out to work the horses. Later, when Micki had gone to Billy's, he asked her if she would just try to get to know him, hang out with him, try to have fun with him so his summer wouldn't "be a total bust," and Micki, very reluctantly, agreed.

That day in mid-August, just before school started, Micki's new friend and closest neighbor Jenny had come over early in the morning. She wanted to ride her two horses down to the boat ramp to play, and needed Micki to ride Hotshot. Sara, Jeff and Brett weren't home, so after securing her stash and most of the money that she didn't take with her, Micki left with Jenny without so much as a note, as she was accustomed to doing. They went down to Jenny's stable and bridled the horses. They rode them bareback, about a mile back down the dirt road from Micki's house. They were going to the pasture first, which belonged to Sophia's uncle

Freddie. They turned down the long fenced driveway that cut through the pasture to the center, toward the small groom's house.

Micki hadn't had a horse of her own since her parents had kept horses in Montgomery. Riding reminded Micki of her dad. She fondly recalled the afternoons and weekends she had spent helping him break them. He had taught her to ride when she was just four. She learned to ride bareback and without a bridle first, holding on to the mane as he led them by rope on a circular path. Sara had initially been apprehensive but Preston had liked to use Micki to break them back then because she was so light, the horses seemed to like her and she was good at holding on. Once they could be rope led, he would introduce Micki to the equation, before finally trying to put a blanket on them. Then came the saddle. It took a lot of dedication, effort, and hard work. Those were some of Micki's fondest memories. Preston would trot next to her leading the horse and she never felt as alive as she did back then.

Her own horse, Snowball, had been fickle. Although she seemed to be trained with Micki, she had been unpredictable for other riders. She had once thrown Brett into a thicket of briers when he was trying to show off. Sara often recalled to her friends the night Micki got Snowball. Preston had been out of town and was coming home late, Sara had told Micki and Brett to go to bed but they were too excited because Preston had told them he was bringing a present home for them. It had been a full moon, and Micki watched out the window while Preston released Snowball into the back field. She was the most beautiful thing Micki thought she'd ever seen. She was so white she glowed in the moonlight, like a silver blanket, animated in the wind. Micki watched her begin to graze and traced her outline on the window in the condensation. Her very own horse. She didn't sleep at all that night, and Preston, let her walk out to the fence and call her horse. He said later that Micki looked "positively ghostly running out to that fence, and that "ghostly looking horse walked right up to her," as if she knew Micki was her new owner. That was the night Brett got his motorcycle.

It had been hard for Micki to lose Snowball. After Richard's death, Preston had told her that they were in a bind, that snowball had to be fed, and he wanted to give her to a friend of theirs who would take care of her. He said that Micki would be able to visit her any time she wanted. Of course, that may have been possible in an alternate universe, but after Preston left, Micki never saw Snowball again. Sara didn't maintain friendships. She said that she didn't have any friends as they had all turned on her and taken Preston's side. Sara could hold a grudge, and when she did, the kids had to live with it too. Her grandparents also had horses when Micki was small, but had stopped keeping them, as well as the cattle, when they had gotten older. She now relished the days she spent in the sun helping Jenny with her horses. Jenny's adult sister Sharon, who Micki sometimes babysat for, lived on the highway. She kept rodeo horses, and the girls helped Sharon with those as well, noting traits, and training them to barrel race. Many people on that part of the lake had them, and it was one of Micki's favorite things about living there. Certainly not the only thing, Micki had secrets, sometimes more powerful than her own reason.

Billy was standing in the yard, watching Sophia mount the horse he'd been running when Jenny and Micki galloped up to them in the small yard. Sophia was laughing hysterically about Danny being drunk and sick the night before. Billy was saying "yeah, he's a lightweight, but he's just a kid." and Sophia pointed out they were the same age but she could hold her alcohol better than him. "Where is he now?" Jenny asked. Billy glanced at her, then at Micki and said that Danny had stayed at the big house the night before. Filling them in he continued to tell them that he had gotten a little drunk with their dad. Micki threw one leg over Hotshot's back and slid off his side, she tied him to the fence rail and announced, "I'm so thirsty, I didn't even have breakfast, Billy? Do you mind if I use your facilities and have a sip of water?" She smiled the smile of a clown. He breathed out as if he had been holding his breath and smiled at her poor attempt at faux cow hand. He said "go ahead, the door's open." Micki went into the house and got a glass from the cabinet. She opened the refrigerator and saw he had made tea again. She poured some in the glass and walked to the window. She looked out at her friends. Billy had been living on the lake road since the winter Micki moved there. He had escorted the girls to many parties since then. He was their buddy and sometimes their emergency ride home, and once he had let Micki spend the night when Jeff was drunk and she didn't want to go home. Of course she never told Billy the whole truth about her life, she never told him about Cameron, who no longer just showed up to see her, who seemed to be exhausted by her, but he knew something was up. They had gotten closer that night, but nobody knew. She was so secretive.

Micki now sat on his couch, and then lay back, closing her eyes. She let the cool glass in her hands rest on her bare stomach. When she heard the door, she sat up straight. "What are you doing?" he asked. She stood up and walked over to him, "I saw you made tea again," she smiled and held up the glass, "Admit it, it's delicious." She took a long drink draining the glass but he looked embarrassed. She said, "I helped myself, I hope that's okay." He was just looking at her, wondering what she was up to, "I was just thinking," she put the glass back on the counter, "I could just slip back and stay here with you today, we could watch movies or I could even help you in the barn." She let her arms rest on his shoulders, and kissed his neck. He put his hands on her wrists, and then slid them down her arms and down to the small of her back. "Micki, we've talked about this, you know that's not going to happen. Why don't you like Danny?" He kissed her forehead gently, "He's your age . . . , you're really hurting his feelings." "He should go out with Jenny." Micki told him. "He doesn't want Jenny, he wants you," When he said that, Micki dropped her arms and backed away from him. "You want me too, don't you?" She asked with a guarded but knowing look, she already knew the answer. She had been slipping down to his house, torturing him, since last Christmas. "I have no right . . . I'm an adult, I could go to jail, is that what you want?" She quickly shot back, "I don't know, do you want me to fuck your little brother? Is that what you want? If I fuck your little brother will you stop treating me like a little girl? Because that's all he wants from me Billy" He seemed to get a little angry. He took her by the arms and appeared to get hold of his temper, "If you were older...I ... Damn, you already know I'd do anything for you." He was twisting a strand of her hair in his fingers now, "But the truth is that although you are not a little girl, you are not a grown woman either. I'm too old for you, Micki. You have no idea what it would mean." He was looking in her eyes again and she felt a familiar tinge of curious desire, she wanted to find out where that feeling was going to lead. "Go to Cal's party with Danny. Try to get to know him. He really likes you, and no, I don't want you to do anything with him but I have no right to say so, and I won't." He took her face in one hand and told her, "Don't be so rude, it's ugly in your mouth," He leaned in and kissed her with the gentle passion she had come to crave from him. First Cameron and now Billy, she didn't know why she needed her secret romances, but she did. Cameron and Billy were harmless and would never take advantage of her. She liked that and knew that one of them would take her virginity eventually but not until she offered it. Today she just wanted to melt in his arms and forget about the lake. She could barely stand to be in the same room with him without touching him. Only hours before Jenny knocked on her door, she had been with him, tempting him as she could. He never kicked her out, but she always left before morning. He was still trying to deny his feelings for her, to be a "good influence on her," he said. But Micki knew that was all bullshit. In the middle of the night, he waited for her knock, with food and music and sometimes wine. He made tea in anticipation of her arrival. No one had ever gone to that trouble for her save her old great aunts who truly loved her. They would talk for hours, and sometimes, he was too weak to resist kissing her. Though he was more rigid than Cameron, she was sure she could break him down. It was just a matter of time. She knew he wanted her. She had known for a while. She wanted to oblige him. Her heart was beating faster now, she put her hands on his chest and he pushed her back a step. He told her she should go with her friends. "Tell Sophia she can just leave the horses in the field when you come back, I'm going to town for the rest of the day." He said as he turned away from her toward the sinks, and started nervously washing the glass she had put there. She just looked at his back biting her lip. He was a little taller than average, lean, with a narrow waist. His white t-shirt fit him a little too well, just like his Levis. The sight of his biceps working, stirred a certain innocent sensuality in her that was still yet to be fully explored. Cameron would not have rejected her, ever, and she missed him terribly wishing she could walk to his house, but he was more than ten miles away, or at work. Her face was hot, and her lips were warm. She could feel tears stinging her eyes. Billy was making her crazy she decided, and without a word turned in frustration and hurried out to retrieve Hotshot. The horse seemed to sympathize with her and was always ready for whatever she wanted to do. He turned and bolted instinctively for the road.

They rode the horses fast down the dirt lake road to the bridge. They barely slowed down to take the left toward the highway. Then charged to the end of the road, where they slowed to a trot and took another left toward town. The girls needed to ride a mile down the highway to get to the boat ramp where they liked to take the horses to play in the water. There was a little fishing bar at the boat ramp, called Minnows. Micki and her friends would hang out there drinking schnapps and shooting pool some afternoons, especially during the off season. Minnows' had just added some new rock songs to the jukebox play list, and the girls loved to play it loud and dance. Buddy, the owner, and married to Jeff's cousin, would make them turn the volume down, but as soon as he walked away, they would turn it back up. There was hardly ever anyone there anyway they would say. Buddy let her sell there, and never told Jeff. He was one of the cooler "anti-relatives."

When they got to the ramp, they waded into the water and the horses started playing. The girls got off and held them by the reigns watching in wonder at the huge beasts playing like puppies. It was a dangerous game, the reigns are short and the horses are heavy. They resemble giant dogs paddling in one moment, and a human child splashing its hands in the water the next. It was an incredible sight, and a lot of fun. Her horse suddenly reared up into the air and came down in a twist, clipping Micki's thigh before she could move. Micki could feel a little sting above her knee and Jenny started to panic. Jenny had been kicked in the face by her dad's horse when she was just three. Micki shook her head to let Jenny know she thought she was fine, although she knew the horses hoof had landed right in the middle of her thigh. She felt it, but it was kind of numb, so she pulled the reigns and walked out of the water to check in no real pain and realized the pressure of the water had softened the blow of the kick. She would be more careful in the future she decided and gave the horse an encouraging nose bump before going back into the water with the other girls and their horses. While they were splashing around, a few boys from school who had been water tubing saw them and rode over to say hello and flirt. Micki knew all of them; they were in a boat that belonged to a boy named Boudreaux. He had been the first person Micki had met at school when she moved there. He had sat behind her and asked her questions about herself, all through class. A guy named Jake and another boy named Mark were with him. All of them except Mark dived from the cliffs and they all lived there on the lake. Mark didn't normally dive, but he did like to ski and tube. They'd been out there since the early morning they said. They were laughing at Boudreaux who had lost his shorts on the tube and had to spend a half hour finding them. The girls laughed about it along with the boys. Boudreaux stood up in the boat and mooned them all before inviting them to go tubing. The girls laughed and declined. Micki needed to get home she said, but did make plans to come back later that afternoon for some diving. Boudreaux, claimed he'd found a rock none of them had ever seen, so Micki, doubtful but interested, made plans to meet them at Boudreaux's dock at three. When he pulled her aside and asked her to bring a stash for him it made her a little uncomfortable, Jenny and Sophia were starting to think she had a thing with every boy she knew. She pulled back quickly but agreed and said she would bring Juanita; another friend who she was sure wouldn't want to miss it. Boudreaux was happy to hear that. Juanita was the prettiest girl in school, he thought. He couldn't wait to hang out with her. Just as Micki thought Sophia and Jenny wanted to know what was going on between her and the guys, but she shrugged it off as nothing knowing full well they didn't believe her. Her business was starting to bleed over into her social life and it scared her a little. She wasn't entirely sure what would happen if the whole world found out she was a dealer. She needed a car she decided but even though she had the money, how could she explain it to her mother?

The boat ramp was just off the highway. Everyone who lived there was accustomed to seeing the girls ride in that area. Cars would give them the right of way as they rode by and wave or blow the horn, sometimes startling the horses. Sophia's parents operated a small store on the corner there near the service road to the ramp. Travelers could buy gas and refreshments, and use a pay phone if needed. There was also a small Laundromat in a separate building there, to accommodate the renters who rented cabins along the lake road. Between the two structures there were a few pine and oak trees with shade to get out of the scorching heat, as well as some picnic tables and an old swing with just one swing left on it. The girls stopped by there to get drinks for the trip home and let the horses nibble at the grassy patches that dotted the little parks otherwise sandy floor. Riding bareback in the hot humidity always left a thick layer of horsehair on their bare legs but they always rode in short-shorts and bathing suits anyway. It was easy enough to wash off and too hot to wear anything else. They laughed at each other's "hairy legs" as Sophia went inside the store to talk to her parents about new school clothes she had seen the day before and really wanted. The new white pocket Levis were at the store in town she told her mother, and soon, they agreed she could have two pair. She got their drinks while Jenny and Micki stayed under the shade trees nearer the back of the store. Jenny asked Micki about Evan, the boy who had been living in one of the lake houses since early June of that summer. His parents were hardly ever home, and being so close to Jenny and Micki's house, they had naturally met the boy who was quiet, pale and a bit awkward. He was tall, even for eighteen, and his dark hair was a stark contrast next to his milky white skin. He was cute, the girls had decided early on, but not boyfriend material. Jenny had asked Micki if she had seen him lately. Micki informed her that although she hadn't seen Evan in a few days, she had seen his parents driving by her house just yesterday, so therefore they had not been found by the Mafia yet. Jenny, giggling, confirmed she too had seen Evan's parents, but not Evan. "He's weird," Jenny said. She was fond of the term when discussing Evan. She clearly wanted to say more, but she didn't. Jenny liked to speculate about the renters and new people on the lake. She was smart and observant with a very creative imagination. She, like Micki, was also an avid reader. Although she didn't like the subjects that Micki liked to read, she was always interested in making one up. Over the year and a half that Micki had lived next door, she and Jenny had concocted hundreds of nightmarish tales for their parents, their teachers, and anyone else who could be manipulated by such a trick. Stories of creeps terrorizing them when they were home alone could yield a break in restrictions that would otherwise interfere with their sleep-over plans.

Micki was okay with the way things turned out. She had put Jeff in check, and no longer lived at the end of an isolated dirt road behind the school. In a way, she had "beaten the devil," she liked to think. She missed Cameron; she didn't yet have the words to express her feelings about their dwindling friendship. It was on life support. He'd been acting crazy, and though she knew it was her fault she needed him and he had been trying to punish her by withholding his attention, his affection. She couldn't bear to be at home sometimes and she had to have an out. It should be Cameron but more and more it was Billy. She knew why she was doing it now. She wanted to be in control of her sexuality. Any night she could go to sleep at home and wake up being assaulted by Jeff, or worse, Brett. She needed to be normal, and normal girls have sex with guys at least close to their age and certainly not a relative. She wished she could tell Cameron how she felt, but something in her was stunted and she was still afraid to go all the way and how could she tell him that's what she wanted but still didn't want to do it. It made no sense. She was afraid of the aftermath.

Now, there were other kids trapped on a dirt road with her. Although their houses weren't spaced closely enough to see each other, she was not alone. Micki sensed the tension between Jenny and herself. It was new. Neither of them wanted it to be that way. Micki, trying to save a worsening situation, said "You should crowd Danny at Cal's party, Jenny." Jenny seemed to get a little uptight but kept listening, "I really don't like him, and if he thought you did, he'd forget all about me..." but Jenny said nothing, "Please." Micki tried again, trying to make things work in her favor too. Finally Jenny blurted out, "Are you kidding me? We made out all last summer. He knows that I like him. He doesn't like me anymore, and if you think I'm going to run interference for you, you are fucking crazy..." Micki laughed gently with her friend, and said "it's his loss." Jenny had been crushed when Danny didn't seem to be interested in her any more. She had gone "all the way" with Danny, she'd told Micki holding back sobs, and he had seemed as if he really cared for her. This summer had been a very rude awakening for Jenny. For that, alone, Micki wanted to break his heart. It would be easy, she thought, if not fun. They both lit a cigarette from the pack Micki had gotten from Buddy down at Minnows and walked over to the store to use the pay phone to call Juanita. She told her that if her dad could bring her to the lake they could dive off some rocks that afternoon with Boudreaux and Jake. Juanita was sixteen and like Micki, had no car. They shared many interests, cliff diving being just one. She was excited to hear from Micki and said she would be there in an hour. She told Micki that her little brother Kevin was staying with one of his little urchin friends and she should spend the night after the diving. Kevin had annoyed Juanita to the point of violence. He developed huge crushes on her friends and constantly harassed them when they stayed over. Juanita would no longer invite company unless he was gone. Micki said she would ask her mom when she got home. As Sophia came out of the store, Micki said "bye," and they rode back to the pasture, where they left Sophia's horse. Sophia went up to the big house to visit Danny and Uncle Freddie. She was going to see if Danny was still hung over, and laugh at him, but Jenny and Micki kept riding down the road toward Jenny's house. Once they had stalled the horses with sweet feed, Jenny said she had to help her dad move dirt for their new patio, and told Micki she was welcome to a shovel. Micki laughed and said, "Maybe later," and ran all the way home to her front door. Jeff was in the driveway sitting in his Dodge Super Bee. He was drunk and listening to "Coward of the County," and trying to sing along in his country gospel bass voice. When he saw her he asked her "you been out smokin pills and takin dope?" he laughed and turned up the bottle of Jim Beam. Micki just sneered at him and went inside. She asked her mother if she could spend the night with Juanita. Sara who wasn't sure how the night might now progress with Jeff already drunk and singing in the driveway, said she could. She gathered some things together and sat by the window. Without telling Sara about the cliff diving, she bolted out the door before Jeff had a chance to embarrass her when Juanita's dad pulled into the drive way. Within the hour, Micki and Juanita were in a boat with Boudreaux, Jake and a new guy named Ken, headed to the pier at Ken's house to catch a good buzz before heading to the big rock. Kens parents had rented a secluded cabin on the Marina side. He said they were staying for two weeks. He was eighteen and looking for entertainment when he met Boudreaux at the Marina. As they drove the boat away from the pier and down the lake, they passed Evan's house. He was there sitting on the pier with his feet dangling off the end above the water. Micki and Juanita stood up and yelled and laughed as they waved to him, and he raised a beer to them. A few minutes later, they were slowing down, turning into a half cove that was nearly surrounded by the closest thing you could get to a cliff in that part of Alabama. Kudzu grew in places on a huge rock that jutted out of the cliff side and created a rock ledge a little more than half way up. Above the ledge the ground looked like it had been cut from a cake, layers of bare earth pierced with a tangle of roots from the trees and plants above it, like so many worms in one apple. Micki figured the land at the top of that cliff had to be somewhere near her house and she determined that she and Jenny would trace the lake up there and find it. It was so close Micki couldn't believe they had never noticed it before. It had to be private property, or there would have been someone here before now. They would have known about it. Her mother would say it looked "snaky." She and Jenny had probably ridden right by it at least once because they rode the horses all over the lake rim in that area. Beneath the ledge, was solid gray rock with only a little bit of wild jasmine tacked to it here and there. Maybe 60 feet to the ledge she thought. That would be a good dive. "Boudreaux, you . . . are the shit," she said out loud as they all uttered varying degrees of approval." Boudreaux smiled and said, "oh yeah," and stopped the boat near the water's edge tying the tow line to a low hanging tree limb. "Okay . . ." Juanita said, "One of the boys needs to make us a trail to the top." Jake laughed and asked if she was afraid of rattle snakes. "Of course I am," she replied, "now get up that hill." The boys took off up the side of the rock toward the top. Occasionally they would cry out as if something had attacked them, but the others knew they were joking, and in just a few minutes, Boudreaux was standing at the ledge with Jake just behind him. "Here we go," he yelled, and ran the short distance into a cannonball off the side making a huge splash in the water below. After he swam back to the newly trampled path, Jake jumped a flip and a perfect dive, surfacing in milliseconds. Juanita, Micki and the new guy Ken, scrambled out of the boat and made their way to the ledge. Cliff diving could be tricky. Hitting the water face first could result in a bloody nose. Body first could produce a blister that would rival sunburn. Diving too close can result in broken limbs and concussions are not unheard of. Cutting through the water, was the trick. Micki had learned to high dive at Lake Martin with her dad. The cliffs up there were generally larger than the ones at Lake Jordan, but this one would qualify as worthy. There was also a pool near Wetumpka called Willow Springs (due to the fact the water was filtered from a natural source and therefore freezing cold, year round) that kept a high dive. The pool was deep, but Micki had scraped the bottom a few times resulting in something resembling road rash. You have to be fast. Micki first and then Juanita, the girls jumped, feet first, holding their swimsuit tops because the force of the plunge from this height could make them come off even though they were routinely double-knotted, they would still slip right off your legs or your head, no matter how you went in. Micki had sworn she would get a one-piece this summer. She intended to buy one and slip it in with her things but hadn't done so yet. She still wore the same brown bikini she had worn the summer before. It was a little small, but she had given up being self-conscious about it. Juanita wore a small bikini too, and nobody bitched about that. Jake was very good at diving, maybe the best on the lake, he had lived here all his life, and knew the water as well as anyone. He did amazing flips and odd twists as he fell through the air before cutting through the water with his fingertips into a perfect dive. Ken wouldn't jump. He couldn't be persuaded. He decided he would rather watch. Looking off the edge of the wall, he said to Micki, "You guys are crazy." Micki just laughed and jumped again. She realized too late that she didn't jump far enough out into the water, and was afraid she was about to hit a shallow bottom. She turned head first so she could try to cut a shallow dive. In a split second she remembered the look on her brother's face after hitting bottom. He would come up with blood and water streaming down his face. She hit the water in a semi-panic, hoping she would be able to cut back upward in time to avoid a head injury. She plunged deep, too deep she thought, this close to the bank, but she never hit the bottom. She started pushing against the water in a panic. She surfaced in darkness and hit her head on a rock. Her head was throbbing and she hoped it was only water running down her face. Putting her hands up she realized she had hit a hollow cave somewhere in the side of the lake. The water was deep there, had it not been for the huge rock jutting out in the other direction, it would have been visible. The underside of that rock was semi-hollow, about ten feet in diameter and maybe as deep in some places, but the bottom, the bottom Micki never found, gave her the creeps. It wasn't easy to scare her, but that day she was at least shaken and no longer wanted to dive remembering all the snake tales Buddy had told them, she quickly dove back down into the water and swam in the direction of the only light available. When she surfaced again, she was back in the sunshine and her friends, who had been frantic when she didn't come back up, were glad to see her. Juanita was wrapped in a towel. She had gotten back into the boat and was crying. Ken who had been nervous about going back down, even on the trail, was still up on the ledge. Boudreaux and Jake were in the water where they had been diving, looking for Micki. They all swam to the boat, and one by one, crawled into it. She told them what had happened and Boudreaux and Jake went back down to explore. Jake came back up and told them it was a deep depression directly under the rock. It didn't go under very far, but there was a hollow cave just past the edge. Boudreaux popped up right after him and said there were no snakes but a lot of slimy stuff was growing under there, and "that hole is deep, wonder what lives down there? This shit is dangerous," he said with a smile and a twinkle in his eye. Juanita wanted to go home, and Micki was relieved to do so. They spent the next fifteen minutes coaxing Ken back down the trail and into the boat. When he went back to Ohio, he would tell his friends that he jumped off the rock, found a cave and made it with two beautiful Alabama girls. The sun was setting, and they headed to Boudreaux's pier, smoking the one joint someone had managed to bring and keep dry.

Juanita's dad picked them up at Boudreaux's, and then dropped them at Juanita's. Her house was on the highway, halfway to town. As they got out, he told them they were getting "too big" and left for the Marina. Juanita and Micki looked confused, wondering what he meant, and set about measuring themselves as soon as they were inside. Hips and thighs mostly, they were terrified of being fat. When they were satisfied that they were of acceptable size and shape, they got some food from the fridge and sat at the table eating and laughing about Ken. The girls shared the same interest in all things creepy and Juanita wanted to do something. Psychic tests, a séance, tell scary stories . . . read each other's mind. Micki agreed it would be a blast and so they got ready for their séance. After trying tirelessly to contact the spirits of dead, they began a round of mind reading. Micki pegged Juanita 8 out of 10 times, and Juanita cried. To Micki, it was all just chance. If she could read minds, things would be far different, she thought. She just happened to know what Juanita was thinking. Juanita talked a lot. So did Micki for that matter. They started trying to move objects with their minds. "Let's make the wind blow!" Juanita said, and she and Micki giggled and went outside. Micki went first and on some sort of coincidence, every time Micki would tell the wind to "Blow," the breeze would pick up. She tried to demonstrate to (now crying again) Juanita that it was just a fluke by telling the wind to periodically stop and start. But no matter how she tried to pattern it, she couldn't predict what it would do. She couldn't miss and therefore could not destroy the impression that she was controlling it. After only making it worse, Micki gave up and said they should stop. They told scary stories about crazed maniacs loose on the lake until Juanita fell asleep in the great room. Micki said, "Juanita, are you asleep?" She got no answer. She got up and went outside on the patio. Her nightgown fluttered in the wind as it picked up and caressed her face, blowing her hair back. She closed her eyes and took a deep breath. The wind comforted her. She went back inside, and curled up on the love seat to sleep. A million thoughts were running through her head. She was playing some pretty serious games, and so far she had been untouchable. People protected her just by protecting themselves, but she really just wanted a normal life. She cried silently as she sometimes allowed herself to do when she couldn't sleep. Suddenly she was outside on the smooth patio and the wind was blowing against her she thought it might knock her down. She moved onto the grass and was standing near a dirt road she didn't remember being there. Unsure where it led she walked along the dirt road without holding the hem of her cream colored gown. The wind was whipping the material and keeping her hair out of her face. As she walked she passed a playground where a bully girl who was round, freckled and strawberry blonde had been taunting a much smaller girl who was frail with black hair so fine it seemed to be plastered to her head. Now some sort of green winged angel type creature was hovering and beating the bully with a pair of drumsticks as if it was playing a song on her head. She watched as she passed but she kept walking. Soon the road turned up and to the left and she thought it was strange that the road went uphill but she kept going. Although the road veered here and there to the left or right, she just kept going straight. At the top of the hill there was what appeared to be a shipwreck. Or maybe a ship that had been turned into a house because there were stone steps that led up to a red front door installed into the side of the ship. A few yards away there was a thin, naked man sitting in a kitchen chair, vomiting into a bucket on the ground in front of him. He did not see her or notice when she went through the door. The ship suddenly became an empty house with windows everywhere. To the left was a small open room so she went to the double doorway to look inside. There was nothing there except for an iron bunk bed that was mounted to the wall. On the bed the mattresses had no sheets or pillows. On the bottom bunk sat a small, very dirty girl of about one and a half maybe. Her thin black hair was matted and gnarled at the back of her head. Micki kneeled down to talk with her and asked her where all her things had gone. In response the girl lifted her finger and pointed to the man outside who could now be seen through the window. A sense of dread hit her in the gut. She panicked and grabbed the girl into her arms promising to take her home. The girl weighed no more than a doll. She ran fast down the hill with the impossibly weightless child in her arms and the man never looked up from his bucket. She rounded the curve to the now empty playground and shot through the woods towards home. She could see the stone walls rising through the trees and then Juanita was shaking her awake, giggling playfully, so Micki hit her with a pillow.

CHAPTER 3

"I watched a change in you, like you never had wings." ~Deftones

When Evan moved in, he was a little reluctant to meet any of the kids nearby. He had been in a lot of trouble before, drugs, fights, some petty theft and burglary. His dad, Jack, never even looked at him anymore and his stepmother, Rita, seemed disappointed to find him there for breakfast every morning. As if somehow it had all been a bad dream, and one day she would awake, married to a man who didn't have a kid, or at least a man who didn't have Evan. Evan's mom had left Jack for another man when Evan was seven. Evan had called him uncle Trey, and had no idea that Trey was anything less than family. Jack was devastated, and closed his law office for a month. Evan became invisible. The housekeeper would make him sandwiches and make his bed. But he had no one to talk to, and no one to play with. He missed his mother so badly, but his dad wouldn't let him cry over her. She wasn't worth his tears he would say. Jack didn't want to coddle Evan; he thought it was important that Evan understood how people really were. "Yes Evan, mothers do walk out on their little boys. It happens every day. One day it won't even bother you." Jack was a defense attorney, a good one. He worked constantly. He was always going and coming. Busy, on the phone, with a client, with his secretary. Evan spent many afternoons sitting on the cool tile floor under a plant stand in the foyer watching people come and go. They were always talking and waiting to talk. In retrospect, Evan felt guilty for not mentioning uncle Trey to his dad, but by the time he understood it, Elise was already gone and Evan was left to sort it all out. Because she abandoned them, she had gotten no rights to Evan at all, not that she wanted any. He hadn't seen her since they were divorced. He did get one letter from her that she had written when he was ten. In it, she told him about her life and that she was very happy in Gulf Shores with uncle Trey and hoped he was too, that she would like him to visit her soon, and left a lipstick kiss over the signature. He saved it and took it out to read every now and then, but if asked, he would say it wasn't that important. Jack's mother had passed away, and sometimes they would visit his dad in the retirement home where he lived. It was difficult because he had Parkinson's disease. Jack was solemn about his dad's condition, and Evan would always just sit quietly, or tell his grandpa something he did at his father's prodding. Jack had been thirty-five when he married Elise. It took him three years to convince her to have Evan. Jack regretted that he was older, and always felt that he had shorted Evan somehow. That it wasn't fair that his dad was too old to enjoy being a grandfather, and his son, isolated in a world of legalistic grown-ups. Jack had faith, and believed that Evan would be fine. For a long time, it seemed to be the case. Jack showered Evan with everything you could expect a boy would want. He had him enrolled in the best private school in Montgomery, and took him to the country club to play golf whenever he could get him to go. It was important to him that Evan was happy, his only child, his only son.

The day after Andrews seventeenth birthday, he approached a girl who had been at his school for just two years. Her name was Jasmine, and she had come there from New York. Both her parents were lawyers who had a joint firm in Montgomery. He had a crush on her when she first started there, but had kept her on a pedestal in his mind since then. He had recently seen her kissing a girl named Candace in the locker room. He was picking up basketballs and just happened to see through the open door. Jasmine had looked right at him in her bra, and smiled. After a day of mental deliberation, he asked her to come to his house and hang out. She said she'd love to. Jasmine liked to take Valium. She had a prescription because she had anxiety. She and Candace would sometimes take it together, and after a while, Evan was taking it as well. The Valium always made him very tired, and he asked a friend he knew at school named Chase, to get him some coke. The boys had done it together before, and Chase lifted it from his dads closet whenever he felt he could get away with it. Evan produced it one afternoon and they would take the Valium and then do the coke a little at a time to stay alert. One afternoon, Jasmine, Candace and Evan were fooling around in the guest bedroom at his house, when Evan had an epiphany. He wanted the whole school to see what he was doing. He had always been quiet, but he was clearly a king, and everyone he knew needed to know that. Jasmine and Candace would make out with each other and he would watch. When he would join them, they would do whatever he asked and it made him feel powerful. He decided it was a good time in his life to throw a party. Jack and Rita were out of town regularly. The new housekeeper, Rosa, barely spoke English and was afraid of Evan anyway. He was a big kid, and could be quite intimidating. She would do whatever he asked he was sure. She never told Jack about the afternoons with Jasmine, even though they left a huge mess every time. He called Chase and asked him to come over. Chase was sixteen, and had been given a Mazda for his birthday. They went into the den and started shooting pool. Evan told Chase about Jasmine and Candace, and how he thought a lot of the girls at school would be just as cool if they only had the right environment. He told him he wanted to throw a party and that he wanted to get a "ton of coke." Chase said that he thought he could probably get his dads hook-up to sell it to him without much hassle, but that it would be really expensive. No way could they spend that kind of money without their parents being aware of it. Evan had his own bank account, but he didn't want to spend the money on coke either, he was saving it for something important and his parents managed his accounts. They devised a plan to break into a neighbor's house, an older woman on Bell Road whose husband had died. Chase said she had tons of jewelry and just a few pieces could finance everything. That they could each take half of what they took to a different pawn shop in Birmingham, and the party could go on. He was in. Later that week, they went to visit Mrs. Bellwether, and asked her if she needed any help with her yard. She told them she had a caretaker, but that they should come in and have some iced teas. Pretending to be interested in her things, they listened attentively and she was flattered to show them her priceless art pieces and thousand dollar gowns she would "never wear again." She was a nice lady whose children didn't visit enough. When the boys left, they had diamond rings and necklaces, an antique diamond and sapphire bracelet as well as a strand of pearls. They took the loot to Birmingham the next day and never heard another word about it. Mrs. Bellwether's children put her in a retirement home sometime later that year.

They bought the coke, and the first party was on. It must have been everyone from his school over twelve that showed up for the party, he thought. People were everywhere, in the house, in the pool. Chase had brought some girl who had "run away from home for the weekend" and she was stripping to "ride on" by ac/dc in the living room. Jasmine and Candace were thoroughly impressed with Evan's new-found coordination skills, and kept him pretty busy during that first party. After that he and Chase had decided it was too risky to actually speak with a home-owner when they were going to rip them off. They made an inventory of all their parents' friends who had anything they thought they could sell. Chemo, the guy who sold cocaine to Chase's dad, also knew someone who would buy guns and "other miscellaneous things of value," he had told the boys at their first exchange. After a year, Evan had made his point. The student body loved him. Nothing happened without his input, and his was most often the final word. He had become the "go to" guy for cocaine and he was doing quite well. He had all but stopped burglarizing homes, as he usually had enough money from selling it to buy what he needed for the parties. A girl named Teresa had a new relationship with Evan and he would trade her cocaine for sex. She could have bought it, but they both preferred the arrangement the way it was. He was careful not to let Jasmine find out, as she had become very possessive and jealous at that point. She would do anything to make him happy. Once when they were high on coke and the three of them were together, Evan told Jasmine he wanted to tie her up for the sex. Jasmine thought about it for a minute and asked him if he wanted to pretend to "rape" them. He said, "I think so. Would you do it?" Jasmine and Candace said okay, and he tied them both up. He tied Jasmine to a desk chair and Candace to a post on the bed. It hadn't gone well, and both girls were pissed off afterwards.

At the last party Evan would ever throw in Montgomery, he was in his room, counting the money he was making selling coke. He was high and his mind was racing. He never let people in his room, not even Jasmine. He came in there to be alone. Suddenly his door opened and a girl named Courtney was standing there. He knew her well. She'd had a crush on Evan since she was old enough to have one. She had been coming to his parties lately. He glared at her but she didn't seem to notice. She was saying Teresa had told her that she could get some coke from him, and she was wondering how that worked. He was pissed that she opened the door, pissed that people were constantly looking for him, tired of people asking for things. He got up and closed the door behind her and said, "Let me show you." He took out the vial of coke he kept in his pocket and dumped some out on the desk for her to try. When she bent over to snort the coke he grabbed her under her dress and pulled her panties down, she stood up and half turned around when he grabbed her hair and forced her down over the desk again shoving her face into the coke that had scattered there. He inserted his penis into her anus and she screamed and cried out. In a minute, it was over. He buttoned and zipped his pants. He sniffed and told her, "That's how it works, now get the fuck out of my room, and don't ever come in here again." He threw a small plastic Ziploc bag at her. She was crying as she slipped her panties back on, picked up the coke and left the room wiping the white powder from her face. He knew he had lost control. He almost felt bad. He waited for Jasmine to come in and tell him what a piece of shit he was. That didn't happen. He stashed the money, and went back out to the party. Courtney was nowhere to be seen. Jasmine and Candace were kissing each other while they danced. He was turned on now. He wanted to have fun with them. He walked over to where they were and let them know he was ready for them. Jasmine said she had to check-in with her mom but would meet them in the guest room in just a few minutes.

When Evan and Candace closed the door, he couldn't wait for Jasmine. He kissed Candace, the way he always wanted to and threw her down on the bed. She was into it, and he got behind her and grabbed her hair in one hand pushing up her skirt with the other. He told her he was going to give it to her the way he gave it to Jasmine. Just when he entered her, she cried out, saying "I love you Evan, I've always loved you." Jasmine was in the room. All the times before didn't matter, at that moment she was sure he was trying to dump her for Candace. They were "behind her back." Jasmine went over to him and slapped him hard on the side of his head. He said "what the hell are you doing?" Jasmine said, "Don't worry; you'll never have to worry about it again." She looked at Candace who was now cowering on the other side of the bed. She told her, "You love him?" Candace immediately said, "No Jas, you know how he gets I was just trying to keep everything going." To which Jasmine replied, "Right, you fucking bitch, you were nothing when I found you, you'll be nothing when I'm done with you." She closed the door, went to her Camaro, and left. Evan assured Candace that she would be alright, and asked Candace to get back on the bed. She said she didn't think it was a good idea. He pulled out some coke for them to do, and after a moment of thought, she got back on the bed. She would tell Jasmine the next day that he had been weird, rough, and when she tried to stop he kept slamming her down on the bed. That he forced her to have anal sex and then oral. They never told anyone else about her humiliating experiences with Evan, but Jasmine had already had enough of his shit.

The next morning, Evan was groggy and hung over when the police arrested him at home. He had a half ounce of cocaine in his pocket and one Valium that Jasmine had given him. He was ready to tell the police that all the sex was consensual, thinking maybe Courtney had told someone about their encounter, but he was being charged with robbery, breaking and entering, selling stolen property and possession of a controlled substance. He was taken to a juvenile detention facility, where he called his dad. Angered at what she considered a betrayal, Jasmine had told her mother everything. It was unexpected.

Rita was in business finance, and was an expert witness for the prosecution in a capital murder case Jack had worked on when Evan was three. By the time he was eight, they were married. Rita hadn't wanted children, but would say to her friends at brunch that she was so in love with Jack she was willing to be a mother to Evan. They would pretend to admire her sacrifice. Evan didn't want another mother, and he thought it was fortunate that Rita had no interest in his life. He would often comment to his friends that she was "full of shit, but no threat." After Evan had broken into the homes of their friends, taken their jewelry and priceless heirlooms to buy cocaine, liquor and whatever else his little band of fiends decided they needed for party supplies, Rita had begun to think she made a mistake marrying Jack. Andrews's parties had been all the rage at the private school he attended. The parties were "legendary" he would say. Now they were the humiliation that Jack and Rita faced daily as they tried to save friendships and professional relationships. Jack and Rita clearly had no clue as to his activities. At first, they defended him, and then, in the face of the incredible evidence against him, they gave in to reality. They agreed to pay restitution to the people he had stolen from on his behalf. Andrews's party guests turned on him, and gave depositions to the prosecutor in order to save themselves. When it was clear he had not been implicated, Chases dad sent him away to boarding school. Jasmine had left his name out. She was angry with Evan, and "tired of his shit," but still thought Chase was cool. Evan never said that Chase was with him, believing it would be wrong to turn him in. He tried to call him once since he had been arrested, but was told by his mother not to call there again. He wasn't bitter. Jasmine and Candace made up, and were closer than ever. They both got counseling because they had been "taken advantage of by a boy with an abusive personality," and Jasmines mother said some "reverse damage" was in order. Evan was the bad guy, and that's how it had to be.

Evan was eventually released into the custody of his father, and at any time his dad could pick up the phone, and Evan's deferred prosecution would come to a screeching halt. After he had been released, his dad said if he got so much as one phone call about Evan being late for school, he would make that call. Evan, distraught and betrayed, decided he was damned no matter what he did, and before the ink was dry on the paperwork, was caught shoplifting at the new mall. The shop owner called his dad, and not the police. His father, well liked and prominent in Montgomery, arrived to pick up his son, paid for the merchandise and didn't speak to him on the ride home. The day after that, Evan got the news about moving to the lake, and within a week there he was. Jack and Rita had escorted Evan on his Honda Enduro, his things packed in the trunk of their car, to the two story plantation style house that sat at the bottom of an off road by the water. The road veered to the left, at a bend in the lake road just past Jenny's house. It was a big house just for the three of them, Evan thought. The other houses on the lake seemed modest in comparison, but his parents had a tendency for extravagance, and hiding from the world didn't seem to dampen that tendency. Everything was painted white and the patio, that joined the house to the walkway leading to the pier, was either marble or faux marble. Evan wasn't sure how to tell the difference. A white iron trellis and other fancy iron work adorned the house in every direction. He moved his things into an upstairs bedroom with a large window that overlooked the driveway. With orders to stay put, his parents went back to the city to close their home, and Evan was suddenly alone. He spent that first day in the yard, on the pier, watching boats and skiers ride by. They never looked over to see him sitting there. After figuring out how to work the satellite TV system, he watched movies until he fell asleep. The next morning he heard laughter through the patio door he had left open. When he stood up, he could see the pier. Two girls, one with long, straight blonde hair and one with long straight black hair. They were tanned, in bathing suits and shorts, and fidgeting with a deep sea reel like the ones he had used in Pensacola, fishing with his dad. He watched them for a while before he decided he should ask them why they were on his parents new pier, and maybe get to find out who they were. If they lived nearby, this might not be so bad after all, he thought. This might be a brand-new start. He lit a cigarette, ruffled his hair and walked down to the pier.

Micki and Jenny had never met anyone so pale on the lake. After watching his parents move the boy in the day before, they decided to be proactive in finding out who these new people were. It was a slow-paced lifestyle, and new people in big houses were exciting. Their collective imaginations were running wild. Curiosity would not be satiated until they knew exactly who they were and why they moved there. The house Evan moved into was normally vacant, and the favorite place for Jenny and Micki to fish. It was secluded, on the edge of a slew that jutted deep into the shoreline effectively hiding the view of the entire house from one side of the lake front, and vice versa. They'd set about investigating at daybreak. They went up the steps to the enormous patio and went straight to the open French doors. Seeing Evan asleep on the sofa, they backed out, giggling. Outside, Jenny suggested it might be better to go and get her dads rods and reels, and fish from the pier till their newest neighbor woke up. They had just gotten back and were changing the line on the reel to a river friendly test. Micki saw him, watching them from the doorway, out of the corner of her eye. She whispered to Jenny without leaning over that he was up and already stalking them. Jenny burst into laughter meant for Evan to hear, and Micki could not suppress her own smile. Without looking back, they listened as his steps came closer and closer. When he said "Hi," they pretended to be startled. "Where the hell did you come from?" Jenny asked as if she owned the lake, and after living there all her life, she might have really felt that way. At sixteen,

Jenny was beautiful, average height and just a little too thin, her dark hair and darker eyes made her look exotic. She was indifferent, in a cool way. This seemed to startle Evan. Micki giggled aloud at Jenny's power to wilt. "I'm Evan," he finally said as if Micki's laughter had let him in on the joke. "This is my pier," he continued, before Jenny cut him off completely by saying, "No. This is not your pier, at best, it belongs to your parents, and you just want to throw some weight around on your first impression. I get it, but it's not your pier. Seriously." Again Evan was speechless, and to Micki he seemed a little fragile. Playing nice, to Jenny's heart crushing, she casually asked him what brought them to the lake. Evan fidgeted, and said his parents just wanted to get away from Montgomery for a while, and this was it. Now with his hands in the pockets of his black jeans and black T-shirt, he suddenly felt like a specimen. It was an alien feeling that he didn't like, he smiled at his self-consciousness and shrugged it off offering them some beer or iced tea. Micki loved tea, and agreed immediately. Rita had been gracious enough to make tea and Tupperware dinners for him. That's how it was with Rita. She went through the motions of being the over protective concerned parent without ever actually having to spend time with Evan. The more time she spent doing things for him, the less she had to actually interact with him. While Evan spent time with and said goodbye to his dad, she spent her goodbyes making food and drinks, folding clothes, opening and closing windows or stacking fresh sheets on Andrews's dresser. Doing what she knew how to do. Jenny seemed genuinely suspicious of Evan, but Micki just ignored it and asked him if he had any music he could play on the stereo. He said, "No, sorry," Micki looked disappointed but said "that's okay," took her tea and went back out to the patio with them. So your parents just want to move, here?" Jenny asked him again when they were sitting at the table on the patio. There was a short uncomfortable silence between them. During that moment, the sound of the blades on the ceiling fan slowly rotating inside the house was the only noise. One revolution, two . . . He wished he'd brought some tapes. "Yeah, they just wanted to move here. People move to the lake right?" He looked at her, leaned forward and narrowed his eyes a little when he spoke and Jenny seemed to back off some, wondering why he was getting so offended, maybe he was really pissed that they were at the pier? "Sure. My parents did, so did Micki's. I'm Jenny by the way, and we live that way . . . "she pointed to the sharp curve where the dirt road disappeared from view."...we saw you move in, and thought we'd be sociable." He said "Cool. I haven't met anyone else." Jenny said, "Well duh, you just moved in yesterday." Micki laughed. Evan could feel his face getting red. He decided he could save this conversation and asked them why they had been on the pier. Jenny seemed a little put off by the question and said, "We fish here all the time; we'll fish here when you're gone." He tried to be casual saying it was cool, but Jenny was clearly irritated "We have to get my dad's fishing reels back in the shed and do some other things before my mom comes home." She said. He nodded his head slowly, as Jenny continued "It was nice meeting you, and we will refrain from fishing from your pier as long as you reside here. Okay then. Come on Micki let's go." Micki got up, smiled and said "see you later." Her smile was warm. He was suddenly embarrassed and had to look down at the glass of tea he had in his hands. As they walked away, he yelled out to them without looking up, "You can fish off my pier any time!" Jenny glared back toward the patio when she heard it and then looked at Micki before bursting into a fit of laughter. Evan realized too late how it had sounded, and feeling a bit burned, just sat there, and never looked up until he was sure they were around the curve. He cursed out loud and went back into the house.

"He's weird." Jenny said. They had stopped around the curve and lay the fishing gear in the road. Jenny had removed a crumpled pack of cigarettes from the pocket of her shorts. As she lit a cigarette she said, "And he's lying . . . why would he have to lie?" Micki thought about it for a minute before suggesting that Evan's family might be in the witness' protection program, and were hiding out from the Mafia. She took one of the Camel cigarettes, and lit it with a match. Jenny pointed out that only bad people have to hide from the bad people they turn in and speculated as to whether or not they could be vampires. "He wasn't burning in the sun light." Micki stated, but Della again pointed out that "what's written about vampires might not be true." Jenny reached down to pick up the gear but Micki just stood there looking at her for a moment, smiling, before reaching for a tackle box. They laughed and decided he was a mental patient who thinks he's a vampire, while hiding from the Mafia. She said nothing more in disagreement. Jenny's older sister Alexis was at home so after they deposited the reels in the shed, they went to Micki's house. Micki's mom didn't have a phone so they could say they had been there all day if need be. They smoked a joint from the last of the weed Micki had gotten from Cameron and made cookies in the new toaster oven, while they continued speculating on the new kid's unquestionably unfortunate reality. That was the story of how Micki and Jenny met Evan.

As it turned out, Evan moved to the lake, but Jack and Rita, could hardly say so. When they did stay on the lake with him, they barely spoke to him before they would leave for their jobs in the city the next day. Evan's dad could have worked from the lake house, but he never did. After a week, they barely came to the lake at all. He was starting school there in the fall, repeating his senior year, and he was to live quietly for a while, until Jack could forget his humiliation.

During that first week that followed their first encounter, Micki and Jenny would see Evan riding his motorcycle along the dirt roads as they were taking the horses through the weave of trails in the woods. They would see him at the store Sophia's parents owned, and once he had come into Minnows while they were shooting pool with Boudreaux and Jake. Micki sold her weed and coke there on the weekends. The motorcycle was noisy, and nobody else on this part of the lake rode one. Plenty of times they would be seen at the Marina, but they couldn't think of even one person who had one on the lake road. He really seemed to bug Jenny, but Micki began to think he was just quiet and deep. Micki thought Evan might be able to make Jenny forget about Danny eventually. She thought they could make a cute couple. One day when they were riding to the quarry Micki said "We should invite him to a party at Cal's house." She was maneuvering her horse through the thick brush trying to avoid getting twigs or bugs caught in her hair. Suddenly Jenny stopped and she got off her horse, Little Bit. Little Bit was a bit on the cranky side and had taken to blowing his body out whenever Jenny tried to saddle him. As she rode, his barrel had shrunk back to normal, and the saddle had gotten loose. She now had one foot on the horse's side and was pulling furiously to tighten the belt. "Are you kidding me? She asked? I can't go to that party. I'm still in shit over that thing at Bobby's house." But Micki, who had no idea what shit she was even talking about didn't think it could be that bad. Pausing behind her with Hotshot, she was determined to go and tried to get Jenny to "get creative and get out of the house." Billy wanted her to go. She decided that she would go down to the mansion, as they liked to call it, and ask Evan if he wanted to come. He hadn't been out much, and maybe she could interest him in

Jenny if the conversation called for it. Either way, they needed to know him better, she thought. Micki and Jenny lived in the water and the sunshine, and Micki figured Evan just needed to be exposed to it, before he could realize he was supposed to be in it. Jenny got back on her horse and they kept riding. When they got to the clearing near the quarry, they made the horses run. From memory, Hotshot and Little Bit, ran the entire range of ravines and ditches, seemingly having fun. When they were finished, they walked out of the trail on the other side of the woods, took the lake road to the bridge and made the left toward Jenny's house.

Late that afternoon, after Micki had gone home, Sam showed up with Cameron, and begged Sara to let Micki come home with her. This was a pre-arranged emergency, but it was half true. She told Sara that her parents were going away for the night and she would be alone when Cameron went out. That she was scared to stay by herself. Sara didn't trust Cameron, but she liked Sam, and gave in. Cameron took them home and showed Micki some weed he had gotten from a guy who had recently moved there from Detroit. While they were smoking, Sam went into a coughing fit and had to pee. While she was in the bathroom, Cameron stared at Micki, he acted like he wanted to say something and she had nowhere to run. He was even better looking now. She wondered what she would do if he kissed her, and then he did. It was warm and sticky. He made her feel all the right things again. When Sam came out of the bathroom, Cameron pulled away and got a glass of water. They got completely toasted. Cameron gave them some of the weed in addition to what he fronted Micki to sell, and then just like Sam said, left them alone. When he was gone, Sam said to Micki, "any boy you want, but not my brother." Micki asked her why she cared what Cameron did. Sam told her that she knew for a fact that he was really into her, and "fucking with his head, is not going to help."

"What if I'm not just fucking with his head, Sam? What if I really like him too?" "No. Not my brother. No hell, no." Sam was really upset "you know he got his girlfriend pregnant?" Micki shook her head no. "That's why my parents really made him quit school and get a job, to support the baby. Her parents freaked and moved away with her, so it didn't matter anyway. They went to Texas or some shit. We don't even know if she had the baby or an abortion, or if it was a boy or a girl." Micki didn't know. She felt ashamed, as if she had done something terrible. Poor Cameron, she thought. Micki decided Sam was probably right, she was in love with Billy anyway, right? Cameron was just temporary nostalgia, no matter how good it felt. It was all so confusing. Sam was probably right; she was fucking with his head. Or maybe he was fucking with hers now. Cameron didn't come home that night, and Micki wondered where he was and why he wasn't there with her.

Cameron was shooting pool at Minnow's. After everything they'd been through he couldn't believe the way she treated him. She had a cold streak, and no matter how much he missed her, he was not going to let her walk on him. She had to understand that. He left at closing time and slept in his car. He'd go home tomorrow. He hoped it had hurt her, but was afraid it didn't.

CHAPTER 4

"It is the nature of truth, as of some ores in particular, to be richest when most superficial." ~Edgar Allan Poe

Evan was home alone again that weekend. When Micki showed up, he was just about to sit down to whatever was in one of the many Tupperware containers Rita had left for him in the freezer. He had the radio up so loud, he never heard her knock, he just turned around and there she was. "Emotional Rescue" was blaring. She seemed older somehow, he knew she was a full year younger than he was, but she looked much older. She was wearing make-up, and her blonde hair suddenly seemed like spun gold. She was wearing a short black skirt and a loose black blouse that was nearly as long as the skirt. She was carrying a pair of black stiletto heels that made him look at her legs. Legs he hadn't noticed much before now, lean and tanned. She informed him that they were all sneaking off to a party at a friend's house down the lake. He sensed a familiar pang of desire. "Why don't we stay here and have our own party?" He asked her. Micki shrugged and laughed. "Down boy, I've got people waiting for me around the corner. Besides, don't you think you should go out with Jenny? I know you like her. She might just warm up to you if you try a little." "Is Jenny coming?" he asked, Micki cocked her head to one side, narrowed her eyes at him and smiled, "No, Jenny can't sneak out this weekend. Maybe next time . . . But you should go, it's the last party before school starts." He said he would. Micki told him how to get to Cal's house and said she would see him there. She then started back up the lake road to meet her friends. He watched her until she got around the corner. Micki wondered if Jenny knew that Evan might be into her but put it out of her mind when she rounded the corner and met Toni and Sophia where they were waiting for her in Sophia's mom's car. Sophia was still trying to get Jenny's mom to let her come out with them. When she came out of the house alone, Sophia informed Micki that she had to stop and pick up Danny and Billy too probably. Micki, who couldn't tell anyone about Billy, said "Great."

Sophia turned the car into the long driveway to Billy's place. The girls got out of the car and went to the door. Without knocking, Sophia burst through the door saying "Let's go, let's go, we don't have all night" Billy was in the kitchen, wiping down the counter and Danny was in the living room, staring into a full length mirror that was attached to the door of Billy's bedroom. He looked at Micki through the mirror, smiled and asked her how he looked. Micki shot a glance at Billy before looking back at Danny and telling him he looked great. Micki picked up the phone on the wall to call Jenny and let her know this was her last chance. Jenny assured her that she had "no chance" of slipping out. Then Micki told her about the encounter with Evan. Jenny laughed about it and said she would come by Micki's in the morning after her parents went to work. Micki hung up the phone and went outside to smoke a cigarette. Danny went to the bar that separated the kitchen from the living area and picked up a case of wine while asking Sophia to open the trunk. Billy said that Cal had called and said they were low on wine and none of the girls wanted to drink beer, so he had picked up a couple of cases from Buster's, a package store on the other side of the lake. As it turned out, Delores had already taken Billy's car to pick up some friends and Billy was definitely going to ride with them too. They all walked to the car together and the boys put the wine in the trunk. Sophia got back in the car and Toni cried "Shotgun" as she jumped into the front seat. She still had a cast on her leg, and nobody would have stopped her. Billy got into the back and Danny held the door in a mock act of chivalry to allow Micki to get in. Micki did and was careful not to get too close to Billy, even though she wanted to. As for Billy himself, he was trying to act normal and not interfere with his brother's good time or give any indication of his feelings for Micki. He had already had a lot of wine trying to maintain his cool. Still he was jealous. Micki could see it, feel it, she liked it.

It was less than a mile to Cal's house but the winding dirt road made it seem much longer. Danny had rested a hand on Micki's thigh and it was so irritating to her she wanted to push it away but she didn't. Danny was saying something about the kids in his school in New Orleans, and the great parties they had. He went on about football, and how the girls there worshipped him and the boys there wanted to be him. Occasionally, he would squeeze Micki's thigh assertively. Danny wasn't trying very hard to be impressive. He was accustomed to being adored by everyone and especially girls. He had no doubt that Micki was happy to be with him and that they would look great together, especially dancing. He was just about to tell her that, when Sophia announced they had arrived. They all got out of the car, and the guys took the wine from the trunk and went into the house with the girls following behind.

Cal's house was adequate for a big party. That's why 99% of the parties they had lately, were held there. It was a split level. There was a basement that had been turned into "funky town" complete with DJ equipment, disco lights a dance floor, and a sign at the entrance. Cal's dad was a good friend of Sophia's Uncle Freddie, and was also divorced. They enjoyed Cal's parties and encouraged him to have them, funding supplies as well as joining in. Occasionally, they would be seen with some of the older girls getting more than friendly, but it was strictly consensual, and nobody ever complained. There were people everywhere, mostly kids that Micki went to school with but some that must have come from other schools and some from as far as Montgomery. The police had been called to parties at Cal's a few times in the past few weeks, but had only told them to keep the noise down. Cal's dad was a good friend of the local sheriff and nothing ever came of it.

When they all walked in, Danny was immediately rushed by a few girls who had been hanging with him at the previous parties that summer. Micki, anticipating the opportunity, grabbed a glass off the table and poured herself some wine from an open bottle, figuring Danny would be busy for a while. She went downstairs where Billy was getting ready to act as DJ. The shit with Cameron was making her crazy, Billy was making her crazy. Selfish fucking men were making her crazy. She wanted to punish him somehow. She walked near enough to him that he could feel the heat off her body, smell her perfume, and leaned against the wall watching people dance. Billy was squatting on the floor putting records in the order he wanted to play them. To Billy, Micki, now wearing the black, open-toed stilettos she had been carrying before, could have easily passed for 21. Something in her face was sophisticated. If he had taken her to New Orleans and introduced her to his friends there, they would never guess she was just a baby, they wouldn't even ask her age, he thought to himself. He loved her mouth most of all. She would smile at him casually with perfect white teeth. Her smile lit up a room. She was smart, and could talk about most anything. Her dad had spent eight years in the Air Force before she was even born, and had taught her so many things about technology. She read all the time and a lot of it was non-fiction. She was so curious about things. Hungry for knowledge as they say, now she was curious about Billy. At this moment, he didn't think he could resist her much longer. He knew he should firmly tell her, but it was too late. He had kissed her, and with that kiss he had betrayed himself, sealed his fate. He kept glancing up at her nervously. When he finally stood up, he said, "You . . . look great." She only looked away and pretended to ignore him. He knew she was playing. He knew her so well now. He started a record by Rick James; a song called "Super Freak" and started trying to get her to dance. She gave in and moved away from the wall, smiling. Billy put his hands on her waist and they began to sway back and forth to the music. "Where's Danny?" he leaned in to ask her, and she told him Danny was "busy being popular" and she smiled. Billy almost said something else, but didn't. Again he was transformed by her smile. She was smiling at him. Only him. He needed more wine. He could feel the anxiety again. He tried to remain cool and when the song was over, he asked Micki if she would "serve" him some wine, she said "Absolutely" and went to get it for him. He went back to the turntable and tried to regain his composure. He knew absolutely nothing would happen between Micki and Danny, and he was grateful. She was perfect, but she was sixteen, and wouldn't even be seventeen till next June. He felt like he was losing his mind. It was all so absurd.

Upstairs, Danny was still talking. Now sitting on a beige chaise lounge in the den, where the crowd around him had gotten bigger. When he saw her, he smiled and waved. She raised her glass to him and went into the kitchen. When she came back out, Danny noticed she was carrying two glasses of wine as she descended the stairs to the basement. Still caught up in the conversation he politely continued to talk to his new friends, temporarily putting off his desire to go dance with her. They had all night, he thought to himself.

Downstairs, Diana Ross was singing, "Upside down, boy, you turn me, inside out, and round and round . . ." while Micki danced with a few other girls she knew from her classes in school. When it changed to Blondie's "Call me," they began singing along in unison. Billy played a slow song. He had been watching her dance, and immediately grabbed her in another moment of drunken weakness and they began the slow dance. It was dark, there were so many people, it seemed harmless enough. He kissed her deeply, and she was excited, it was the first time he ever kissed her in public, she kissed him back and he embraced it, taking control. While Foreigner sang "I've been waiting, for a girl like you to come into my life..." Micki felt light headed, butterflies danced in her stomach. Billy told her he loved watching her dance. She could feel his breath on her neck, in her hair, she could smell the wine in his head. She kissed his warm skin softly, and he turned and kissed her mouth again, deeper and more passionate than before, he took her head in both hands as she put a hand on his chest, he kissed her harder. Swooning, she relaxed in his arms. He suddenly stopped. He just looked at her. She was breathing a little harder and her lips were bright pink and numb from the kiss. Her lipstick, now just a memory, she looked at him as seductively as she knew how, and he said she was one of the most beautiful women he would ever know, "one of a kind, a broken mold, fine skin like vanilla cream," he said. As he told her this, she was flattered and would have fulfilled any desire he could ask of her, but he didn't ask. His heart ached. No matter how much she wanted him, she didn't really know what to do and he wouldn't. It was frustrating. Billy leaned in and paused beside her face for a moment and she could feel the heat from his skin. He kissed her cheek and put his forehead against hers with his hands on her neck holding her taught jaw and caressing her bottom lip with one thumb. Then he went back to the turntables, leaving Micki standing there. She went across the room and sat down on the leather sofa that was there and tried to regain her composure. After he set the records to play on time he couldn't resist but to go to her. He had already removed his shoes and the wine was working. He sat down and in less than a minute he had laid her back on the sofa kissing her and caressing her body. Micki felt his erection in his pants pressing against her where he was laying. Her knee across his thigh where he'd slipped his hand under her skirt into the hem of her panties. She was happy that she could give him an erection and was enjoying the way it felt against her. They forgot about everyone else in the room and later people would say "there was soft porn in the basement." Things were definitely out of control; he got up and went out the back door to get some air telling her to stay there. She got up and straightened her skirt, thankful for the black strobe lighting in that corner and pushed her hair behind her ear, checking to make sure her earrings weren't tangled before she left the basement via the stairs to the kitchen.

Evan arrived and started looking for Micki. He had assumed that she would hang out with him at the party. He didn't know anyone there and he had hoped she would introduce him to some of the other kids on the lake. He was so sick and tired of being stuck at home alone. Once, he had ridden his bike into Montgomery to try and talk to Jasmine, but she didn't want to speak to him. When he finally got her to come outside, it had gotten ugly. She told him that he was an emotional vampire, that she had done everything she knew how to please him but he always wanted more. Angry, Evan told her she was just a whore, and that she would always be a whore. She had slapped him then, and he slapped her back, nearly knocking her to the ground. She told him he was a monster that used people up. She'd wanted him to be cool but now he was just an asshole. That he deserved everything he got and that she hoped he would go back to jail just so he could be ass raped, that he would probably like it since he was so fascinated with it. He moved to hit her again and she cringed but he stopped at the last moment, breathing hard, looking around hoping no one had seen, and started backing away. "That's right, she said, get the fuck out, go back to your cage and rot, whatever it is, it's too good for you freak!" It was definitely over. If she had told her parents about that he might go back to jail. But she hadn't as of yet. Or they chose to let it go, doubtful. He didn't care anymore.

At this party, no one seemed to notice that he was a stranger. They hardly noticed him at all. He just walked in the house without speaking to anyone thinking how different it was from the parties he had thrown in Montgomery. He went into the kitchen and got a beer from a cooler. It was all so casual, and nobody was selling coke in the kitchen. He was pretty sure they were selling it somewhere, but not in the kitchen. Still, if his parents had known he was here he might be in a lot of trouble, but after sitting around the lake house with no one to talk to for weeks, he couldn't resist the opportunity. Evan began to look around. This was a nice place, nicer than his house, but he decided that he could modernize the faux mansion with some new stuff and make it just as cool as the wide screen TV and the contemporary furnishings seem to set this place off. His dad would never agree to let him party there. He'd be too afraid Evan would start using coke again, but he could have small gatherings without much problem he was sure. After walking around the wraparound deck to get an idea of the layout he went below and went inside the door there to the basement where people were going in and out. He could hear music blasting. He crossed the room to the stairs and almost went up when he saw her. She was slow dancing intimately with a dark-haired guy. He looked older, maybe nineteen or twenty even, he thought. He had his hands all over Micki, sliding up her skirt. It was dirty. He felt like he was doing something wrong by watching them, but no one seemed to notice. He couldn't believe what he was seeing. Micki was definitely a girl he wanted to get to know better. Maybe she and Jenny might want to play with him sometimes. He stopped himself from thinking about it and sat down on the bottom step at the doorway for a moment. They parted long enough for dude to go work the stereo and then continued their escapade on a dark red leather sofa against the back wall, nearly in a corner. The black light over there was pulsing on and off so it was hard to see through the dancers and the disco lights but he saw enough to know they didn't just meet. As soon as the guy sat down they started kissing, and he couldn't tear his gaze away. It was sexy, she was beautiful. He was a little jealous of that guy for a split second and then he decided he had no reason to be, still, it nagged him a little. He loved the way her face looked right then. Her voice had startled him the first time he heard it. Smooth and a little deeper than most girls, it was a woman's voice. Now watching her open mouth and closed eyes making sex faces he knew he would never look at her the same way again. Her leg was now adorned with the black stiletto she'd been carrying earlier and the gold nail polish on her fingers and toes glittered in the strobe light. He almost went over there, he wanted to, but resisted the urge. He'd been watching for some time, and he wasn't the only one. He noticed every solo person down there was watching intently. It was quite a show. He decided it wasn't cool just to watch, he'd never been a voyeur exactly, just on occasion. He was definitely aroused so he figured he would go back upstairs, cool down, get another beer and try to meet someone on his own. He could hear a lot of laughing and talking in the den off the kitchen so he went there to see what was happening. Several people were crowded around one guy. He was talking about New Orleans, and how great it is to live there. Everyone seemed to like this guy, but Evan was a little put off by him. When Danny started bragging about his football success, Evan laughed out loud. Insulted, Danny turned to him and demanded to know who the fuck he was. Evan introduced himself and said that he was supposed to meet a crazy sexy bitch named Micki, but that seemed to have fallen through so he was just mingling. Danny was really pissed off now and Evan wasn't sure what was going on. The crowd around Danny was quiet. He had just finished telling them about his date with Micki. She was probably wondering where he was by now he'd just said five seconds before. He'd said he should go and find her. He'd said she was the only girl he could even think about this summer. He now glared at Evan, speechless, humiliated. After several moments of uncomfortable silence, Evan said, "What dude?" Danny was sure this clown was just fucking with him out of jealousy and he informed him, "Micki is my date. You must have gotten the wrong idea somehow, she's very nice, I'm sure it was just a casual invitation; I don't know why you think she'd be meeting you here. I can't see that happening." Danny's voice was even measured. Evan laughed at the slight and said "Good one, real mature, well," He scratched his head before he continued. "...she invited me for sure, and I'm pretty sure she was flirting with me when she did it," he glared back at Danny, "and...if she's your date, you might want to tell that fucking guy downstairs who has his tongue down her throat and his hand up her ass." At this, Danny lunged at him but Evan moved out of the way. A couple of guys came and held Danny back as they told Evan he should go. Danny was screaming at them to let him go. They released him and he headed for the basement stairs. Evan flipped Danny the finger, and went outside, but didn't leave. He wanted to finish his beer. He grabbed another from a barrel of ice on the deck and sat in one of the chairs that faced the lake. He wasn't ready to give up on the event. He sat on the deck drinking his beer, enjoying being away from his new prison. He thought about Micki, "what just happened?" he wondered, "she's so fucking sexy, I'd fuck her silly. What will happen now?" His thoughts were scattered, the anticipation was killing him and he stayed alert listening for anything.

She went upstairs, unsure what to do with the feelings he had just brought out in her. She could find him and start again but she knew it would end the same way. It was the most responsive he'd ever been to her. He treated her like someone else, he'd marked her as his. More wine, she thought, and poured herself some. She didn't notice that Danny was no longer in the den, she forgot all about Danny. Her mind was racing. She was going to see Billy tonight after this party, and he would have to throw her out, or finish what he started. She was tired of playing this game.

Freddie had been warning Billy about "weakness." Micki was "too young," he had said, Billy shouldn't even consider "spending so much time with her. She'll hate you for it later." Tonight, Billy's defenses were down, the wine and the music, Micki looking so sexy in her little black outfit and high heels. Those lips, her mouth, she wanted him to kiss her, a lot, was it so wrong? He just wanted to ravage her. Show her the difference between a boy and a man. He didn't of course. Billy was a young man of strong character. That's why Micki liked him, he knew. She could explore her own feelings without the danger of assault, or even follow through. But he wanted to, more than anything else at that very moment. She didn't realize what she was playing with. He tried to keep that in mind, but he was afraid the damage was already done. He was losing control. He didn't need to drink so fast. He went back inside and saw she was gone so he had a girl named Cindy go up and get him some ice water. He knew she'd be back, and she'd be touching his shoulders and taking his hand, touching his chest, pressing her body close to him. Standing there, fucking gorgeous, tempting him, teasing him relentlessly. He needed a clear head tonight. "Where is that water?"

Micki was drinking more wine, and now she had to pee. The two ground level bathrooms were occupied so she had to go up the main stairs to get to the bedrooms. Bobby, her friend with the vintage acoustic guitar was sitting there with his girlfriend Anita. He had taken some microdot acid and was convinced he couldn't breathe. He was near hyperventilating. Micki told them she hoped he felt better soon, and then continued upstairs and found an empty bathroom. She had dropped microdot before with one of her many cousins in Talladega when she was only twelve, it was her fee for not ratting. She'd liked it. She wanted to do it again sometime. She wanted to do it alone. She liked being alone. She did it the first time alone, and was pretty sure she saw God. She hoped Bobby would see God too.

No way could she be with Danny, she thought, as she entered the bathroom. Not tonight, or any night. She didn't like Danny. She only came to be with Billy and she wished she had told Danny that before they ever came there. She was feeling a little drunk and was sucking her bottom lip into her mouth. She began to resent being there as his date. What the fuck is Billy doing? She thought. It was almost like he was rubbing Danny's nose in it. After washing her hands and patting her face with water, she went back downstairs to the mid-level kitchen and took a shot of peach schnapps off a tray on the counter and drank it. She put down the shot glass and grabbed another. As she drank, she began to feel looser. She wanted to dance. She went downstairs and started dancing to a song called "Leather and Lace" with a guy from her school. He seemed to be psyched that she was dancing with him and kept trying to put his hands on her butt. She had to stay alert to keep him off her body. There was an older girl talking to Billy, and it bothered Micki. She watched them for a moment and then walked over to where they were and put an arm on his shoulder and a hand on his forearm before she looked at the girl and then back at Billy. He was a coward she thought. He just kept smiling like an idiot and looking at the floor. The girl said "Oh, Okay" and walked away. Billy didn't seem to mind and reached behind her to squeeze her ass a little making her smile. She played with the hair at the nape of his neck, it was black and straight and neatly cut. When he leaned over the turntable again she kissed him just below and behind his ear. He stood up and grabbed her pulling her close and moving side to side as if they were just dancing close and he said to her. "If you were older, I'd be asking you some questions by now, but you're not and something bad is going to happen to you if you don't stop turning me on, I am just a man after all, just like any other man...Micki are you listening to me?" She was, he was acting weird again she thought, but then he grabbed the back of her head and kissed her mouth so hard she thought it might bruise or even break the skin on her lips forcing her mouth open wide to receive his tongue and offer him hers. He stopped kissing her after a few seconds but didn't move away keeping his face close to hers, looking into her green eyes, trying to connect with her so she would get it, his guard was down, he would not stop tonight. She of course, didn't care. "I'm coming over tonight," she told him and then ran upstairs before the next song ended, feeling a little bit panicked. Billy watched her go, pretending not to. He turned back to the turntable and took a deep breath while the girl she'd chased away found her way back over. She was talking but he couldn't hear her. He was about to play "waiting on a friend," he put it on the table and readied it for the change. He took a drink of his wine and hoped she would come back down, but she didn't this time. He decided that was probably best.

Micki noticed Danny was gone, and figured he was still entertaining. It was possible that some girl had taken him away from her. That would be the coolest thing that could happen tonight, she thought. She went into the den and sat on the lounge. Kena, an older girl from church who had befriended Micki right after the Jeff incident, was on the sofa with Jim. Jim was Jeff's little brother, he was about 25 at the time. He had served a couple of years in prison when he was just 21 years old for armed robbery. When he'd gotten out, he'd come looking for Jeff, and had stayed with Micki's family for a few days. Kena had started dating him a few months before that party, and they both seemed to be very happy about it. Kena would confide in Micki that she thought Jim drank too much, and they would regularly dispose of his alcohol. Kena was sure Jim was the "One" and she swooned over him all the time now when they would hang out and Micki had lately been confiding more of her own secrets to Kena, she was one of Micki's best friends even though she was 24. She smiled at her trying not to laugh as she dropped onto a huge chaise lounge already occupied by three other people. Micki leaned back and started watching "Casanova" or "Sex on the Run" on Cinemax. A friend named Shelley, that she knew from school, came up to her in the den and said, "Hey, didn't you come with Danny?" Micki told her she did, and then Shelley said "He's been asking people to find you and ask you to come outside, he's really pissed." Micki was a little drunk, she smiled as if she was confused and said "Really?" For some reason Micki thought this was funny. Shelley, who wasn't laughing, just stared at Micki wide-eyed. Micki thought she could pass for her mother's daughter. She looked more like Sara than Micki did; red hair, freckles everywhere, and everything else. Her blue eyes always seemed a little unstable. She said in a low-voice that wasn't quite a whisper, "he said he saw you kissing his brother." Micki sold weed to Shelley, and she sold weed to her brother but Shelley was never to find out. They had smoked pot together a few times but they were both committed to discretion, and here, Micki's date was making a scene. It was so uncool. She moved a strand of Shelley's dark red wavy hair from her face thinking her mother must have looked like that when she was young, and Shelley said in almost a whisper ". . . he's really pissed Micki." Micki took a deep breath and drained the glass of wine she had just poured. She set the glass on a table by the door and stepped outside feeling a little more than tipsy. Danny was out in the yard, hands folded, and leaning on his dad's car, glaring at her angrily. She shrugged and walked toward him. At first he didn't say anything, and then he told her to get in the car. She didn't move, but he went and opened the car door and glared at her impatiently. She got in and he closed the door and got into the driver's seat. He was smoking a joint and he passed it to her angrily. She hesitated a moment before taking it from him and taking a long drag. He asked her why she came to the party with him. He had seen her with Billy but didn't want to humiliate himself further by intruding and causing a scene and preferred to talk about it out here. She truly didn't have an answer. She hit the joint again. "Damn, I like you so much...you are not at all who I thought you were." He was leaning on the steering wheel and rolling his face from side to side. "Shit!" he screamed and hit the wheel with open palms. Micki started to talk but he cut her off, angrier now, "I could have brought any girl I wanted to this party, it didn't have to be you." He was staring out the window now. Micki said, "We're not dating Danny, go. Go and be with whomever you want, I don't care, I came to the party with you because Billy asked me too." He looked at her, shocked that she would make it sound like a charity date. "You are the girl I want to be with, I thought you wanted that too." Suddenly he had actual tears in his eyes. Micki couldn't believe he was so emotionally invested with her when she felt absolutely nothing more than friendship toward him. It was too hot in the car, she felt like she might pass out. She passed the joint back to him but he wouldn't take it. She laid it in the ashtray and got out of the car closing the door behind her. She was dizzy and leaned on it to catch her balance. The wine was making her woozy, and she needed fresh air. She breathed in deeply as Danny got out of the car, humiliated beyond repair. He walked around the car and leaned so close to Micki's face she could feel his breath and said, "I saw you in the basement kissing my brother, my brother Micki, you were all over him. Like a whore! You couldn't wait till I was gone? You had to do it here? Everybody knows! You made a fool out of me." It stung, and now Micki had tears in her eyes. "Well now you know how it feels don't you," she thought but didn't say it aloud. Instead she said, "Why can't you just go and have fun Danny?" He looked really angry. When he had arrived in Alabama he'd told them all he was "here to have fun," Now it seemed to him that Micki was mocking him, and maybe she was. Something flashed in her eyes and new anger flashed in his. She was afraid and trembling just enough to give herself away. She could still feel his breath on her face. She was nauseated. He was still leaning into her, like he was thinking about what to say, or do, next. Having experienced domestic violence as a witness to her mother's volatile relationship with Jeff, she was somewhat detached and had no inclination to fight with him. He was clearly as drunk as she was. People who had been outside were now gathering to watch them and he relaxed a little. She took that opportunity to break away and started to walk back toward the house but Danny grabbed her and snatched her back so hard she would have fallen if he hadn't had her by the arm. "Don't walk away from me, Micki." She couldn't believe what just happened. She looked around at all the faces watching them, so many people, she knew most of them. She'd sold weed and or coke to half of them, and some of them would never imagine she even smoked pot. He was holding her arms now so tightly she was sure it was going to bruise. He slammed her against the car and she saw Cameron in the crowd, just over Danny's right shoulder. Their eyes met cruelly, and then he was gone. Danny leaned in and said, "It's okay, we can still be together tonight, just don't do it again. Tell me you won't do it again." Micki had closed her eyes for reasons that had nothing to do with Danny and everything to do with Cameron but she said to him, "Danny, let me go, you're drunk, and you already did something a decent man would regret. Just let me go back inside." Danny put his head down and said, "With him? No. You came with me, you should be with me." He sounded weaker, almost beaten. Out of nowhere Billy showed up and told Danny that he was drunk and he should "Back off," but Danny only turned his rage toward Billy, who hit him once in the face. Micki didn't stay to see what happened next. Everything was spiraling out of control. Her whole life was unraveling. They'd be talking about this, about her. Everyone who mattered was going to know everything. She ran inside to the kitchen and taking a quick inventory of the bottles of liquor on the counter, grabbed a half full bottle of whiskey she figured was Jim's and went upstairs where the bedrooms were. She found Cal's room and locked herself in his bathroom. She cupped her hands under the faucet and let the water fill them to put her face in. She didn't rub because she didn't want to smear her make-up any worse than it already was. She opened her hands to drop the water and let it drip off her face into the sink for a minute. She took a hand towel from a rack and patted her cheeks under her eyes, careful not to touch her eyelashes, and then she patted her forehead and chin. She put the cover-girl stained towel on the counter casually and then sat on the floor. She took a drink of the whiskey straight from the bottle. Billy would be in trouble over this. Everyone heard Danny call her a whore, she just wanted to die. She was most sorry for Cameron; he was the sweetest one of all. Her first real crush, she had pursued him wildly. She still had a soft spot for him, still cared for him, but Billy made her feel something else. He was smart, and that didn't mean she thought Cameron wasn't. She felt ashamed for the way she'd let Cameron think everything was the same all this time, but she knew he already knew it wasn't. Billy, the top secret love Billy. The untouchable, but so available Billy. She took a drink from the bottle and set it down on the tile. She opened a cabinet to the left of the sink and took out a box she knew Cal kept stashed there. Inside the box she found what she was looking for. She took out the weed and broke a little up on the floor. She found a rolling paper in the box and managed to create a small joint. She put the rest of the weed back into the box after removing one cigarette from the pack that was in there along with a lighter to make it all burn. She closed the box and put it back under the cabinet before she lit the joint. She took deep drags and let the smoke drift slowly form her mouth while she was thinking. He's just twenty-one, he was only twenty the first time they kissed. It had been so sweet. He was gentle and caring, he was warm and inviting. When he kissed her, he made the world disappear, and she needed her world to disappear. It was an ugly world. She needed his kiss. She needed more. Why was it such a big deal? The rumors. The Jeff incident had been traumatic. She wasn't sure if she could endure being called a whore all over town again. She knew she was too young to be feeling this way. "I'm just a kid," she thought to herself and took another drink. By the time she'd finished the joint and the cigarette, the whiskey was gone and so was she.

After Danny went ballistic, Evan felt a little responsible, and excited, it was awesome he thought to himself. He stood in the shadows at the corner of the house and watched the two brothers argue. After Danny had made clear to Billy that he could "go fuck himself," by restating that point, Billy realized he wouldn't be able to make it all right after he'd admitted in the name of honesty that he'd been seeing her "some, a little" and Danny was furious that Billy had not disclosed that previously, and now he felt like a fool. Billy felt bad for hitting him, but it was too late. "You want her?" Danny finally asked angrily, "Take her." Danny got into a car with some girls, who had come to the rescue of his ego, and they left. Billy watched them drive away and then realizing everyone outside was still looking at him, went back inside to find Micki. Evan suddenly felt sorry for her. After his own experience with Jasmine, he felt a certain kinship to Micki. If he had known, he wouldn't have busted her out. He thought he knew how she felt. He didn't understand why Jasmine had gotten so jealous, mad enough to send him to prison over a little bit of sex. Or even a lot of sex, it was just sex after all. She'd liked the sex as much as he did, he knew, as well as the sex that included Candace, but for some reason when she found them doing it without her for just a second she'd lost her mind and ruined his life. "A fucking cunt," he had called her on his recent trip to Montgomery. Of course, no guy wants his girl kissing another guy. Micki was just confused. But he agreed, "Why couldn't they just have fun?" When it was quiet outside again, he got on his bike, and went home to masturbate.

When Micki woke up in Cal's room, the sunlight was shining through the drapes. She immediately noticed that she was naked. She vaguely remembered Kena turning the shower on her while she lay in the bathtub, her clothes still on. She couldn't remember much else after coming upstairs with the whiskey. She rubbed her eyes and sat up in the bed. Billy was sitting in a chair by the window. He didn't look as if he'd had much sleep. She tried to remember what happened that she would wake up with him like this. He didn't say anything. He just brought her a stack of neatly folded clothes, her blouse, skirt and panties from the night before, and said. "I would have dressed you, but it would have been wrong." She was so hung over she could barely sit up. He kissed her forehead and said "Get dressed, I'll be right back." He disappeared out of the room and she began to get dressed. When she was finished, she went into the bathroom. Billy came back in, walked in the bathroom with her, and sat on the counter. He was drinking ice water from a jar and offered it to her. "Drink" he said, "You're dehydrated from the alcohol." She took a big gulp from the jar and then went to the sink and threw water on her face, drying it with a new hand towel. Billy told her that Danny was "going back to New Orleans early, today in fact." Micki said she was sorry but she "just couldn't do it." Billy continued telling her that Kena and Jim had discovered her in the locked bathroom when they came up to Cal's room to make out. He'd been worried after she disappeared and waited around for her. When Kena finally got the door unlocked, they found Micki, lying in a puddle of vomit next to Jim's empty (save for the cigarette butt in the bottom) bottle of Jack Daniels. Kena, amused by the whole thing, had thrown Micki into the shower and taken her clothes off. She dried her with a towel and put her to bed. Billy agreed to sit with her, and Jim and Kena went downstairs to stop anyone from going into that room and to watch TV. While Micki slept, Kena washed, dried and folded her clothes. Having been informed of the emergency use of his home, Cal's dad was heard at the party making a joke about having a naked girl upstairs. It was all in good fun. The party went on well past day light. Billy had sat in the chair by the window, all night, waiting for her to wake-up. Micki listened to all of this without speaking or even looking at Billy. The events the night before had been sobering for both of them and they were still reeling in her head. She didn't know what to say yet. When she finally looked up at him, he was holding the empty bottle she had drank the night before and said "this is poison Micki, you could've died." He then asked her if she was "proud of herself?" She got angry, how could he ask her that. How could he, still, be so damn patronizing? She wanted to lash out at him. "This is your fault," she said, "You did this. You should have told Danny I was not the right girl for him when he asked you. You wanted him to see us, he always gets the girl and you wanted him to feel that." she accused him, "You wanted him to see, you danced with me, you kissed me, and that was not a brotherly kiss, Billy. It was dirty. It was great. Every cell in my body trembled when you touched me, but you did it this time, in front of everyone and you loved it. I'm not stupid and I am not a child! You didn't want anything to happen between me and Danny. What would you have done, if you had seen me kissing him? This is your fault Billy, just admit it! You never wanted me to be with Danny." He just sat there looking at her, still distracted by her mouth. Even angry and hung over she was still so sexy. She was dripping with an unintentional sexuality, unaware of her own power but testing it more and more. Now it was his turn to be speechless. She moved for the door saying "You are such a liar . . . I need to go home. You can preach to me later." Without knowing what else to say, Billy said "Fine," and followed her out of the bathroom, her words spinning in his head. He told her Kena was downstairs and was waiting to give her a ride. He gave her a short hug that she did not respond to, and told her she should go down first. He needed to think. "Right." She said, knowing full well he was ashamed of his feelings for her in the day light. She left the bedroom as he sat down where she had been sleeping. She wiped angry tears from her cheeks, and went downstairs.

Evan had gotten up early, oddly invigorated by the events of the night before. Feeling more confident, he decided he would visit Jenny. He could tell her about Micki's problems at the party. Play the concerned friend of a friend, and maybe get some information. When he got there, Jenny was in the back yard, helping her dad with the horses. She stopped what she was doing and walked out front to see what Evan wanted. Jenny thanked him for stopping by but told him Micki was a "big girl" who had been taking care of herself for some time now. The last thing Jenny needed to hear was how fucked up Danny was over Micki, but Evan could not have known that. As she started to walk away, he offered to help her finish her task in the yard. She just said, "That's okay, we're almost finished," so he asked her to come over to his house and hang out. He had gotten so lonely, and last night he had remembered how good it was to have friends around. He wanted Micki and Jenny to start coming over. He needed to figure out how to make that happen. She told him she might stop by later and then went back to start helping her dad finish getting the ground ready for a patio. They were placing the boards that would hold the cement. Evan went back home, sure Jenny would come over, excited to have some company.

Kena was in a great mood, she always was. Micki had never met anyone so happy. It was because she was overly emotional. She said she had a blast at the party. She was laughing and joking about cleaning up the vomit in the bathroom, and Jim's face when he saw she had taken his whiskey. Kena, wrapped up in Jim, had not been present for the drama with Danny outside the night before but had heard her upstairs yelling at Billy and asked Micki point blank what was going on between them. Kena's friendship with Micki was ageless; she always spoke to her like an adult. She didn't "have time for bullshit," she would say, "Life's too short." Kena would pick her up after school and they would do coke together, shop and talk about guys. It was a little weird when Kena started dating Jim, Micki was never sure if he would tell Jeff, and thereby her mother, about her secrets. He never did. Micki broke down and told Kena about her feelings for Billy.

Last December, just before Christmas, she had left her house in the middle of the night because Jeff and her mom were tearing up the house in a fight. She had just been looking for a quiet place to get some sleep. Jenny's parents would have freaked if she had shown up there that time of night, and Billy's was the closest house. She knew Billy and had no qualms about asking him to let her sleep there. He let her in; concerned that she would be out so late in the cold. He asked her why, she told him some of the truth, and he was sympathetic. They talked for hours about religion, history and literature. Billy had a record player, and lots of old cool albums. Pink Floyd, Heart, Led Zeppelin, he played them for her. She liked Pat Benatar and a really dirty song by a band called Berlin. She danced playfully when it played. She had told him briefly about the Jeff incident that night, something she rarely shared with people, mostly because everyone knew, but also because it was humiliating. Micki drank his wine and ate his food. He was a perfect host; he even made her iced tea when she asked. She told Kena how, after that night, she had been sneaking up to Billy's house a lot. She said that he seemed to be waiting for her after a while, and that although tired, he had been especially sociable at that time of night, that he was really interested in what she thought, and even asked for her opinion. He always made tea for her now before she even arrived. They had gotten into the habit of lying on opposite ends of the couch while they talked and he sometimes rubbed her feet when he was talking. Then eventually, a few weeks before, they were sitting on the floor together leaning against the couch watching a scary movie and he had kissed her, really kissed her. She'd dreamt about it a hundred times before, she said, but it was even better than that. Kena's eyes were wide as if she had been watching a movie, "What is he, like twenty-five?" Micki smiled and said, "Twenty-one." She said she had never met anyone like him, that he was amazing, and made her feel the most amazing things.

"He makes me feel wild and free. He was the one who started acting weird after the first kiss." And it was true. He had called it "a moment of weakness," and said he forgot how young she was for just a moment, and that he would "be a better influence in the future," but that, "it wasn't going any further." Since then, he just kept pushing her away, and she kept trying to recreate that night. "Last night," she said, "it could have been perfect," but it wasn't. "It was all wrong." They were sitting in Micki's driveway now. Kena leaned over and gave her a hug. Smiling sympathetically she said, "You, poor thing." Kena then told her that while Billy might be just as amazing as Micki thought he was, that she hadn't lived long enough to know if he was the one or not. That she had no one to compare him to, and Micki reminded her of Cameron and admitted she still had strong feeling for him as well. Kena said it was normal but that "while losing your virginity sounds like fun, it isn't neat. It's not like love stories in books," she told her, "and you should really consider the fact that if you have sex with him, it will make him a weirdo. It's called statutory rape. How will you feel about him then?" Micki looked out the window at her house and said, "I know. I don't care. I want to choose who I have sex with. I'm tired of feeling like a victim. It's pathetic. I can't explain it to you Kena. He makes me feel . . . , normal." "I'm not sure it's normal for a sixteen-year-old girl to want to sleep with anyone." Kena said frankly and looked at Micki seriously. Micki said, "Well. I don't want to be afraid of it, I know that. It's going to happen to me, Kena, I should choose when and where, and who, right?" Kena didn't say anything. While she understood Micki perfectly, Micki was still a child. It was a complicated issue. Snapping out of the drama, Micki said, "Thank you for helping me, and for being such a good friend, tell Jim I'm sorry about his Jack Daniels." Kena smiled at her and said, "I'm glad he didn't drink it, he's just too much when he's drunk." She was laughing again. Micki smiled back at her and said "Me too," and got out of the car to go inside.

It was quiet, and no one was home, Micki was grateful for this moment of peace. She went into her room to change clothes and lie down on the bed. Her mom would be home later and she was certain to be in deep trouble. Jeff would be gloating and worst of all, the party had come and gone and still she couldn't stop thinking about Billy. There was a knock at the front door. Micki got up and went to the hallway to go up the stairs to the living room and answer the door. It was Jenny. She came in telling Micki she had already heard about the party, "from Evan of all people," and that Evan seemed really concerned about her, inferring that Micki was mistaken about whom Evan was "in to." "Where is everyone?" she asked while she looked around. "I don't know," said Micki, "probably out buying my cage," she said without smiling. Jenny had followed Micki and sat down in the kitchen. She slapped one of Micki's story folders down on the table top telling her that her "grammar sucks, and there's no worry that you'll be a literary genius any time soon, therefore the world is safe . . . for now." She smiled wickedly and Micki unfolded her middle finger for her. She almost absently said "Heartless bitch." before smiling back at her, but Micki had a lot on her mind. She had a joint, and lit it. Micki got up and opened the back door so the smoke could escape outside. Then Jenny blew a shotgun for her. It was a thick stream of white smoke and Micki coughed a little before doing the same for her. They always got the shotguns out of the way first, because the joint got too warm on their lips when it was short. Micki sat down and passed the joint back to Jenny. "You really blew it with Danny," Jenny said, but Micki just glared back at her saying "not everyone is into Danny." Jenny put up a fight, certain that Micki really liked him but pretended not to because she knew about Jenny's feelings for him. Micki said, "Some of it was for you. I mean I was drunk and Bill and I were dancing, it was purely coincidental, But when he said that I made a fool of him, it felt good, I thought of you. I wanted to rip his heart out. I did too; it was located in his ego." Jenny was half-laughing, half-crying "That's so funny, I shouldn't laugh." "Yes you should." Micki couldn't take it anymore, and she finally told Jenny, "I'm in love with Billy." "What?" She asked. Micki smiled and said it again, "I'm hopelessly, and desperately in love with Bill. Is that dramatic enough for you? I want to have sex with him." Jenny got up and walked to the back door, blowing the smoke from the weed into the air. "You decided this last night?" she asked. Micki said, "Since Christmas." Jenny raised her eyes and looked at her quizzically. Micki said, "Okay. It was cold. I needed a warm place to sleep. You were a zombie. His is the next closest house." Micki was hitting the joint hard now. The way Cameron taught her to get high. She never held the smoke since he'd told her there was no point. It felt good to tell Jenny about Billy. All the tension that had been between them was gone as fast as it had appeared. "It makes sense," she said aloud to Micki, "I can't believe I didn't see it before. Why didn't you tell me?" "You didn't see it because he's older," said Micki. "And I didn't tell you because at first, I thought it was nothing. But then it just kept happening, I couldn't stop, but I didn't want anyone to think badly of Bill. You can't tell anyone. I remind you that you didn't tell me the whole truth about Danny until day before yesterday." She raised her eyes at Jenny. As it sank in, Jenny seemed to have an epiphany. "So that's why you didn't let me ride up front in the plane, you were being seductive." She said the word slowly and smiled. "Oh my god" Jenny said, "He's a pervert." "No," said Micki smiling, "I did it. I wanted him to kiss me, and he did. It was so sweet, but he's too freaked out by my age to go any further right now. I lead him to the water and he refuses to drink. You know?" "Oh," Jenny said, "Bummer, You know, Danny wouldn't have been so fickle." Micki shot her a dirty look. "It's not just the sex Jenny. I want it to be Bill. It's about the memory..." She rolled her eyes and threw her head back to stare at the ceiling when she spoke and then hit the joint again. "Is he a good kisser?" Jenny asked. Micki smiled and closed her eyes thinking about it. "It's incredible. I just want to touch him for hours. He's so firm," she said out loud. Jenny laughed hysterically as she took the joint and said "oh my god." and Micki giggled, showing her age.

Evan decided Jenny wasn't coming. He was bored, and lonely. In Montgomery he had been popular. Everyone knew him and liked him until he was busted. They would do whatever he asked. They all wanted something from him, something only he could provide, a certain validation that they were worthy. An invitation to his party had been like an invitation to the Playboy Mansion. All the finest girls were there, getting drunk and naked and whatever else he wanted them to do. He loved the power he had. On the lake, things were different. Everyone was tanned and busy. All the kids there were part of a tight-knit little group that he had been unable to penetrate thus far. His parents, who claimed they had closed the house on Bell Road, were spending an awful lot of time there. He would be alone for more than a week at a time. His dad told him it was just easier to get to work if he and Rita stayed in the city. Not that it mattered. The kids on the lake had no idea who his father was or how much money they had. Further, they didn't seem to care. He knew this was his exile. He missed Jasmine, he missed the sex. He wasn't sure why she couldn't get over the thing with Candace. He could forgive her for ratting on him, if she would just call and say she was sorry. She hated him now, and since the day he had tried to talk to her, he had been worried she would get him in even more trouble. He should not have slapped her. He regretted it, but at the time he couldn't control himself. He had gotten into the habit of calling her private line, and hanging up when she answered. He could hear the clock ticking and he decided to turn on the radio. He took Jasmine's picture out of his wallet and looked at the back. It read:

To Evan,
the love of my life, 4ever and always
love Jasmine   Age 16

He smirked and walked to the kitchen. He put the picture in the garbage disposal in the sink drain, and turned it on. "Bitch" he said out loud and turned the switch off again. He needed to find a way back into his dad's good graces. He wasn't going to wait for anyone any more. He decided to go and explore the lake. He went outside and started up the road. When he came to the bend that, to the left, went toward the lake road, and Jenny's house, he went to the right. This part of the road was barely used. He had seen Freddie, Billy and a bunch of girls, including Micki, Sophia and Jenny, taking a big raft down there a few days ago. Freddie had a jeep, and had backed skillfully down that incline, with the raft going first. Evan had noticed the little road before, thinking it would be fun to ride his bike on. Now was a good time to take a look. He walked down the steep twisting little road taking note of deep ravines that had been cut into it by rain running off into the lake. Because of the landscape, he couldn't see his house from here, but he knew that the slew with his pier was just on the other side. The road veered to the left, and then back to the right before ending at a drop off into the lake. He was happy he had walked here before bringing his bike. The distance to the water from the last turn was only about 20 feet, he might have landed in the lake had he been riding. The huge raft was tied to a tree, homemade from plywood and Styrofoam blocks underneath keeping it afloat. It was more like a floating dock. Sophia, her sister and some other kids from the lake, were playing on the raft. Jumping in and out of the water, laughing. They didn't look up to see Evan, and he didn't want them to. He noticed a trail that went into the woods off to his left. He started in that direction realizing that this must be a part of the trails where he had seen Jenny and Micki when they were riding the horses. There wasn't a soul here now, so he figured he should get to know the trails a little better.

Micki was starting to feel a buzz from the pot, and decided that if she cleaned up the house, she might be able to avoid some trouble. She didn't know what her mom knew at this point, so she and Jenny cleaned Micki's house. Jenny confessed that she now had a crush on Brett. Micki was completely grossed out by the thought of it. They laughed and Micki said, "He's so stupid, and he's such a pussy. Remember King?" Jenny laughed with her as they recalled the year before, when Jenny had spent the night with her one night. That afternoon they had caught a big old King Snake behind Micki's house, near the creek. He was surely over five feet long but he didn't like to stretch out so they couldn't be sure. She'd owed Brett. They had kept it in a huge glass jar but had taken it out to play with it. In the middle of the night, knowing how terrified Brett was of all snakes, they snuck in his room where he was sleeping and Micki let "King," as they named him, crawl across Brett's torso onto his chest. Brett had awakened in terror and at first didn't move but said "Get it off me," but then, as the snake got closer to his face, he jumped out of bed, backing and crouching into the corner of his room, screaming at them to "Get it away from me," But they just stood there laughing, holding the snake. All the noise had woken her mother and she came in and made the girls, and King, exit the room. They had put the snake back in the jar and covered it with pantyhose, telling him "night, night." The next morning the pantyhose were still there, but King, had escaped. They told Sara about it being loose. Sara told them not to tell Brett, but they told him anyway. Jenny had taken Brett's cigarettes that night. They laughed about it now, but Jenny wanted to "console him," she said smiling. Micki laughed at her and said she was "so bent," and that Brett was probably terrified of her. Micki would have told her more about Brett, but she just couldn't bring herself to spoil Jenny's mood.

Evan had followed the trail till he wasn't sure where he was. Several times the path had come to a cross section where he had to make a choice. He avoided the trails that were certain to lead him to the water as he was more interested in where the others might go. He had come to a deep quarry. It was an old quartz mine. There was a sign about trespassing, but he didn't want to jump the fence. The water was so clear he could see the rock bed at the bottom of the deep pool. More deep ravines like he'd seen on the road were here as well, too wide to jump across. This would be a good place to ride his bike he thought to himself. The elevation was higher here, and the air was crisp and fresh. He heard some people talking and moved behind the remnants of an old metal shed. Three guys about his age were jumping over the fence to dive in the quarry. One of the boys was Brett, Micki's brother, he was sure. He thought it might be cool to walk over and introduce himself. But that didn't work out so well at the party last night, and besides, everyone here wore shorts and no shirts. He thought it was clearly uncivilized. Dressed in his signature Calvin Klein black jeans and t-shirts, he stuck out like a sore thumb, but he wasn't about to change now. He slipped into the woods and made his way back to the trail that brought him here. He didn't want to risk being met on the trail the other boys had emerged from, but resolved to explore it later. Backtracking, he came to the last intersection he recognized, but wasn't sure which path he had come from before. He took the one to his right, and figured it would lead somewhere. A little way up the path, the trail crossed a dirt road. With more uncertainty, he crossed and continued to follow the path that continued there. There was a creek with big stones edging it every few feet, and piled in some places. A black salamander with white spots slid off one and jumped into the water as he walked nearby. That stream had to lead to the lake, he thought, and might be useful if he became lost. The trail turned a sharp 90 degrees to the left and Evan was getting nervous. When he finally came to the end of the trail, he could smell pot and wondered where it was coming from. He looked around and realized he was standing in thick woods, directly behind the back corner of Micki's house. He moved through the trail until he was at the edge of her yard. He never liked to smoke pot, it made him feel dirty, and it was a nasty habit. "Beer was better," he always said. Stoners were just too wrapped up in their own little lives and usually couldn't see the forest from the trees, he thought, laughing inside at his coincidental phrasing. Evan did realize that pot was a valuable commodity and when he had been burglarizing homes, he would always take the weed. He could sell it or trade it for something better, like cocaine. Now there was a drug. He could hear Jenny and Micki talking. He could see her back door from the trail, it was open. Careful to stay hidden, he moved further toward the back of the house along the edge of the woods. He could hear them a little better now, picking up a few words here and there. They were talking about someone, a guy. Evan wondered if they were talking about him. He thought it might be funny to jump out and scare them, but Jenny always acted like such a bitch, and he didn't want to be confronted by her again. He was embarrassed that she hadn't shown up today. He tried to move a little closer but was afraid they might see him from the open door. They were giggling and laughing, he supposed Micki thought it was funny that Jenny had stood him up. He sat down behind the house and tried to listen to them for what seemed like hours until finally, he clearly heard Jenny say she was going home.

Forgetting all about visiting Evan, Jenny left after making Micki promise to come and help her catch little pigs for her dad the next day. He had about ten of them, and they all had to get rings. They were just little things, but were rooting the fence line. Micki promised she wouldn't leave her to do it alone, and when Jenny left, she took a shower. Afterwards, she started shaping beef that had been thawing in the sink, to make a hamburger steak and gravy dinner for her mother, brother, and Jeff, if he made an appearance.

Jenny went out the front door and took the road. Evan took the trail that conveniently picked up on the other side of Micki's house. It led straight to the edge of the road and Jenny's yard. He watched her go inside. He saw her dad in the backyard and decided staying would be too risky. He knew he should go home, it was getting late in the day, but there was no one waiting for him. His parents wouldn't even call over a weekend like this. He went back to Micki's house, to watch her through the windows. When her brother pulled into the driveway with the same two guys he had seen at the quarry an hour or so later, Evan finally slipped back down the trail to Jenny's, crossed the road, and went back home.

When Jenny got home, she had some iced tea and remembered she had said she would visit Evan. She decided she would go and come back before it got dark. She headed the short distance downhill on the off road, around the bend, and she was there. She walked up on the patio and went to the French doors. One of the doors was open so Jenny went inside calling his name. There was no answer so she called out to him again. When he still didn't answer she started walking around the great room and she saw the food and drinks on the table. A bowl of ice had melted, and the sweat from the bowl was leaking off the table and onto the floor. She headed into the kitchen, "Evan, are you here" still, no answer. Jenny walked over to the sink and noticed the shreds of what appeared to be a picture of a girl. The shred was too small to tell much about the photo or why someone, Evan? Would have destroyed it this way? She wondered why his parents were never there. "This is just creepy," she said aloud. She stood there for a moment, wrinkling her brow. Jenny turned and went out of the house, quickly taking the left toward home. Fall was coming, the wind was picking up like it always did this time of year. Although the days were still unbearably hot, the evening heat had subsided somewhat. All the leaves on the oak trees were still green. Jenny wondered what had happened to Evan. Why would he make all those snacks and then just leave it there? It was too weird. Something about him was off. She was certain of it. She ran the last 20 yards to her front door and once inside, locked it.

Dinner was on the table, and Micki was reading The Exorcist in the living room when she heard her brother's car pull into the driveway. He was eighteen and after failing to pass, had recently quit school to get a job, supposedly to help his mom with the bills. Micki knew he just wanted to quit school and helping mom was a bribe for her to go along with it. Since then he had been pretending he was an adult and developed a tendency to get somewhat bossy with Micki. He came in the house, with two friends of his, James and Johnny. He marched right over to Micki and tore the book she was reading from her hands, he ripped it into pieces and threw them into the air. "What is your problem?" She screamed in shock. He pulled her to her feet, and started screaming at her about the party, someone had told him everything. He said she made a fool out of herself in front of everyone. Micki was humiliated that he would talk to her like that in front of his friends. Furious, she began to rail back at him. Micki's mom must have pulled in the driveway right after Brett, because she was now trying to get him to leave his sister alone. Brett was yelling and Micki started denying everything, "Who told you that? It never happened. You're a liar!" With that, Brett slapped Micki hard across the face, she lunged at him and he ran down the steps into the hallway to his room and locked the door. Micki, angry for too many reasons, kept hitting the door, calling him a pussy, until her mother made her go to her room. His friends were laughing hysterically as they left. Micki locked her door, turned on the radio and threw herself on the bed. Def Leppard's song, "Too Late" was playing. She loved that song and closed her eyes and let the music work its magic. When her mother knocked on the door later and asked if she was going to eat dinner, Micki told her to go away, that she wasn't hungry. Sara didn't want to believe that Micki had been at that party, it didn't sound like Micki at all. They had her confused with someone else, Sara had told Brett.

She was lying flat on her back not sleeping. She had turned off the radio so she could hear what was going on in the house. She heard someone say her name, "Michelle", a deep, monotone voice that seemed to be coming from someone next to her in the bed. She opened her eyes but could only see a light above her head, it seemed miles above her, everything else was darkness. The light seemed so far away. "Michelle", the voice said again, clear and closer. Startled, she jumped up quickly and ran out of the room. "Who's there?" She asked, but no one else was around. She figured she must have been dreaming, without realizing she had fallen asleep. She went back into her room flipping the light switch, and lit a cigarette from the top drawer of her dresser. She decided to count her money. All the drama at the party had distracted her from her routine. She took a treasure box from under some clothes in the bottom drawer and opened the lid. Inside she had a stack of cash totaling $2430. She had two more eight balls and about an ounce of pot. It was nearly time to pay Cal and re-up with Cameron, if he was still speaking to her. She was anxious and decided to visit Billy.

Evan had gone home. He cleaned up the food and melted ice on the coffee table and tried to watch some TV. He couldn't stop thinking about Micki now. She was actually perfect for him, he thought. He watched TV for a while and ate some stir fried rice from the freezer Rita had made. He went back to the TV and called Jasmines line again. "Hello?" She said in a sleepy voice and he just sat there. "Please stop calling me," she said and hung up the phone. He wondered if she knew it was him. A few hours later, restless and bored, he went outside and started walking down the lake road.

She quietly slipped into the kitchen and out the back door. The moon was full and it seemed more like a dark day than a bright night. She went up the road to the pasture. Unaware that she was being followed, she made her way across to the house, and knocked on Billy's door. A girl named Tammy opened it. Tammy was 20, and already had a baby from a relationship that didn't work out. She was supposed to get married, but the guy took off with someone else before the wedding. Tammy had the baby a few months later. Everyone said he was a beautiful baby, and hoped she would find someone new. Micki wondered why everyone seemed to think that Tammy had to "meet someone new" to be happy. She said hello to Micki and opened the door wide and let her come in. There were a couple of more women that Micki didn't know. Uncle Freddie was sitting at the breakfast bar with a bottle of wine and a glass in front of him. "You come to party with us, young Micki? Have a seat, have some wine." He was looking down at his cup and speaking slowly, but seemingly unsurprised at her arrival. Micki had the odd feeling she had been a subject of conversation tonight. Billy was sitting on the couch watching a girl who was clearly into him, dance. The girl seemed to be drunk and so did Billy. Micki took the seat next to Freddie and the wine that he offered her. He was watching her watch Billy. He moved in closer to her and put an arm around her shoulder, he smelled like sour wine and stale cigarettes. He told her "You know, when you're 18, you are going to have so many men all over you, you'll forget all about Billy. He knows that, you're so beautiful and sweet, that's why you're so hard for him to resist, it's killing him, you want him, but it isn't right, and when it is right, you won't want him." Freddie took her face in one hand and looked her in the eye to tell her, "When you're 18, you won't be safe around here...around me." Micki, startled by that comment, jumped up and said she had to get back home. Billy, seeing something in her eyes that told him this was it, last dance, went after her. Even though he knew he should let her go, he couldn't stand the thought of hurting her, it couldn't end like this. He was drunk and perhaps a little emotional himself. He cared so much about what she thought of him. "Why?" He wondered. He called out for her to stop and wait just as she was about to jump the fence to cross the pasture. She told him he shouldn't come after her. It would only make things worse. He had to run to reach her and pulled her back down off the fence. "Come on, we didn't finish our talk," he pleaded, "It doesn't look like we have anything to talk about..." she shot back. "You know Micki, you know my dad, he's just trying to help, he thinks I might have some sort of perversion for young girls, everyone has heard how I was 'molesting' you at Cal's house, Jesus Christ can't you see what's been happening here?" Micki told him she didn't feel like a child, that not since the incident with Jeff had anyone treated her like a little girl. Women didn't trust her with their husbands, the preacher wouldn't counsel her. Everyone treated her like a hot tramp except for him, she told him. "I just... I just..., I just want you...." She knew it was wrong but couldn't help herself. She broke into streaming tears and sat down in the grass. Billy sat down next to her and put his arm around her shoulders. She sat there crying but he didn't say a word, he just let her cry. She had somehow overcome the Jeff incident, but it was true. People did treat her differently he knew, he had heard the talk. He loved how strong she was. No matter what happened she was always the stable one. He understood that Micki had been through a lot. That she had matured emotionally in a way that girls with better homes didn't. She could also get the wrong idea in a way that girls with better homes didn't. Boundaries had been crossed. He knew she really felt something for him, and he really wanted to reciprocate. But that desire alone was enough to make him pause. What was it about this sixteen-year-old girl that made him want to throw caution to the wind and defy his own reason? He had never been attracted to women even as young as he was before, and now this sweet, neglected, virginal girl was making him weak, like he was the sixteen-year-old. He wanted to protect her, but from whom did she need protecting? If he treated her like a woman wouldn't she be horrified? He had shown her passion and patience, maybe even love. What would she do when he showed her pure lust and sex drive? Maybe he should, maybe the house of pleasant cards would crumble under the weight of the reality and the destruction of the fantasy. Maybe, or he might not be able to get over it at all, he might be fucked-up forever, and what would it do to her in the long run. He thought he knew what she wanted from him, he was pretty sure it was some psychological reaction to the Jeff incident. She was "safe with him." Text books were full of such theories. As for him, she made him feel needed, at a time in his life when nobody really did. He wished he had never kissed her that first time. It had made it so easy to kiss her all those other times. It was some sort of hero worship he was certain, but if he kept crossing the line with her, and was no longer a nice guy who wouldn't take advantage of her, what then? They heard Freddie and the other women laughing as they were leaving the house and getting into Freddie's car. Freddie was singing. As they drove down the driveway, Billy told Micki to go inside. "I don't want to." She began to protest but without looking at her Billy said, "yes Micki, you do, now go inside, get yourself together." She got up sniffling, thinking she actually could use a restroom right now. She liked the force in his voice and so did he.

Evan watched Micki go back inside the house after the other people left. He was astonished at the antics of this girl. Part of him knew he shouldn't be stalking her but the more he watched her, the more he wanted to watch her. When Billy went into the house, Evan slipped in a little closer. Moving around the back side of the house where he saw Billy through a window, sitting on a bed. Billy was staring out as if he were looking right at Evan, but Evan knew he couldn't see him for the trees that grew back there. Then he leaned forward with his elbows on his knees and his face in his hands. Evan crouched in the pine straw and waited to see what would happen next.

She went straight to the bathroom and threw water on her face. She had been crying so much lately, She said "You are such a fucking crybaby." to herself. In the mirror, she noticed the deep green in her eyes and realized she had never really noticed it before. They reminded her of the lake. Mascara was streaked across a red hue on one cheek where Brett had slapped her earlier. That was the first time he had ever done that. He had been such an asshole since the Jeff Incident. She looked flushed. Before, she had just wanted to die. Now, she just wanted to die in Billy's arms, from overwhelming emotional exhaustion. She used tissues to get the make-up off her face and left the bathroom. Billy wasn't in the living room or the kitchen. She went to the fridge and got herself some tea. She called his name and opened the door to his room. There he was, sitting on the bed staring out the window at the night. She knew him. She thought to herself, he was good. He worked with the horses, he had an associate's degree, he had a pilot's license, he came here to train horses. He was a nice guy and she wanted to monopolize his time, devour his mind. She wanted to carve him into her deepest, most precious memories, into her soul, forever. She crawled across the bed on her knees, leaned against his back and put her hands on his shoulders. He was so warm. She put her legs beside his and kissed his back. She put her hands inside his white t-shirt and caressed his skin slowly, raising the shirt so her lips could touch his spine. Billy was tired, he had been fighting this for so long it seemed. He could feel the shape of her body against his back. She was warm. Her hands were relentless, and he reached behind him to catch them, and bringing them to his lips, closed his eyes. What evil was it that made him feel so much strength and so little will power at the same time? He stood up and turned to face her. Before she could speak he pushed her back on the bed and kissed her more passionately than he ever did before. He tasted like sweet red wine and she loved the smell of his skin. This time he let his hands find her body, he slid them underneath her t-shirt to her waist and lower back. She moaned softly when he touched her, it thrilled him and he became extremely aroused. He grabbed her arms and held her down flat as he pressed against her hard so she could feel his full erection. He looked her in the eye and asked in an urgent voice, "Is that what you want?" and kissed her again before she could speak as he continued to press his groin against hers. She couldn't breathe, she wanted to, but she was frozen in the moment. She couldn't even close her mouth completely. All she could do was look at his sleepy eyes. The seriousness in his face, the way he looked at every inch of her as he touched her. Her chest was heaving from her breathing. He touched her face and kissed her gently before he released her arms and embraced her again saying close to her ear, "You make my dick so hard I can feel it crack, did you know that?" She couldn't believe what he just said to her and was shocked into breathing again. She tried to speak but only managed to moan softly as she ran the tips of her fingers through his short cropped hair and kissed his neck passionately. "Is this what you really want? Do you think you look like a kid to me?" His hands couldn't move fast enough over the frame of her body. He grabbed her leg, kissed her ankle as he slid his hand the length of it down to her thigh and wrapped it around his waist before descending on her again. "Do you even know what's happening here? I'm not made of stone. You don't know what you're playing with." She was caressing his back inside the waist of his jeans, barely audible saying, "Please, please don't stop. I need you, please." She kissed his neck and face. He was leaning into her kiss, saying, "Oh my god, I am so weak, you were right today, I am a liar. Everything you said was true. I'm not a hero, or a saint, or even a good guy. I'm just a man who wants you so bad I made an ass of myself." He said as he backed off to furiously pull down her shorts. She didn't try to stop him and he threw them on the floor. She already felt as if something was missing where he had just been; warm, on top of her and she said, "I don't care about that, it's what I want . . . you know I do . . . you know I want it to be you, I still love, because of you." She was breathing harder now and she thought her heart might burst through her chest. She was scared, but only of the unknown. She felt as if Billy would do everything right. She didn't want to stop. She had never seen Billy act in such a way, even at the party he had been somewhat reserved, and it was thrilling and frightening all at once to see him like this. She liked it. She got up on her knees to tear at his t-shirt, and pulled it over his head to let it fall to the bed behind her. Again he pressed himself against her warm body. He could feel her hands all over his back, in his hair, on his chest and stomach. He grabbed her ass in both hands, then lifted her and pushed her back again. He found her hands and held them down above her head as he kissed her neck, and then her throat. She cried out and he smothered her mouth again with his. He slid his hands beneath her back and lifted her until she was nearly sitting up. She tugged at the button of his jeans and his kiss became more urgent. She had never felt so light before. Micki told him she had never wanted anything so much in her life than to have him make love to her right then. He had to be the one. It had to be now. He pulled her to her knees again and helped her out of her t-shirt to reveal her bare breasts, pausing for a moment to look at her body. Up on her parted knees, only in her panties, she was just too sexy. He had seen her naked before. She had stripped in front of him once, thinking that alone would destroy his resolve. He hadn't really looked at her then, but he was looking at her now. That was not the body of a child. With her long hair scattered all around her shoulders, hanging straight down her back. She stood up on the bed and turned around for his pleasure. He found it impossible to believe she was just sixteen years old. Sixteen, his brain kept screaming the number inside his head but when she pushed her hair back behind her ear he gave in to her warm, smooth skin, and pulled her down to press his body and his mouth hard against hers in yet another moment of passion. She loved the way his bare skin felt against hers, she was in ecstasy. She wrapped one leg around his and put a foot down on his calf, sliding it back and forth in an unconscious motion like a cricket singing. He lifted her body up just slightly by the small of her back to hold her groin firmly to his and began kissing her breasts. She put her hands on the side of his head and told him she felt "the most amazing sensations," like being more stoned than she had ever been. He pulled away and ran his hand from between her breasts down slowly across her firm stomach and to the edge of her panties and put his hand down between her legs and let it rest there for a moment before turning her over to kiss her back and neck. He pulled her up in front of him and took her hair in one hand and kissed her shoulders. She leaned back into him and he dropped her hair taking a breast in each hand still kissing her neck the whole time. He pushed her down on her back again and fell on top of her in a fit of passion. He put his hands inside her panties now touching the skin on both ass cheeks. She was so fucking soft. He wanted to take those panties off, to taste her, to make love to her, to make her feel all the things it is a woman's right to feel. He knew that if he continued he would never stop. If he made love to her tonight, it would be every night, once would never be enough, not for him. How would that work? He hadn't yet satiated this moment and he was already anticipating the next." I'm a fucking grown man dammit," he said to himself, furiously kissing her body. She didn't know. She was too young to understand what it meant to be in an adult sexual relationship. She was just playing, experimenting. He felt an aching in his gut. He couldn't. He groaned, frustrated, and collapsed on top of her, wrapping his arms and legs around her so tightly she couldn't move and could barely breathe, he was nearly out of control when he groaned loudly and tore himself from her arms, erection bulging in his unbuttoned jeans, and left the room, saying "Get dressed," as he slammed the door behind him. Micki just lay there, breathing heavily, stomach quivering, hoping he would come back, even though she knew he wouldn't. She began to cry a little as involuntary tears rolled down her cheeks. She touched her lips with the tips of her fingers. They were still stinging from the friction of his kiss. Beads of sweat had formed on her lip and the brushed it away. After a little while, she got up and put her shorts back on. She found her t-shirt and then sat on the bed. His bed, the bed she would never share. It was over.

Evan was still watching Micki through the window. Aroused by what he had just witnessed. Her naked body was just fucking perfect he thought. The t-shirt she was wearing was slutty, and those cut-off shorts, hip huggers from the 70's to start with, were just rags. He knew she didn't like to wear a bra, but her tits were big and firm, it was like porn watching her walk around in daylight. He couldn't believe the way she dressed. He couldn't believe he had just watched them like some freak, but he felt a thrill a lot like the one he got when he was burglarizing homes, and no way could he stop now. When Billy had come outside to catch one of the horses, he almost walked up on Evan as he made his way to the fence behind the trees. Evan was so caught up in watching Micki; Billy was almost on top of him before he heard him whistling. Evan moved just in time. Billy, in a world of his own, went over to the fence and climbed up on the bottom rail, let out a louder whistle and a dark horse the color of mahogany ran up to him. Billy grabbed the horse's mane, threw one leg over the barrel, and then rode off toward the stable. Evan had to pass the stable and the barn between the pasture and Micki's house when he had crept behind her. Evan was thinking what a wuss Billy must be. He said "pussy" out loud as he watched him ride away. He was now excited. He wanted to give Micki what she wanted. She cried! He hadn't had sex since he'd moved here, and it seemed to him that Micki at least, was open to the idea. She was a beautiful girl and a sex kitten. She knew a lot of people too. Tonight was no good of course, not like this. She had to want him too. He moved into a better position to see the window, saw Micki sitting on the bed dressed again, and waited.

She finally pulled herself up off the bed. She went outside and saw him in the moonlight, riding one of the horses in the pasture, he was so beautiful to her and the sight of him like that stirred familiar pangs that were almost unbearable. Simulating a barrel race, he was riding bareback in only the jeans she had only managed to unbutton. She was sure now that he had told her the truth. If she was just a couple years older, she'd have to beat him off with a stick. She'd liked that side of him, but decided if he could break away at the moment he did, then he might never give in to her. Tempting him further would not make it happen. He had shown her strength. She stood there watching him until he rode over to the fence, held out a hand to her and told her to get on. She did as he asked without a fuss. She wrapped her arms around his waist tightly but didn't say anything. She just lay her head on his back. They took the long way around the pasture to the gate on the farthest side and made the trip down the driveway. It was a long easy ride walking the horse in the moonlight and Micki was grateful for what she was afraid would be their last intimate moment. The dirt road was dry and dusty, but seemed wet in that light. Micki wanted to say she was sorry, but she wasn't sure what for and wasn't even sure that she was sorry. The desire she felt for him was still very much alive inside her. Billy pulled on the reigns and the horse stopped at the edge of the woods just out of sight of her house. She kissed the back of his neck before getting off and started to say something to him but he stopped her and told her that if she still wanted to tell him in two years, he couldn't wait to listen. He turned the horse around and rode away. Micki stood there for a few moments watching him before she crept up to the back door, snuck back inside the house to her room and fell into her bed.

Evan watched them take the horse down the driveway before he went inside the house. He went straight to the bedroom to look for something, anything of hers. But there wasn't anything. He sat down on the bed and picked up the pillow she had lain on. He bunched it in his hands, held it to his face and breathed in deeply. It still smelled like her. He got up and left quickly so he could take a shorter route to the trail behind the stable. When he reached the edge of the trail he saw Billy coming back toward the stable. He watched him put up the horse and cross the field back to his house. He thought he might want to kill him, but wasn't sure yet. He admired Micki for her stealth and fearlessness. It would be intense to break a girl like that. He was going to go all the way for Micki. Resolved, he went home. Everyone was so normal, but Micki had secrets. When he had first met her, she'd seemed so ordinarily young and dumb. But now, he understood that Micki was not just any girl. She had a dark side. He liked that about her, and began to devise a plan to get her focus aimed at him. How hard could it be? This was red neck hell, and Micki clearly had taste. Jenny didn't seem to trust him and she might interfere. He might have to think of a way to come between them, he wanted Micki for himself now. He wanted her. He needed her. She would make him feel better. She had to.

Billy rode the horse back down to the stable and put her in the barn. He felt dirty, like an animal. To think what he wanted to do to that girl, what he almost did. She really was right. He had been honest with her about that. He didn't want her to be with Danny, or anyone. At the party he had been so worried she would actually like Danny, and never look to him again. He was thrilled to see her come downstairs without him. Maybe still, deep down, he did want Danny to see them together. He had kissed her long and hard, and it hadn't stopped at a kiss. Plenty of people saw it. She was right about him. He was a liar. He was in love with her, or as close as he could get to being in love with a girl her age. Although she looked the part, he knew she still had the mind of a teenager, no matter how well she hid it. If he had finished her tonight, she would have hated him years from now when she finally grew up. That's what

Freddie said, it's what Billy told himself. Maybe she was going to hate him for the things he had already done. That thought made him sad, it had been exquisite. He began to think maybe he should go back to New Orleans, but he knew he wouldn't, he couldn't, not yet. It wasn't finished, not while he still couldn't stop thinking about her. He had lived with his girlfriend while he was in college in Lafayette. They had been in love. She was beginning her third year when he met her. He was enrolling for the next semester. It had been a torrid love affair, "full of passion and bullshit," he liked to say on those rare moments when he actually talked about it. When he earned his Associate's degree the following year, she was being awarded a BA in Behavioral Science. She had graduated Cum Laude and was offered a job in New York. She was so excited about her new job, she forgot to be sad about leaving him. He had intended to go back the following year, but ended up in Alabama taking some time off instead. If nothing else, his adolescent affair with Micki was healing his wounds even if she was merely creating new ones in their place. It was new, fresh, he felt alive. He made his way to the house, went inside and took a long hot shower.

CHAPTER 5

"We loved with a love that was more than love in our kingdom by the sea". ~Edgar Allan Poe

School started the next week and except for Toni, who still wasn't ready, according to her mother, all the girls wanted to go together the first day. Sophia had, by then, been given her mom's old car, and they unanimously decided it was better than the bus. Micki had spent the night with Jenny and they got ready at her house. When Sophia showed up they smoked and laughed in Jenny's room until it was time to go. They were all excited about school.

When they pulled into the parking lot, lots of people they knew were there. It was "greet time" and they all got out to speak to someone they hadn't seen much over the summer. Micki went straight to Sam, who was still sitting in Cameron's car. She said hello to Cameron, but he was a little standoffish. Sam got out and he drove away. Micki walked with Sam but was only half listening to her. She was really concerned about Cameron. Things were getting weird, she thought. She'd never felt so wrong and out-of-control before.

Micki noticed Evan in the hallway and smiled at him. He caught up to her and walked her to her first class trying to think of something to say in order to strike up a conversation. She seemed sad, but thanked him for walking with her, and disappeared inside the library. Evan was a senior and his classes were on the other end of the school so he hurried off in that direction telling himself he would offer her a ride home at the end of the day.

Micki was a smart if not a good student. She was rarely challenged by her teachers and they knew it. She had lost interest to a certain degree. Still, she took pride in being an A student without much effort. She made the occasional B that was due to a lack of effort, but she was destined to graduate early. There were kids in her classes that did nothing but study, the smart kids, she and Jenny called them, but Micki was always first. Her papers and tests were always handed in first with a high degree of accuracy on the material. Micki liked that idea that even stoned she had more memory power than some of the most diligent kids in her school. Micki liked to read a lot. She read her textbooks for fun, but not always the assigned material. It paid off in the classroom either way. She could talk about the subject at hand and was happy to do so. She was excited about being back at school, she did enjoy the atmosphere. Micki would sometimes skip classes in the library posing as an aid. Even the principal thought she belonged there. There was no better day to do it than the first day she decided. Micki was writing a story about the school, a scary story as a gift for her friends at Halloween. It was called "Demon High." In the story, the teachers became possessed by demons, of course, and she was going to hand it out a chapter at a time, in separate folders. The library provided a quiet place to write. Her friend Teresa was back this year. She didn't live on the lake. Her dad was in the Air Force and hers and Micki's friendship only existed at school, but it was a good one. Teresa was a happy teenage alcoholic, and brought vodka to school every day in her thermos. She came into the library and shook the thermos with a smile on her face in Micki's direction. She always shared with Micki the year before, and she learned to skip in the library from Micki. She liked to read, or catch up on homework. Sometimes, Danny, a football player who liked to flirt with them, would join them for some vodka as well. He was the real library aide. His mother was a nurse who taught student nurses. She had been trying to get Sara enrolled in classes so she could get a better job. Danny was very popular, but few people knew him the way Micki and Teresa did. His image was as safe with them as theirs was with him. Many people in that area worked at the military bases in Montgomery, and there were kids born in Germany, Iran and Turkey who attended that school. One girl, Katie, whose dad was a fed, always had really good weed. She had just moved there from Germany when her dad had changed careers from the military to the DEA, and she and Micki hit it off immediately. Micki liked people and culture and she was a friend to most everyone who wanted her friendship. The year before there had been a small skirmish at the smoking area, but just that once. A girl named Tina who was Brett's age, as well as his friend, was threatening a girl named Jamie. Jamie was Anemic and fragile. She had always been sickly. Jamie was also a long-time friend of Brett's. Micki interfered and told Tina the only way she would ever lay a hand on Jamie, was to come through her first. At that moment, another girl named Ella, who had always been the school "bad ass," stepped in with Micki and told Tina there wasn't going to be any "ass kicking" going on that day. Tina backed down. That was it since middle school, when she and her friend Shauna had fought daily in the sixth grade until they became good friends.

Evan waited in the parking lot after school but Micki never came out. When he saw Jenny and Sophia walking toward Sophia's car, he ran over to Jenny and asked her where Micki was. Jenny informed him that Micki checked out early, and why did he want to know. Evan offered Jenny a ride, but she just looked at him like he was out of his mind. "Right." he said, and went back and got on his bike wondering why Micki checked out. He pulled on the fingerless gloves his dad had given him, and started his bike. Nobody wore a helmet around there, and neither did he. There was so much he didn't know about Micki, what began as curiosity, was becoming an obsession. He had asked around about her but nobody really told him anything, "Yeah, she's sweet," or "Yeah, she's pretty hot this year," was not the kind of information he was looking for.

Kena knew that Micki had been depressed since her episode at the party with Billy and Danny, so she decided school would probably be a drag. She waited until lunchtime, locked her desk and then went to pick up her young friend. Even though Jeff wasn't really married to Micki's mom, since Kena had been dating Jim, she liked to think of herself as Micki's aunt. That's what she told the office lady when she went to check her out of school. When she got into the car, Kena handed her a vial of the coke Micki had sold her at the party. She was happy to see her and took a bump. Kena informed her they would be shopping for the rest of the day, and perhaps have some drinks later in the afternoon. Kena worked for her father, and didn't have many friends. She had met Micki at church where her parents went. She had been raised in that church and knew everyone there, but could hardly stand to go any more. Everyone was such a hypocrite. Micki was always available for her when she needed a comrade, which was often over the last year. She liked being a friend to Micki, it made her feel needed as well. She asked Micki how she was doing and she said she was okay but still wanted to have sex with Billy, "if that's what you're asking." She finished laughing. "I'm not 'cured' or anything." Kena laughed and said, "I'm not sure there is a cure." Micki told her about Billy's unexpected visit the day before. He told her he had waited up for her every night that week to be sure he wouldn't miss her, but she never came. Concerned, he had stopped by to see how she was doing, or just to see her. He said he missed her. Micki missed him as well but hadn't told him that. Her mom had been there and was more than a little curious as to why this obviously grown man was visiting her daughter. As strange as it seems, Billy actually looked older than twenty-one. It had been awkward. To lighten the moment, Kena laughed and said, "Damn Micki, he's sick with it, what are you doing to this man?" But Micki just stared out the window. "Maybe you should visit him again, give him some closure, let him off the hook." "No." Micki said, "I don't want to let him off the hook, that's what you do with fish you don't intend to eat." At this, Kena burst into laughter and told her to just give him a blow job then and really sink her teeth in. Micki laughed deeply at the visual. After a few hours of shopping at the mall in the city, Kena drove to her parent's house, and they drank tequila. Kena's dad had one of the coolest lakeside stone patios ever constructed by man. Kena worked as his secretary but dreamt of much more. Kena shared Micki's interest in the macabre and religion. They usually had a lot to talk about, but today, Micki and Kena sat there watching the sun set, talking only about Jim and Billy. Micki talked to Kena about Cameron, and to Kena, Cameron sounded like the one. Micki didn't want to hurt Kena's feelings, but Jim was an alcoholic like Jeff. Any future she had with him was uncertain. She loved Kena, but never took her advice when it came to boys. She never took anyone's advice about boys. She was raised by her father to have her own opinion, and that it was always a legitimate one, because it was hers. The lake was calm and peaceful that afternoon. Micki said she needed to get home before anyone else, but called Cameron and asked him if he wanted to come by and get her high. Kena, a little tipsy from the tequila, told her she was "wicked and shameless." Micki said she knew "all about it." Kena dropped her off at home with a hug goodbye and hurried back to have dinner with Jim and her parents.

Evan had been waiting on the trail for a while when the blue 280Z pulled into Micki's driveway. Finally, he thought, crushing out the fire on his cigarette in the pine straw, wondering what awful thing she had been out doing today. His mind had been wandering. He had gone to Billy's but no one had been there. All afternoon it had been eating at him and he finally settled down on the trail to wait for her. It was getting late now, and the sky was a periwinkle blue. He had watched as all of three cars had come down that road in the last hour and a half; Jenny's dad coming home, Jenny's mom coming home, Jenny's mom leaving again. That had been it. He saw her get out of the car and he felt excitement setting in. He couldn't believe he was doing this, but didn't want to stop, couldn't stop. She was standing there, talking to the girl in the car. Then she closed the car door and started walking toward the house. Evan put his face down on the ground. What am I doing? he thought to himself and rolled over facing the sky through the canopy of tree limbs. Micki let herself in the house. Kena went around the drive, and turned back down in the direction she came from. Evan was about to get up and leave when a green pinto pulled into the drive, and Micki ran back outside and got in the car. Evan rose up on his elbows like a commando. The car didn't start up or drive away. They just sat there. It irritated Evan that he didn't understand what he was looking at, but this was just one more guy Micki appeared to be fucking with. He had to fight the urge to go over to the car. He lit another cigarette and waited.

At first, Cameron didn't seem to want to talk to her, but when Micki asked him to come and get her high, he said he would. He related to Micki easily. She knew a lot about music. She knew the words to all the good songs. She wanted to get high, and he was happy to go there with her. He wondered if her mother would ever let her go out with him. He wondered if she would. The party, it all had to be a misunderstanding. He realized that he should have stuck up for her, he wanted to apologize, but if she was upset about it, it didn't show. He didn't want to just have sex with Micki. She might be "the one," he had thought many times. A serious relationship can take years to develop, he had read, and since Micki was still young, they had plenty of time. They never talked about that night, the year before, when she started all this, or anything else that was between them. He wasn't sure she was ready, he wasn't sure he was. It was more than a year ago now. He had been very drunk, but when she got into his lap, he felt things he didn't think he'd ever forget. She had startled him. "It's not every day you realize your little sisters friend has taken your balls," he had told a guy at work once. He had passed out, but he hadn't forgotten. He just didn't know how to bring it up and she never did. But now, that shit at the party, he was starting to feel like he might miss his chance. She had become even more beautiful since then, and he wondered if she knew. She wasn't like other girls. She could talk about a lot of stuff, so he never knew what she was thinking. Micki wanted "more," and though he had no idea what that would mean later, he was willing to wait it out, see how it ended. He was patient. If she decided that she wanted to take their relationship further, he would be there. If not, that would be okay. He had plenty of girlfriends, but there was only one Micki, he thought. The kiss last week had been awkward he was sure, and he hadn't heard from her since. He had waited with Sam that morning, mostly so he could see her. He wanted to confront her and then decided he might be wrong about everything. When she had walked toward his car that morning, he changed his mind, and just wanted to leave before he said something stupid. But she called him today. Today, she was his, just for a little while. He had two joints rolled and offered her a shotgun which she accepted. She leaned a hand on his chest as she took it in, and he fell in love with her all over again.

To Evan, it seemed Micki was over in the driver's seat making out with this guy. His heart was pounding in his chest, he was sure anyone could hear it. Then she sat in the passenger seat again. They were talking and then she did it again. The car window was rolled down about an inch and smoke streamed out of it. They were getting high. Evan was disappointed. He knew she smoked pot, but the loser in the pinto was almost too much to bear. He put his face down, but had to look back again, he couldn't stand it.

She told Cameron she was cooking dinner for her mom while they smoked a second joint. He had a new sticker on his dash that read, "Ass, gas, or grass, no one rides for free." When Micki noticed it, she suddenly stopped talking and looked at him with narrowed eyes and a funny grin. He seemed embarrassed, but said he thought it was funny. Cameron wanted to tell her how he felt, but again, he just sat there wondering how she couldn't know, wishing she would kiss him again, wanting to kiss her. Some days, like this one, the urges were harder to conceal. She must have sensed something because she suddenly stopped talking about the night at Juanita's house, and told him he was one of the sweetest guys she ever met. She kissed him on the cheek and then just got out of the car. He hoped it wasn't for the last time. Cameron really liked Micki and he was content with her friendship. He was afraid, if he made any more moves on her, that she would reject him, and he would lose her friendship. If he was down, he could spend five minutes with Micki and feel great. He would be cooler from now on.

After the Jeff Incident, Micki had begun to hate Sara a little. Jeff had convinced Sara that Micki, maturing, had come on to him, and upon his rejection, ran away in shame. He had told his entire family and circle of friends the same story. Jeff said that Micki needed counseling. That she had a thing for older men and she was going to be raped if Sara didn't get it under control. That's why Sara had stood at the door watching Billy like a hawk the day before. Micki hated the way it looked. Jeff was an asshole, but he wasn't stupid. Sara had been looking at Micki differently since then. As if she didn't really know her at all, maybe she didn't. Micki was sure it wasn't her mother's fault. She had said so numerous times to her own friends. Micki just didn't want to have to think about it anymore. Micki fooled her mother easily, and had for a very long time. That's why her mother couldn't believe her now. She put "Toys in the attic" on the stereo, a record she had borrowed form Cameron long ago, and went down the steps into the kitchen. She pulled some pork chops out of the sink and set out making dinner. She had been feeling so strange lately, she couldn't explain it, as if she had forgotten something. When dinner was finally ready, Micki wrapped it all up in aluminum foil, and left it on the table. She was suddenly and uncharacteristically tired. She went into her bedroom and turned on the black light on her dresser. She found the cool, dark, blue light to be soothing. What had just happened with Cameron? She wasn't sure. She knew how much he liked her now, but wasn't sure how she could be so in love with Billy, as she was certain she was, and still feel the things she felt with Cameron. She felt bad when she thought about that kiss. Was she leading him on? This was all so confusing. She lay all the way down on the bed and as her head hit the pillows, she was suddenly paralyzed. She couldn't move. To her left she could see a cloaked figure, chanting something she couldn't understand. It was moving toward the foot of her bed. She couldn't scream, inside she was struggling but her eyes were working fine, she kept trying to adjust her vision, to scream. "This is an illusion!" Her brain kept screaming. She couldn't move or speak. The figure was taking sparkling dust from a pouch and tossing it on her body as it passed by. She continued to struggle and just one second before she would have seen the face of this mysterious figure, she was free. In one motion she came up off the bed and was out of the room. She opened the door so fast it had bounced off the wall and back into the frame with a slam. Once in the hall, Micki turned back to the door of her bedroom, and put her hands on the door. Her heart was pounding and she was breathing very hard. Slowly she turned the knob and opened it. The electric blue light filled the hallway and she stepped inside. How long had she lain there before she couldn't move. It seemed like it had only been a few seconds.

No longer tired, she wondered what had just happened to her. She wanted to research it and find out if had happened to anyone else but there were no books to read that she knew of, no reports. If she mentioned this to anyone, they might think she was crazy. What if she had a tumor? She lit a cigarette and went out the kitchen door so her mother wouldn't smell it, but there were no cars in the driveway. Her mother was a staunch non-smoker. She loved to brag about it. She didn't drink either. Micki liked to smoke, her grandfather smoked, and he was awesome. She understood why some people didn't drink, the taste was terrible. Micki had never been able to drink beer or much liquor without being sick afterwards. She did like wine. She had grown up drinking it with dinner at her grandparents' house. It was also the remedy for any headache or body ache she had while at their house. They had a farm, and when Micki was there, she worked on the farm, drank homemade wines and brandies and read books by the fire with her grandmother till the wee hours of the morning. This was one of the few summers Micki hadn't gone there for at least a week. It was because of Billy. She went to the edge of the woods at the back of the house and sat down on a log that had broken there. Maybe it was the tequila she thought. She had only tasted it recently with Kena, and hadn't had enough to be sick from it yet. She knew that tequila wasn't the same as other liquors. She had read that it was made from a drug. Maybe that's why she had the delusion in her room. Her mom's car pulled into the circular drive. Micki put out the cigarette, and rushed back inside to her room before her mother could unlock the front door. She no longer wanted to talk to her mom. She wondered if things wouldn't have been better in North Alabama.

CHAPTER 6

"Zoom, Zoom, Zoom. As I sit in my Four-Cornered Room." ~ WAR

Over the next few weeks Micki tried very hard to stay away from Billy. Busy with school and Friday night football games as well as other school functions, she was grateful to have something to take her mind off of her unrequited love. When she ran into him at the stables she would say hello and leave it at that. It was excruciatingly difficult. She knew by the look in his eyes that he was still thinking of her. He took a little too much time sometimes, helping her with the saddle and other tack. He seemed tired, beaten. He told her he missed her once, but she pretended not to hear it. He never spoke to her about it again, and she never asked. She wanted to be normal, just for a little while. She was still trying to decide how she felt about Cameron. At school Micki, Sam, Jenny and Sophia, had taken to calling each other "bitch," as a pet name. This year, Sam had been hanging with them more at the smoking area, a courtyard at the center of the school surrounded by classroom windows where teachers could watch them. It was also by the basement entrance. The caretaker knew they all got high and wouldn't tell if he caught them smoking weed on the steps that led down to the furnace. It was a great spot. One day Micki was going to be late for class, because she was going to finish her cigarette. Sophia and Jay were still embraced against the brick wall, unable to tear themselves away from each other. Brett's friend Tina, perhaps a little pissed at Micki's interference the year before, came out after the bell rang. She walked up to her and said "give me a light bitch."

The tone in her voice irritated an already uptight Micki and she slapped the cigarette out of Tina's hand. Tina tried to take a swing at her but Micki grabbed her wrist and twisted it behind her back. She wasn't sure why she was really doing it, but told Tina, "You don't know me, don't ever talk like that to me again." Suddenly, Coach Johnston, who must have seen from a window, was pulling Micki off Tina, who was clearly surprised at the force she'd used. Coach told Micki to go to class, and then looked after a shaken Tina. Sophia and Jay were giggling. Sophia whispered, "Kick her ass Micki," as she walked by and Micki almost laughed, though she didn't really feel that way. Sophia was too much fun. Micki was coming unglued.

Sometime in late September the police came to the school and picked up a clean cut, A-Class senior named Steve Sawyer. He dated a girl named Kelley that everyone knew. They were both very popular, homecoming king and queen their junior year. As has been said, they all partied together. He was a star athlete on the football team and everyone knew he was university bound on a full-ride scholarship to Alabama. The days before he had gotten into an argument with Kelley on the way back from a gathering at the lake. Steve had a few beers that day but no one had thought he was drunk. They, and Steve's best friend Mark, had pulled off to the side of the road because his driving was becoming erratic and Kelley wanted out. Steve and Kelley had gotten out of the blazer and they were arguing. Many rumors and speculations circulated later on about what they argued about and what happened next. Some said she was pregnant and wanted an abortion, some said she was pregnant and the baby wasn't Steve's, some said she just wanted to break up; the story seemed to change often. Whatever the conversation, Steve had beaten her to death with his baseball bat that afternoon while Mark watched in horror. Two days went by before he couldn't take it anymore and told authorities what Steve did and where to find her body, just dumped on the side of the road where they had argued. Steve was taken out of school in handcuffs and the police were searching his gym locker. A hush came over the entire school that lasted for weeks or months. The brutality of the murder had been stunning. The whole town was in a trance. Gradually, people were able to put it out of their minds, or at least stop thinking about it every day, but something had changed. The atmosphere was dark.

Micki had accepted the fact that Billy was bound to meet someone. Only Jenny and Kena knew about her feelings toward him. She couldn't bring herself to tell Sophia, who was quite protective of her family and friends. When Micki moved here Sophia and Jenny had been really close, and they still were, but because Micki lived much closer to Jenny, they naturally spent more time together. Sophia was Catholic, and attended Mass nearby, but Jenny and Micki attended the Baptist church on the lake road together. Occasionally, for bible school, holidays, revival or some dinner event, they would all attend one church or the other together; they sang non spiritual songs in the church and studied Revelations together. They loved to push the limits and would even ride the horses to revivals. Jenny's mom always made a Yankee pot roast on Sunday evenings and Micki rarely missed one. Some weekends the three of them would stay at Jenny's. Jenny's mom was always bringing home books, tapes and old records from yard sales and the girls loved to look over the plunder. Micki really liked Sophia, she loved to dance and sing and she was always in a jovial mood. Sophia was always ready to smoke weed, even had some occasionally and she never, ever, betrayed a friend. As of late, they had spent a lot of time on the trails with the horses. Even though the weather was still quite warm, the temperature in the lake had dropped as it normally would that time of year and swimming had become a rarity. Sophia was in love. She and Jay were so into each other their grades were dropping. Sophia was sure she would one day marry him, and the girls giggled about it a lot. Micki thought Sophia probably would marry him. She couldn't think of a more perfect couple. She wished she had a normal life, and normal feelings, but somehow, the incident with Jeff had left her with an emotional stunt. Or maybe she was just fucked up at birth, maybe there was something about her, something Jeff recognized and no one else could see. Maybe she was toxic. In the afternoons they would mostly stay at Jenny's house till her mom came home. Jenny's mom kept a bookshelf in the hallway with a lot of different books. Micki and Jenny liked to sit in the living room reading stories and then would tell each other about them. Jenny had been helping Micki edit "Demon High," and they generally had a good time together. Aside from school, Juanita hadn't been around since the séance, but had told everyone at school that Micki could make the wind blow. Boudreaux had already asked Micki to do it again, but Micki just laughed at him and told him he was crazy. She had decided she really, really liked to get high, and on some afternoons, Cameron would come by and Micki would get weed from him or they would sit in his pinto and listen to Pink Floyd. They once listened to the entire 8-track of Dark Side of the Moon without speaking. They had a connection, Cameron had said, that didn't need words. When she got out of the car that day, there was so much smoke inside, it looked like the car was on fire. Brett told her he was going to tell her mother as she walked by him at the picnic table. She turned and looked at him and said. "Fine, tell her." She just stared at him and he became uncomfortable, she knew he was afraid of her on a level that was hard to explain. He said, "Maybe I will, maybe I won't, you don't know do you." But she knew that he wouldn't. Micki flipped him off and went in the house. Micki spent the night with Sam later that week, Telling Sara she missed her and wanted to hang-out. Cameron got high with them and they gave each other make-overs and fell asleep happy. Micki slipped into Cameron's room after Sam went to sleep but he was sleeping too. She just kissed his forehead and went back to Sam's room. The next morning was Friday, and they dressed in their school colors and got Cameron to give them a ride. Sam ran into the school but Micki stayed back to get one more shotgun from Cameron. She knew she had deep feelings for him now, but wasn't sure where it might lead. She still thought of Billy every day. She was so nervous with him lately. He put his hand on the back of her head and kissed her long and deep. He pulled back and said he would see her later. She just looked at him, breathing heavily, before getting out of the car, shaking her head "yes" as a response. Cameron was feeling pretty good when he drove away headed to work. He was late, but it was worth it. Jenny and Sophia, teased Micki about her friendship with Cameron when she walked by Sophia's car. Micki stopped and sat in the back seat. They said he had been bounced on his head when he was a child and that's why he was so dumb. It hurt Micki's feelings when they talked about him like that, but she usually just shrugged it off and walked away. People were generally cruel she thought. They had been that way so long they were desensitized and careless. Cameron wasn't dumb, or slow. He was just wrapped up in his world, and that sometimes made him slow to react, giving a false impression. He knew everything about good rock and roll, and weed, two of Micki's favorite things. Sophia was looking at her in the rear-view, "he is pretty cute though" she said. Sophia had been one of the few people who liked that Micki had put Danny in his place. "It builds character," she had said. Believing it had all been about getting even for Jenny, she was genuinely surprised when Jenny said, "I thought you were in love with Billy." Micki gave her that thanks a lot look. As Sophia said "Billy? My cousin Billy? He's grown right?"

She was still looking at Micki in the rear-view. "It doesn't matter," she said to Sophia, he's not interested." She got out of the car and walked quickly as she was known to do. She was buzzing from the ride to school, and went straight to the library to write. She would check-in officially sometime later. Jenny was sorry she brought it up. Sophia was still in shock. They got out of the car and she went to find Jay.

At school Evan had stopped trying to get Micki's attention, she was always on her way somewhere, or coming back and going again. It was exhausting trying to keep up with her and keep his schedule. He decided to stop. He had felt so out of control, he had to stop. He was sure he was making a fool out of himself now. He had to stop. He was in class one day, when he noticed the girl next to him had a bright yellow folder on her desk that said chapter 2 at the top in big letters. He noticed it because it had Micki's name underneath the title, "Demon High." He asked the girl if he could read it and she said he could and that he should be sure and pass it around when he was done. After school that day, he sat down to read her imagination and decided it was a good way to connect with her intellect, and maybe figure out a new way to get her attention. It was a story she was writing about their school and it's teachers. In it, the coach has discovered some weird object buried in the baseball field clay and he became sick, and then all the teachers were affected. The students had to fight the demonic presence in each teacher. There was some "gruesome shit in there," Evan thought. He felt a deeper connection with her through her writing and felt like he knew her now on a more personal level. He kept the folder in his backpack until he found another chapter and then would trade folders. It was a weird way to read a story but it wasn't boring and it kept him from obsessing so blatantly.

One afternoon, Jenny and Micki had gotten high and thought it would be fun to visit Evan, and see if he "took the stick out of his ass yet." When they arrived, he was on the pier, throwing beer cans up in the air and shooting at them with a handgun. They asked him where he got the gun, and he just told them it was something he had picked up and decided to keep. Micki and Jenny weren't startled; everyone on the lake had guns for the most part. They themselves were quite apt at breaking bottles and piercing cans, but they had pretty much grown out of that sort of destruction for the sake of destruction type behavior. When Micki was ten, in the woods behind her grandparents' house, she swore to herself she would never shoot another squirrel, or any animal, just for the sake of killing it. She had stood there watching a squirrel wriggle in panic after she had winged it with a .22. So they weren't the least bit put off by Evan's antics, girls mature faster, right? Evan invited them in and started asking them questions about what they had been up to as of late, then saying he had seen them on the trails the days before. Micki said he should try horses, that they were "cooler than motorcycles." "And not nearly as noisy," Jenny added. They giggled. Jenny asked him, when he had seen them because they had not seen him on the trails. "Yeah," he said, "you were too far away to yell out, so I didn't, I was going to the quarry." He was hoping that sounded convincing. Kids went to the quarry all the time to smoke pot and hang out. He had been there many times. Micki got up to use the bathroom and while she was gone Evan turned to Jenny and asked her why she was always so suspicious of him. "What?!" Jenny asked, truly surprised. "Yeah, you always ask the strangest questions, like you think I'm hiding something, and you know what, I was sick of answering questions before I moved here so, get off my ass." Jenny who had no idea of the trouble Evan had been in, looked at him wide-eyed and said in a thick sarcastic tone, "Well, okay there buddy, I'm sorry I stepped on your dick." Evan, clearly pissed, said, "You know, when I first moved here I thought you were great, you're so fine and . . . " he held up a finger and pursed his lips as if telling her to wait "though I am used to a higher maintenance type girl, I wanted to date you, but now, to me, you are just the biggest bitch. I don't see how Micki can stand to be around you. You're just like my ex-girlfriend. A fucking cunt." he smiled. Jenny, who looked genuinely hurt, and shocked, was speechless. No one had ever talked to her that way. She just looked at him and let out a short breath as if she had been holding it to say something, but had lost her train of thought. Micki came out of the bathroom and Evan was still smiling at Jenny. It was a creepy smile. Jenny told Micki she really needed to get home, Micki said okay, they said goodbye to Evan. Even though she wanted to, Jenny didn't tell Micki about that strange confrontation. She just reiterated that he was "weird," on the way back to her house. After the summer drama over Danny, she just wanted things to be the way they were before. It's not like they ever had to go back to Evan's. If Jenny didn't suggest it, Micki never would, she knew.

Evan waited till they were around the curve, and then went after them. He watched them go inside Jenny's house and waited for a while, until he was sure they weren't coming back out. He watched them through Jenny's window, singing, and dancing. And coming back in with their hair wrapped in towels after a shower. First Jenny, and then Micki, he watched them each get dressed and dry their hair. He liked the way it felt. He was seeing them, when they didn't think anyone could. It was hard to break away from the sight. Micki was staying the night there. He finally went back home to read chapter 5 again. Chapter 5 was his ticket into Micki's life. After he read it over twice more, he called Sandy, the girl who had given it to him. She was a girl at school who always sat alone. Evan wasn't sure she had any friends, but he knew he didn't have any friends.

Sandy's grandmother ran the Marina. A bar and actual marina, located a couple of miles down the highway from the lake road on the marina road. It was another lake access point for visitors bringing their boats. There were places to swim there, rental cabins and boat ramps. There was a small parking lot near the water. A huge parking lot sat up higher on a more level patch of ground where bikers would sometimes loiter around fires in drums. Sandy had befriended more than a few of those bikers, and would retell their stories when the girls were at the Marina. There were also the rumored Satanists. Maybe they were Satanists. The only thing Micki ever witnessed was a bunch of people running naked through the trees alongside the lake there. She had been out with Kena sometime around the Halloween before, people had been saying the Satanists were renting cabins on the lake and they went to see if the rumor was real. They had parked in the lower parking lot and shut off the car. They got out and went to sit on a floating dock that the marina used to accommodate customers. Kena was drinking a beer, and they were both smoking weed, talking about life. Nothing was happening and Kena just blurted out that she had lost a baby two summers before. Micki was stunned and didn't know what to say. Kena said she and her boyfriend at the time had gotten into a physical fight and that she gotten really drunk and didn't really remember much after that. When she woke up, she was bleeding, a lot. She said she knew, but she went to the hospital anyway and sure enough, she had lost it. Jim didn't even know she had ever been pregnant. She just hadn't wanted to tell him. Kena was about to cry but she had to laugh, she said. She could be very emotional and Micki was a great listener. Like a lot of people Kena was afraid. Afraid she wasn't loved, afraid she would never get out, afraid of perpetual loss. Micki wasn't bad at consoling people either; she had been to a lot of funerals.

That night there'd been a small gathering of people standing around a fire burning in a drum, a little too far from Micki and Kena for them to really see what was happening. Other than the glow of the fire, and the shadows moving around it, they'd decided the rumor was bullshit when suddenly and without warning, all of them started taking off their clothes and began to run toward the woods. They ran within ten feet of Micki and Kena, but never saw them sitting there, or pretended not to. Neither of the girls made a sound as they ran by, they sat there, frozen. After the last one disappeared into the trees, the girls ran to Kena's car and drove away, laughing hysterically. Some of the members had been old, and they kept their socks on, Kena speculated that they were old people who just wanted to be dirty old people and Satanism offers that. Micki said there were no real Satanists, because Satan doesn't work like that, and Kena said. "Well, how the hell would you know, Satan might get off watching old people porn on Halloween." Micki laughed and snorted and Kena laughed again. That was her Satanist story.

This summer Micki and Jenny had been proud of themselves for swimming from place to place as opposed to always taking the road. They were excellent swimmers at this point, and would race any boy across the lake. Micki and Jenny knew Sandy's grandmother because, often, they swam to the Marina. She would sometimes let them drink in the bar if there was nobody there. Few people really knew what was going on with Sandy. She was attractive, sixteen, she had stringy reddish colored hair, and she was so much more. She had a tattoo on her back of a broken heart with a hissing snake coming out at the break. Micki always said it was "bad-assed." It was her favorite word for cool things. Sandy did party tricks she had learned from Bikers, like putting cigarettes out inside her mouth, with her tongue, and she always carried a knife.

She was very serious, and rarely smiled. She had a reputation for being easy but Micki had never seen her with anyone. The real story was far more sinister. The year before Sandy had gone to a party in a town nearby with a boy she had just met. The rumor was that she had gone to a party in Wetumpka, and let the boys there "run a train" on her, as they called it. The truth was, Micki and Jenny knew, that the boy she had gone with had gotten her very drunk, and then he and his four pathetic friends gang raped her over and over again for hours. When they were finished, he brought her back to the lake and dumped her on the deck. She wanted to press charges but she soon found out she didn't even know his real name. Sandy had told them the story one day when they were there. She had been watching the bar for her grandmother, as she sometimes did on lazy days. Jenny had been so angry at the thought that people could get away with such a thing. Micki had chill bumps listening to the details Sandy shared with them. She said that ever since then, guys would visit her, or ask her out, but they all just wanted the same thing. Micki asked her why she kept going out with them, and she said, "Every time I screw someone of my choice, that's one more between me and the assholes. It's me, taking my sexuality back, taking my life back." Micki's eyes were wet. Jenny said, "That's beautiful." Sandy poured them all shots of Glenlivet after she finished telling them. They had a secret bond and had shared many such shots over the summer.

Evan figured Sandy would probably be most grateful for his attention. As it turned out, she actually seemed to be. She took a boat right over to his pier when he called her. She came inside, and they listened to his stereo. She asked if he had any weed and he told her he didn't smoke it, but offered her a beer. He told her how cool he thought her tattoos were. He wanted her to teach him the cigarette trick, but he kept burning himself. He showed her his gun, and let her hold it. He told her she was his only friend and he was glad she came over. He sat next to her on the sofa and put his hand on the back of her head, playing with her hair. Sensing his intentions, she asked him if he wanted a blow job, "Yeah Sandy, that would be cool." She smiled at him and said, "You must give in order to receive." and started getting undressed. When she left, she was hurrying to get the boat back to the Marina before her grandmother noticed she was still gone.

At school the next day Evan had decided it was time to make a more aggressive move toward Micki. When Sandy saw him in class, she went and sat next to him. He was somewhat standoffish. Later, in the hall after school, she asked him if something was wrong, to which he replied, "No, nothing's wrong," but kept walking. The look on her face made him stop and tell her, "Look, we had a good time, right?" She nodded her head but something had changed in her face.. "Maybe we can do it again sometime, but right now I just need some space, okay?" She just nodded her head again, this time more slowly. "That's why I like you Sandy, you know how it is...Right?" He didn't wait for an answer. He just hurried out to the parking lot. She watched him run out to the lot to catch up with Micki, thinking what a typical asshole he was.

Evan spotted Micki while he was talking with Sandy and rushed out to catch her, waving chapter 5 in his hand. Stopping her, he asked, "You wrote this?" Micki, stopped, always happy to talk about her writing, "Yes, I did." She smiled, "Do you like it?" He told her that he loved it. He had read it so many times now he had practically memorized it, and had no problem convincing Micki that he did, in fact, love it. Jenny and Sophia were calling her, telling her to "come on," from the car, but Evan said, "Let me take you home, I really want to talk to you about some ideas I had for this book," Micki thought about it for a second, and then waved to Sophia, yelling for them to go ahead, that she would ride with Evan. Jenny wanted to stop her, but she fought the urge and got in the car and left with Sophia. Jay was following them in his old mustang.

Micki had not been on a motorcycle since Brett had one. He and another neighbor of theirs used to ride the smaller kids around the block. Once she had been riding with Marty, and had burned her leg on the exhaust. She still had a faint scar in the shape of a star. She actually enjoyed the ride to her house that day. When they got there, her mom was home. She asked Evan to wait outside while she took her things in, because her mom would freak if she saw him smoking in the house. She went inside and Sara asked her who it was that brought her home on a motorcycle. She told her it was Evan, a new guy on the lake. Her mom told her she thought she had seen him in the woods late at night. "It's not a crime is it?" Micki asked. "I guess not." her mother said, "but it just seemed a little weird." To Micki, who spent a lot of time in the woods, even at night, it didn't sound strange at all. She was happy, happy to be doing something normal. Happy that Evan was interested in her story. It was another of her favorite subjects.

Billy had been in the pasture training the horses when he saw the bike go by. He recognized it as belonging to the boy who had moved into the mansion. He was sure that long blonde hair on the back belonged to Micki. He stopped for a moment, unsure what to do, but then rode to the gate and went out, the horse ran to Micki's house and Billy stopped in front. Billy was holding the reigns tightly and the horse was neighing, perhaps sensing Billy's agitation. He just looked at Evan, standing there in the yard, Evan smiled and waved. Micki came outside and Billy glared at her, then back at Evan before nudging the horse to run back in the direction of the pasture. Micki watched him ride away, "I think that guy was a little surprised to see me. Is he your uncle or something?" he said, fucking with her. Micki started walking to a picnic table in the yard and motioned for him to follow, "He's not my uncle, he's Sophia's cousin, and just one of my many jealous lovers." She smiled, but he didn't seem to get the joke, so she explained to him that she was only playing. Still, he didn't seem amused, so she sat down with the parts of her story she had at home, changing the subject by asking him what great ideas he had for her to put in the story. He said, he loved the idea that the demons knew all the inner desires of the students. He asked her if the girl in Chapter 2 had been based on her. She said it wasn't, that she was in Chapter 1. Laughing now, she told him that all the characters were loosely based on real people. "Write me into the story, I want to be in it," he said. She thought for a minute, and asked him, "How would you like to be the anti-hero?" He smiled and said, "Micki, dammit girl, that's exactly what I want to be."

Billy freed the horse in the pasture and went inside the house. He knew he shouldn't be upset but he was. He grabbed a beer from the refrigerator and began pacing back and forth. There was probably nothing going on anyway. Micki had it bad for him, he knew for a fact. The way that cocky little brat waved and smiled at him infuriated him. It made him feel like a kid in school again. Evan was creepy he thought, dressed in all black like the weird Satanists who came down to the lake every year. But he didn't feel that way when Micki was dressed in all black. He was just jealous. It was eating at him. Maybe Micki had taken his advice and decided to date someone her own age. The thought of it made him throw his beer across the room to the kitchen wall, wet suds slid down like Windex. He went outside and got into his car. He was going to the Marina, for beer and dancing. That's where he needed to be right now, with grown-ups. He turned the car around in the yard and sped out of the driveway, kicking up dirt as he went.

Evan and Micki were laughing over the different ways the students had to defend themselves against the demon-possessed faculty, apparently, there wasn't a priest to be found and the kids had to be thrifty. Each chapter contained a different teacher and a different victim. It would culminate until the last chapter in which an anti-hero would save the survivors in a final battle of evil vs. bad to the bone. Evan was feeling pretty good about getting this far with Micki. They were laughing together and she was comfortable with him. It wouldn't be long he thought. His life was about to get a lot better. He was looking at her and thought it might be the right time to kiss her. He loved the way she looked him in the eye. He was about to make that move when her mom came out and said it was time for her company to go home. Evan knew if it had been Jenny or any other girl she wouldn't have said so, but he was trying to make an impression, even though he didn't think much of Micki's mom. He thought Micki was great, so he left chapter 5 with Micki, and she gave him chapters 1 and 3. He said goodbye to her mother and told Micki he would see her later. He waited for her to say okay before she slipped inside the house and then he got on his bike and headed home. He was feeling pretty good. He slowed down in front of Jenny's to take the sharp left toward his house. He saw her in the yard laying out in the sunshine. He flipped her the finger when she looked up, just as he made the left in front of her house. When he got home, he called Sandy and asked her to come over.

Micki went inside and went to her room to do her algebra homework. She hated homework, and in the past had skipped it, a lot. This year she had vowed that she would do better, and so far, she hadn't slipped. One more year and she'd be headed to college, she had to get serious. She took a long shower afterward and went straight to bed. She had the radio on and "Hell is for children" played in her room, bouncing off the walls and in her head. Music always made her think of Cameron. She wondered what he was doing right now. She tried to imagine him in his room, but she couldn't. She could only remember the kiss at school that morning, and Sam's voice telling her "no." Of course she wasn't sleeping. As hard as she tried to sleep her thoughts kept going back to Billy. The thought that he was jealous of Evan made her feel good. She had never seen him act that way before. She decided he probably just happened by and was surprised to see Evan in the yard. She still couldn't shake the feeling that she was missing something. She was restless. She lay there, anxious, until she was sure her mother and brother were asleep and then slipped out the kitchen door headed to Billy's house.

Billy, was intoxicated. He had temporarily forgotten his frustration. He'd run into Tammy at the bar, and they had a nice time together dancing and drinking. There was a live band and though the music was terrible, Billy was actually relaxing. When Tammy offered to let him come to her place, he started to say no. Tammy looked at him and said, "Hey, it's not a marriage proposal, I'm not expecting you to make breakfast in the morning or anything. I don't want to go home alone, do you?" He said, "I'm pretty drunk. Probably useless" She laughed and replied, "Oh, me too, I had hardly noticed . . . Come on," Billy went with her. Tammy had a trailer that was set up on the edge of the road that went to the Marina. The baby was with her mother for the night, she told him when they got there. When they went inside, they didn't talk. Billy followed her down the long hallway to the bedroom, and let himself go. He was thinking about Micki, naked in his bed the weeks before. He just closed his eyes, and let his thoughts run free. For Tammy's part, she enjoyed his company. He knew he would feel bad about it later, but he was too mentally exhausted to fight the fantasy. He was thoughtful and passionate with Tammy. No one ever need know the source of that passion, he thought. Afterward, Tammy slept like a baby.

When Micki got to Billy's house, she noticed his car was gone. She hadn't been here in three weeks like this, but she went to the door anyway. It wasn't locked, it never was, so she let herself in. She wasn't sure where he might be at this hour, but no way was she going back home, not without talking to him first. She walked to the kitchen and noticed the crumpled beer can on the floor. It still had beer in it, she tossed it into the garbage, thinking it was unlike him. Maybe he really was jealous. She looked in the refrigerator and took out an open bottle of wine. After taking a plastic cup from the cabinet she poured herself a small amount, and drank it down in one drink, letting the warmth of it settle over her. Thinking maybe she should just go home, she sat on the sofa and turned on the TV. She flipped through the channels, but not really being into TV, gave up and turned it off. She went into his bedroom, and sat on the bed for a few minutes before getting up and closing the curtains. She turned on the radio and an old Van Halen song called "The cradle will Rock" was playing, she loved that song, but didn't turn it up loud. She wanted to hear him drive in the yard. She remembered Cameron had this album. Then she took off her clothes and got into his bed. This was the first time she had ever done that. She still thought often of the last night she had been there, and wanted to feel the sheets against her bare skin again. Eric Clapton started singing, "Cocaine." She lay there, wrapping herself in those sheets, listening to the only rock station around. When she was finally calm, she fell asleep.

Billy was trying to find Micki, he was barefoot and shirtless, running. He had looked in every house on the lake and feared the worst. He was running down the lake road not sure where he was going. There were barking dogs chasing him. Suddenly he was at the old mansion running up the steps to the patio. He ran inside and there she was, lying on the floor. Blood was running from the corner of her mouth, and the whites of her eyes were purple, there was so much blood, her legs were covered in it, and it was crusted on her nose. A black snake slithered protectively across her body, and then it was gone. He got down on his knees and was trying to wake her up, shaking her, calling her name. He said he was sorry when he realized he had done this. What? He realized he was dreaming and immediately woke up. It was still dark outside. It took him a minute to remember where he was. He wasn't in the habit of sleeping with women without being involved with them, and he felt a tinge of shame. Tammy was sleeping next to him. If he had been calling Micki's name out loud, Tammy didn't hear it. He got up and found his pants. It was dark and he wasn't sure where he had left his shoes. He felt around on the floor by the bed and finally located them. After searching unsuccessfully, he decided to leave his shirt behind. He quietly tiptoed through the trailer carrying his shoes and then putting them on at the door. As he left, he took the time to lock it behind him. He went out to his car, looking for his keys in his pants but they weren't there. He was afraid he would have to knock on the door and wake Tammy up to find them. He glanced in the car window and there they were, in the ignition. He got in and started the car and headed down the Marina road to the highway. The dream was fresh in his mind. He couldn't even sleep without this obsession burning in his brain, he thought to himself. How would he ever get over this? He slammed his hand on the steering wheel. He was at the breaking point. When he got to the highway, he didn't stop but took the left going a little too fast, the car fish tailed but he regained control and was turning onto the lake road just a few minutes later. When he got home, he sat in the car for a while before getting out and going inside. He was so tired of that little house. He was tired, mentally. He should have never kissed

Micki the first time, or maybe letting her in that first night was the mistake. Maybe coming to Alabama was a mistake. He got out of the car and went inside. Billy, meticulous, noticed the plastic red cup on the counter, but didn't see anyone in the house. Maybe his dad had come down and had a drink while he waited, he thought. He washed the cup, dried it with a paper towel and put it back in the cabinet. The beer he had thrown earlier was now in the garbage can. He took a bottle of cleaner and wiped the wall and the floor where it had been. The sky outside was turning a bright blue. It would be daylight in a couple of hours. He went into the bedroom to get some sleep. He didn't turn the light on. He just took off his pants and got in the bed. Before he laid down, he noticed the closed curtains and he didn't remember leaving the radio on. Micki. He turned on the lamp and turned to look around. There she was, sleeping, naked. An unexpected sense of relief came over him, and he turned off the light. The radio played "Refugee." He decided to go ahead and get some sleep. He could talk to her in the morning. As he lay down, she rolled over close to him and one arm fell casually across his chest. He knew he should wake her up then, tell her to go home, but he couldn't. He let her head fall onto his arm and he gently held her there. The song changed to "Comfortably Numb" after the DJ informed them that it was already 77 degrees outside, it was going to be "a scorcher," he said. He smelled her hair, and she instinctively wrapped her arm around his waist. He was a dead man he thought. He should have showered. He should make her go home. His thoughts were in free fall. He just didn't want to move now. He'd have to wake her up to get out of bed, and she might leave on her own. He didn't disturb her. He liked the way her head felt on his bare chest, her naked body against his. "Brass in pocket" was drifting from the radio now playing the "classic rock Friday Show." After a little while, he fell asleep too.

Someone was knocking on the door. Billy was startled awake. The bright sun was coming through the slit in the curtains. He remembered Micki was there next to him and wondered if he had dreamt it. He looked over and there she was. She had rolled over again and her long hair was cascading down her bare back. The sheets were just barely covering her from the waist down. Bob Seger was singing "Fire Lake." The clock on the radio said it was after ten. He took a deep breath, pulled on his pants, and went to the door. It was his dad. Billy was supposed to be up already. "These horses won't feed themselves," said Freddie, without coming inside. Billy made an excuse about not feeling well, because it was unusual, and Freddie might be sympathetic. "I got a little too drunk last night and I just couldn't get up. I'm feeling a little nauseous" Freddie said he would handle everything for him that day. Billy said thanks, and Freddie told him to go back to bed. "Yeah," Billy said, "I intend to." He closed the door and after thinking for a second, locked it, afraid Freddie might come back and let himself in. He stood there for a moment thinking. What if it had been Micki's brother, would he have told him she was there? Would they even come looking for her? He went to take a shower. He was in there for a while, not sure what to do next. When he got out, he wrapped a towel around his waist, brushed his teeth and went back into the bedroom. Micki was still sleeping. She must have been tired he thought. He stood there for a long time, thinking and listening to the radio. "Crazy little thing called love" was playing, appropriately, he thought. He walked to the dresser to get some clothes out to get dressed but then he stopped. He walked over to the bed to wake her up and stopped again. He went to the window and looked out the little crack in the curtains. Then he dropped the towel, and got back into bed with her. He didn't touch her at first, he wanted her to roll over, back into his arms, it had seemed so natural, so right. She didn't, so he began to trace his fingers along her back, down to her hips, he put his hand down on her hip bone and squeezed it gently. She turned over, startled, and saw him. Without a word, he began to kiss her, and she kissed him back. He caressed her body and she caressed his. She pushed herself closer to him and found him aroused. Completely naked, he was vulnerable. She, naked as well, didn't want it to end this time. She took his hand in hers and placed it between her thighs, letting him feel the warmth there. "Red skies at night" was playing on the radio, and Micki thought the music was perfect. He raised up and pushed her flat onto her back into the pillows. Her legs spread around him, it was over, there was no stopping now. He leaned down and kissed her stomach, and then lower. She groaned and said "Oh my god" when he put his mouth on her. "Oh my god," she said again in a weaker voice when his hands explored her body further. When she was just about to climax, he stopped, "No, no don't stop this time, I miss you so much, I need you. Just finish me." She said, and then he was inside her. He watched her face as he entered her and thought she looked radiant. She had a misty look that made him think of magic castles and every fairy fantasy ever dreamed. For Micki, It hurt a little but it felt so good she didn't care. It felt like she was on fire inside, and she needed him to put it out. Is this what I've been craving? "Yes" she said softly but out loud. The feeling was so powerful she was suddenly squirming as if she was trying to get away. He asked her if she was okay, and she said she was, it just felt so good she couldn't be still. He tried to take it easy but the moment was so intense it was difficult to control himself. The tension between them had grown till this moment and it was almost too much for him. He was sure he was being too rough with her, but she kept saying it was great. She cried out a lot and squeezed his skin in her fingers. She was moving with him, as if they were one body. He kissed her shoulders and then her face. They were wet with sweat and the slickness of her skin only excited him further. He had to hold her firmly. She kept groaning and he hoped no one was around to hear them. She felt so good, he told her, he was holding her head in his hands, her hair in his fingers, "you're so sweet" he said, kissing her face, and her mouth. He didn't care about tomorrow, neither did she. Right now was all that mattered.

Micki's mom, Sara, didn't have to work that day, she slept in. She had been so tired lately. Jeff had come in late and drunk. She wished he would stop drinking because he always wanted to argue when he was drunk. She loved him, and she still believed he would one day divorce Jane, and marry her, but she could do without his drinking and his attitude. She got up without waking him. Brett had been moved to the night shift at his new job to get more pay, so she didn't bother waking him either. She went to Micki's room and saw that Micki was gone. Her bed hadn't been made. She must have left in a hurry, she thought, assuming Micki had gone to school for some early function. Micki was like that. Ever since she was a baby she had tried to be independent. She never wanted Sara's help with anything. If Sara did try to help her, Micki would just blow her off. Micki was smart, her smartest child, she knew. She had been reading and writing when she was just three and had never stopped. People didn't understand how hard it was to raise such a smart kid. A kid you can't even educate because she is beyond everything you ever knew. She closed Micki's door and went back to bed with Jeff.

When she didn't show up at Jenny's house to catch a ride with Sophia, Jenny was a little concerned. Micki was unpredictable, she could be anywhere. She had a lot of friends that didn't all run in the same circles. The last time Jenny had seen her, she had been with Evan, and then later he had flipped her off on his bike, but he had been alone then. She had seen Evan leave on his motorcycle earlier, just before Sophia pulled up in the car. Maybe Micki rode with him to school she thought. As they rode by Micki's house there was no one in the yard, it looked quiet. Hopefully everything was okay. Jeff's car was in the driveway. Jenny had never forgotten the night last November, when Jeff had broken Sara's arm. Micki had spent the night with Jenny, but woke up in the middle of the night, completely panicked, saying she had to get home. Jenny's parents hadn't wanted her to go out so late, but Micki, clearly upset, had convinced them that something was wrong and she had to go. The "something wrong," was Jeff. In a drunken rage, he had beaten Sara. Sara was tired of waiting for him to leave Jane and had told Jeff she was going to leave him and go to her parents place in Talladega. He had used her body to break furniture. Broken pieces were strewn everywhere, even in the yard, and Sara was in the hospital. It had been a miracle she had only sustained a broken arm. Jenny tried to put it out of her mind. She had her own problems, and whatever was going on, Micki would tell her about it later. The girls were listening to the radio and Jenny liked the song playing, she turned it up, and they all started singing "Hit me with your best shot."

When Evan got to school, he sat on his motorcycle and waited in the parking lot for Micki to show up. When Jenny and Sophia pulled in without her, he got a little nervous. When Jenny walked by him, he grabbed her arm to stop her. "What are you doing?" She asked snatching her arm away as if he had plague. He said he was sorry for startling her before he asked her, "Where's Micki?" Jenny looked at him coldly, "Maybe I should ask you that." Evan put up his hands defensively and said, "When I left her, she was with her mother," Jenny looked at him coldly for a moment and then turned and went into the school yard, headed for the side door. What if she's sick? He worried. He started his bike to go find out why she wasn't there. He went straight to her house and knocked on the door. Sara answered and he asked if Micki was home. Her mom said, "Micki is in school, shouldn't you be there too?" He said "yeah, I was headed there now. I just thought she might want a ride." Sara told him that he was late already, and that Micki didn't like to be late, "She left early." As her mother closed the door, he could feel the blood rushing in his face. He knew where Micki was. He knew it. She only went to one place before the sun came up. That fucking duplicitous bitch. They almost kissed yesterday but apparently, it had meant nothing. He saw the way she looked at Billy on that stupid horse, and that comment, about jealous lovers, what the fuck was that. That fucking whore. He rode his bike back home and went upstairs to his room. He was pacing back and forth but couldn't calm down. He wanted to find her. He paced more, cursing Micki out loud. He took a shoebox from his closet and took the .45 out. He took the loaded clip he kept in the box and put it in the gun. He put it in the back of his jeans, under his shirt. He went downstairs and stopped in the great room. "What am I doing?" He said aloud and started pacing back and forth again. He groaned and walked out of the house lighting a cigarette. He was walking toward the trail. He knew it well now. He had spent so much time on these trails he could get anywhere. Even on the trail, it was a good distance to the pasture. He was walking fast but not fast enough, he thought to himself. He would have ridden his bike but it was too noisy. He finally came to the back of the stable and quickly went around the pasture fence. He didn't jump it till he was sure he was behind the house. He then crossed the pasture, jumping the fence again when he got to the trees, directly facing Billy's bedroom window. The curtains were almost completely drawn this time, with only a couple of inches available to see through. He just knew Micki was in there, but he wanted to be sure. Part of him didn't believe it, the part of him that was certain he and Micki were soul mates. She had to know by now. She had to see in him what he saw in her. Yesterday, he had seen it. He knew she felt something too. They just needed some time together. If she was in there, he didn't know what he would do. She could have been with Kena, but he had to be sure. He slipped out of the trees, taking a big chance in the broad daylight, and went over to the window. He carefully peaked inside. The lights were off and the only light in the room was shining through the curtains. He didn't want his shadow to startle anyone who might be in the room, so he backed away before he could see anything. He slid down to the ground and slowly raised his head just enough to see through the bottom part of the window. She was there all right. They were clearly having sex. He watched long enough to watch them roll over a couple of times and actually saw her face. There was no question, it was her. His heart sank and he slid back down the wall of the house. He was shaking his head back and forth and he hit his own forehead with his palm and then rested his head in his hand. Billy was doing to Micki, what he had been fantasizing about since the party at Cal's house. His stomach turned. He felt like he had been hit in the gut. He moved away from the window and put his hand on the gun in the back of his pants. He was gritting his teeth. He got up and started walking fast toward the door. After he went around the corner, he heard a man with a slight Cajun accent say, "Can I help you?" He took his hand off the gun and turned around. There was an older Italian looking man with salt and pepper hair and a thin mustache standing there drying his hands on a rag.. "I was looking for the guy who works these horses?" Evan covered his intentions a little. "These horses are mine. What you want?" Freddie had always sounded short when he spoke, it was just his way. Evan, who was quick with an answer, said "Well everyone around her rides, I was going to see if maybe I could get some riding lessons." Freddie waved for him to come and walk with him. They walked away from the house down the driveway as they talked. Freddie was seeing him out. "We don't train people, we train horses." Evan who wasn't ready to give up glanced nervously back at the house, "What about all these girls I see riding all the time? Where did they learn to ride?" Freddie laughed and said, "Oh I see, you want to meet the girls." Freddie was still smiling at him, "Well this is no good. All those girls? They been riding since they were little tiny girls. They know horses, you know, they help train them. They like da ornery ones, you know." Freddie laughed and Evan pretended to. As they reached the driveway Freddie stopped and said, "I'm sorry we couldn't help you. If you get yourself a horse, you can put it here. We can train it to let you ride. You could be part of that, and I'm sure you would learn a lot." Evan said he would give it some thought, thanked him and headed down the lake road toward home. Freddie watched him until he disappeared around the bend and then went to the stables. He had seen Evan walking around Billy's house and had come over to see what he was doing there. There was something he didn't like about it, about that kid. He was sure he was lying, but he'd be watching, that was sure.

Billy was trying to pace himself. They were both enjoying it so much he didn't want it to end too abruptly. The feeling was building and soon he wouldn't be able to stop. He tried to think of flying, but she kept moaning and something in the tone of it touched him inside, and he wanted to hear it again, over and over. When he was about to explode inside her, he waited till the very last second and then pulled out, catching his semen in his hand. She was writhing in the bed. He got up and went to the bathroom, washed the semen off his hands and took a condom from the medicine cabinet, and put it on. He couldn't wait to be back inside her. He went back toward the bedroom and saw his reflection in the mirror on the door. Not now, he thought. He closed his eyes to it and went into the room. She was lying very still, staring at the ceiling. Eric Clapton was singing on the radio and he thought she really did look wonderful. "Are you okay?" he asked her. She turned to look at him. Her eyes were beautiful he thought, like the deepest ocean on a sunny day. "I'm okay," she said, "Is that it? is it over?" He got back into bed and said, "No, that's not it," He kissed her face and asked her, "Do you want to stop?" She said she didn't. There was blood on the sheets and between her thighs, hymen blood. He was strangely aroused by the sight of it. He kissed her again, and this time, it was slower, not as urgent, he made love to her for a long while. When it was time, he exploded inside her. He had wanted her to feel that. She started to climax and he kept pushing. She cried out again as if she was in pain and threw her head back like she was having a seizure. He put his arms around her back placing his hands just below her shoulder blades and held her firmly as her body pulsed on his. She was hitting his shoulders with the palms of her hands. He felt her begin to relax in his arms. This is ecstasy, he thought. She fell back in a stupor. He fell down next to her exhausted. After a few minutes she pulled herself up and went into the bathroom without a word. Billy knew what he had just done was wrong, criminal even. He still wanted her, even now. A girl he couldn't date publicly. He wasn't sure how he would make this work but he wanted to try. Maybe her mom would come around in time. Micki was sweet, sexy and beautiful and she needed and loved him. He hoped she always would.

It was sticky. Not like period blood, it was thinner. It was drying on her thighs. She got into his shower and turned on the water to wash it off. She felt like a cracked egg but she liked the way it felt. She sat down under the warm shower stream and let the water wash over her. Finally, she had something that might be stronger than the memory of the things Jeff had done to her. No one understood what it was like to have to look at him nearly every day, snide and rejected. Her mother actually thought Micki wanted her married, alcoholic, abusive boyfriend. He was a snake who betrayed her, but now, now she might be able to forget, or at least ignore, the past. She felt like she had when she was baptized in the Baptist church, sanctified. She smiled at the wicked thought. She got out of the shower, took a towel from the rack and dried herself. There was a little bit of blood on the towel, so she put it in the hamper in the corner. She hadn't gone home, she hadn't gone to school and nobody but Billy knew where she was. She didn't want to think about that right now. She wanted this to last forever. She went into the bedroom and got back into bed with him. He was almost asleep again. It was nice that he wasn't aloof or pretending not to want her. All the apprehension was gone. She loved him at that moment, truly and deeply, as much as a sixteen year old girl could love anyone. He had given her something nobody could ever take away. She moved close to him and wrapped one leg across his. He was almost asleep, but he put one arm around her and kissed her face as she put her head on his chest like she had the night before. They fell asleep together. It was the best sleep Micki ever had.

Evan was cursing, walking toward his house on the lake road. As he passed Micki's house, Sara was in the yard talking to a guy sitting in a car. Micki's dad? It bothered him that there was so much he didn't know about Micki. He hadn't had time to make her like him yet, and that little fucking whore was up there fucking Billy right now. He guessed this was how Danny must have felt that night at the party. This was just a setback, he tried to reason, if Billy could take her from Danny, he could take her from Billy. That's the way it was with girls. He just had to figure out a way to make her realize he had what she wanted. Micki's mom looked at him strangely as he walked by. He just smiled and waved. He was so angry. He could bury her right now he thought. What would mom say if she knew her sweet little angel was down at Billy's getting her brains fucked out. He wondered if her mother knew what a whore Micki was. He wouldn't tell her though, no. Micki's secret might ultimately be more valuable than a moments revenge, he couldn't blow this. He passed Jenny's house without looking up. When he got home, he went inside and upstairs to his room and ditched the .45 in the shoe box in the back of his closet without unloading it. He had stolen it from one of his dad's friends. He should have sold it probably, but he just loved the way it made him feel when he carried it. He knew he would have used it on Billy today if that old jerk hadn't popped up. He would get another chance, of this, he was certain. His parents were supposed to be bringing food and some other stuff this afternoon. He was glad he had ditched school, this place was a wreck, and he didn't need to hear any shit from Rita. He busied himself cleaning up the mess. That's when it hit him. He would invite Micki to a party. An exclusive party, right here in this house. He smiled and wondered why he didn't think of it before. He started whistling as he finished tidying the room, then he went downstairs and watched TV.

When Billy woke up, Micki was still sleeping. He looked at the clock by the bed, 2:07. They had slept most of the day. He got up and put on a fresh pair of underwear and pulled on his jeans. He went into the kitchen and made coffee. Micki preferred tea, so he checked to see if there was tea in the fridge, there was. He had been making it for her when she visited regularly, but lately she hadn't been around. He had kept making it just in case. He took it out and set it on the bar. He was starving, and decided to make them some sandwiches. He was anxious. His head was spinning. He felt like everything was dangling by a thread and today, it had all come tumbling down. He was scrambling eggs for their sandwiches and absently burned his hand when he grabbed the skillet without a potholder. "Shit!" He said. He turned off the eye, and let cool water run over his hand at the sink. His feelings for Micki had not changed, but he had gone too far. "I couldn't help it" he told himself. His thoughts were spiraling. She wouldn't have stopped until she had broken him down completely, he told himself, and he was broken. He thought again of the first time he had kissed her. That's when she understood how much he liked her, and she had used his affection for her against him ever since. He wasn't blaming her. They understood each other at least. He had not lied to Micki. He had broken her too. What would happen now? Could they really embark on a relationship? He cut the sandwiches in half, and put the plates on the bar in front of the bar stools. He washed his hands and dried them on a towel, and went in the bedroom to wake her up. She looked so peaceful, he wished she didn't have to leave, but what would happen if she didn't? He sat down on the bed and started caressing her back. She groaned a little bit and rolled over, hugging the sheet to her. "What time is it?" she asked. "Late," he said, "after two." She sat up now, "Damn...I have to go home...I might be in a lot of trouble this time." She was rubbing her head, her legs felt like jello and her mind was rushing. She started to move off the bed and he took her head in his hands and kissed her, he wanted her to know nothing had changed. "I made us some food." He told her, just looking at her, and then he left her to get dressed, and went back into the kitchen.

Rita and Jack brought more than food when they showed up that afternoon. Jack had been feeling a little nicer toward Evan, who, so far, had been quietly living on the lake. Jack wanted to reward him for staying out of trouble these last few months. When Evan saw the boat, he was completely stoked. It wasn't a huge boat, but it was newer and brighter than any of the boats the other kids rode around in. His dad had driven the boat from the ramp at Minnows and docked it at their pier. It was the last thing Evan had expected. Jack told him that he was proud of him for being so good, and he thought country life must suit him. Evan was thrilled about the boat. He barely heard his dad's voice. This was going to make living here a lot easier. Wait till Micki sees this, he thought. Rita had brought him some new clothes and towels and was putting them away inside. His dad was telling him that soon, he and Rita would come there to stay but that it wasn't easy trying to move your whole life around. Evan told him "Dad, it's okay.. really." and patted him on the arm. Jack thought that was kind of strange but he shrugged it off. His son was trying to grow up, he thought. Rita made them all dinner, and they sat on the patio and ate together. Evan told them he thought he met a girl they might like. Rita smiled at the notion and told him he seemed "positively reborn." and that she "hoped it worked out to meet his expectations." He said he hoped so too, but was "certain that it will." It was the best time he'd had with Jack in years, and the best he'd ever felt about Rita since he could remember. He was feeling better now. He had an idea. He wanted to make this happen. A "coordinator," that's what Jasmine called him. He wanted to prove that theory. He decided during dinner that he wanted to do cocaine again. He missed the mood it put him in. He had laughed so much when he was high. He was reminded of the feeling laughing with Jack and Rita. When dinner was over, Rita cleaned up and Jack played chess with his son in the great room. He drank 100 year old scotch with him, and they smoked cigars. Rita cheered them on for a while and then tried the satellite system. She found a movie and curled up comfortably on the sofa. When the game was over, Rita had gone to sleep on the couch. Jack decided they would stay the night and woke Rita up to go to bed. Evan sat on the sofa after they went upstairs completely amazed at himself. Rita's face lit up when he mentioned a new girlfriend. He supposed that would be a sign that he was moving on.

What if Jasmine had been telling them that he was calling her? She had no proof it was him. Besides, she had changed her number now and he couldn't call her anyway. He wondered if she had told them about his visit. He wished he could tell her he was sorry. He wondered what she would think of Micki, and decided she would be jealous. She would call Micki "white trash." There was nothing wrong with Micki a new wardrobe wouldn't cure, he thought and smiled. Her family seemed like a bunch of hicks, but they were oddly cultured to a degree he was accustomed to. Micki knew how to act. She was pleasant. She knew all the right moves. She could be an incredible asset to him. It had to be fate. Rita's reaction was another sign. It meant something. Everything that had happened until now was all just a long string of necessary events to bring him to this moment. He felt good, really good. Micki's thing with Billy was just a setback. He could overcome this. He would overcome this, he corrected himself.

Billy was eating, but saying she wasn't hungry, Micki only drank cold tea. She was nervous, he could see it, fear. Micki was scared to go home, and scared not to. She was chewing one nail and tracing the rim of the glass with the other. He loved the way her eyes looked when she was lost in thought. He didn't want to be another source of confusion in her life. He wanted a stable relationship. He thought about how absurd that sounded under the circumstances. It was too late, he had to try. He didn't want any secrets between them so he stopped eating and broke the silence when he told her, "I was with Tammy last night." Micki stopped rubbing the rim of her glass and looked at him. He felt shame and turned away, "I wanted you to know because I care about you, I didn't want you to hear it from someone else." Micki nodded her head, still lost in thought. "You were 'with' her?" Although she was pretty sure what he meant, she was looking for clarification. Not wanting to drag it out, he said, "I fucked her, Micki, That's why I wasn't home." She just stared at him. "After I saw you with that guy . . . I just had to get away from here for a while. I didn't go there to do it, but I got drunk and it happened . . . It didn't mean anything." Micki seemed to ignore this, "How am I going to get home Billy, I can't leave now without taking a chance on being seen, I can't stay till dark, my mother will kill me. What can I do?" Billy didn't know what to say, "Are you going to see her again?" She asked him. He looked at her and smiled a little, "No, there's only you babe. It was always only you. Even when I was with her . . . I don't know what in the hell we are going to do, but it's just you Micki." He took her sandwich and started eating it. After thinking for a few minutes he said, "We'll get in my car, and drive by, if the coast is clear, I'll let you out there, if not, I'll let you out at Jenny's." She said okay. "Will you come back later?" He asked her. "I don't know. I'll try." He felt a little pang thinking she might not come back to him tonight, every night, he needed her now, he needed the feeling she gave him. He needed her and didn't know what he would do if she didn't come back. "I'm sorry about Tammy," he said. "I know ...it's okay," she assured him. She finished her second glass of tea, and stood up to go. She walked around the bar and put her arms around him from behind. "It was magical," she told him, referring to the day they had together and she kissed the back of his neck. He put one hand over hers, and was relieved that she wasn't angry. He hoped she really wasn't. Sometimes it was hard to tell, and she could go from happy to pissed in a split second. "Rapid mood swings" he recalled the term. He got up from the bar, turned around and kissed her. Just in case she didn't make it back. He finally released her and grabbed his keys. Without a word, he went for his car. He pulled it right up to the backdoor, and she half crawled in from the door. He had to get out and close it just in case Freddie was about. She was laughing then, and all seemed well. He turned the car around as she lay down in the seat with her head in his lap, she was looking up at him smiling. He loved her. There was no doubt.

No one was home when Billy pulled up to Micki's house. She got out of the car and went in the kitchen door. Billy went around the drive and pulled out going back home. He hoped he would see her later. When he pulled back into his drive, Freddie was there and asked him if he was feeling better. Billy, looked guilty, and something in Freddie's tone said he knew something was up. Billy said he thought he was feeling better. Freddie didn't press him, but invited him to dinner. Billy said "that would be great," and they walked to the big house together. Freddie was worried about his son, but knew he had to tread lightly.

Micki wasn't sure how she felt yet. It had been great, that was a certainty. Aside from some minor physical evidence, she didn't really feel any different than the day before. She was trying to sort out what it all meant, if anything. The afternoon passed uneventfully and no one even asked about her day. She made dinner and cleaned the dishes so her mom could go to be and get some "much needed rest." Micki told her. She was definitely going back. That much she was sure of. When she was sure her mom had gone to sleep, Micki slipped down to the pasture again. When Billy opened the door, he seemed to have cooled a little. He closed the door and embraced her, but she sensed he was holding back again. "What's up?" She asked. "Nothing," he answered. She told him he was lying. He told her about his dinner with his dad. Freddie made up a hypothetical story about Billy and Micki in order to prove a point. It wasn't so hypothetical. It had left Billy with a bad feeling. He said, "I should never have encouraged you to sneak out of your house in the middle of the night. I should never have done a lot of things. I've been selfish and childish. I'm sorry." She lit a joint she had brought with her and said. I was sneaking out of my house in the middle of the night, long before I met you Billy. Now, when I sneak out, I have a friend to visit, and a warm bed. Before, I only had the ground and the wildlife, and 'even good people are inherently selfish,' or at least that's what my father said. It made sense at the time. I'm not sorry and you can't make me sorry, so stop trying. Blow me a shotgun." She passed him the joint and he did. He was completely diminished. After they smoked the joint, he took her into his bedroom and retrieved his manhood.

Billy walked Micki home on the road before Brett came home from work. Worse things were going on in the world, Micki had told him. She was right. Jenny's own sister was dating a man ten years older than she was. His own cousin Delores hung out with some older guys. People only looked at Micki differently because of the Jeff Incident. She was right. Although she didn't seem to know it, Billy himself had looked at her differently after she told him. They were going to have their relationship, like normal people, or as normal as they could get, even if they had to slip around sometimes. They said goodnight and she slipped in the backdoor as usual. She had no trouble falling into a dreamless restful sleep. Micki woke up happy in her bed. She was even nice to Jeff as she ran out the door on her way to Jenny's house. Her dad had a cement mixer, they were going to mix concrete with tiny pebbles and finish the last section of the patio. It was fun.

The next morning, Rita made brunch and told Evan she was looking forward to meeting his new friend while Evan promised they could all have dinner soon. She was actually smiling, not pretending to. It was amazing. Even Jack seemed to be happier because she was happy. While Rita took the dishes in, Evan said, "Dad, I uh, I could use some extra money. It's not easy trying to impress someone, and my lunch money budget isn't helping." Jack didn't get a chance to say anything before Evan finished. "You don't have to trust me, I know I fucked up, but if you did, I promise you won't regret it." Jack said. "I hope you don't talk like that to your new friend," and Evan said "of course not." Jack continued, "I was going to give you this before I left." He handed him his old account cards and check-book. "I thought you used this to pay the court costs?" Evan looked puzzled. Jack said that he had only confiscated his articles and told him he closed it, to be sure he wouldn't try to access it. That he had paid the fines and restitutions out of his own savings. He told Evan that he was proud of how well he had adjusted and looked forward to meeting his new friend as much as Rita did. Rita stepped back outside and asked Evan if he wanted her to hire a maid for him a few days a week, or even a live-in. "Definitely not." he said and smiled. As soon as they were gone, Evan went to Montgomery. He had some things to buy. He was on top of the world.

CHAPTER 7

I became insane, with long intervals of horrible sanity. ~Edgar Allan Poe

Evan couldn't wait to show Micki his boat. They needed to establish some things first. He decided he wouldn't follow her any more. He didn't need to now. He had a new strategy. The following Monday she showed up at school with a perfect note she had written herself. Micki could forge anyone's handwriting, and was the absolute "go to" girl for an excused absence, a check-out note, or a smoking pass. The latter being her specialty. A parent had found out once that her kid was smoking at school, and when presented with the consent form with her signature on it, thought she must have absent-mindedly signed it. Micki was very good. Evan hadn't needed a note from Micki, Jack had signed the consent form upon Evan's enrollment. He knew Evan smoked, and didn't like the idea of him sneaking around to do so. Still Evan was aware that she had this talent. He liked that about her, and that she was willing to do it, for free. She just did it so everyone who wanted to could join in. She was either generous to a fault, or stupid he used to think. Now he knew neither thing was true. She was unique, priceless.

Just so he could hear her lie, Evan asked her why she wasn't there the Friday before. She told him she hadn't been feeling well and had stayed home. Unready to stop the game, he told her he had gotten a new boat and wanted to try it out, that she should come over because it was "bad-assed," using Micki's favorite word with a smile. He said he knew she was going to love it. She told him she would try to get by there as soon as she could but that she had a lot going on now. He immediately thought of her with Billy, "I'm sure you do Micki, but you really should make time to have some fun with me." Micki didn't really understand the comment. She had never ridden in a boat just to ride in a boat, there had to be a purpose, "Where do you want to take it?" She asked him. He said he wasn't sure, that she knew more about the lake than he did. Micki told him that he should ask Boudreaux, that he was really into the boating thing, and he could show him all the coolest spots. Evan looked visibly upset, and said, "Okay, I'm sorry I asked," She hadn't intended to hurt his feelings and put a hand on his arm saying she was sorry. He knew it, she was sensitive. When she touched him, he thought his heart skipped a beat. She said that she really didn't think she would have time to come by any time soon. Another lie, she was such a fucking liar. He told her he stopped by and talked to her mom last Friday, and Sara had told him she left early for school. Micki looked stunned and wrinkled her brow as she got her books from her locker. "You talked to my mom?" He went on "Yeah, I stopped by to see if you wanted a ride and she said you left early." Micki closed her locker and told him, "I skipped. I do it sometimes with Kena, a friend of mine who's out of school." She was still in a hurry and told him she didn't want to be late. "Is the library making you bring a pass now?" He asked. He wasn't smiling any more. He looked at her seriously. "I saw you." She stopped, what did he just say? She managed to ask "What?" He said "See me after school." and he turned and went down the hall toward his class. Micki went to Math class and didn't even pause at the library. Ms. Brown acknowledged her as she entered "Well Micki, we're so happy you could join us this week." She took a seat next to her friend Wanda. When the bell rang, she rode with Sophia and Jenny. She told them what Evan had said to her, and then she told them where she had been. Sophia said, "How do you know he's even talking about that. He could be talking about anything. He probably saw you selling something. It's not like putting it on my cousin is the only wrong thing you're doing." She laughed. Jenny agreed it was probably bullshit. Sophia said she was paranoid, and anyway, who cares. Sara would never believe some jerk who just moved there. Micki was being paranoid. They all agreed. Micki got out of the car at Jenny's and left her books there while she went down to see what he was up to. Jenny wanted to go, but still a little nervous, Micki didn't want her to. She walked down the off road toward the mansion carrying her purse, believing she knew what he wanted.

Evan saw her coming from his bedroom window. He picked up a box from his bed and took it downstairs. She knocked on the French doors and he let her in. She came in and he asked her to have a seat. She sat in the chair by the sofa. He sat on the sofa and looked at her smiling. "I think I know what's going on," she started and he waited curiously to hear her thoughts. She opened her purse and pulled out a quarter ounce of weed. He looked at it and shook his head. She put it back and pulled out an eight ball. He looked surprised, but interested and she told him that she would sell to him "cheap" if he would just keep it quiet. He was amused at her attempt to guess what he'd seen. He hadn't known about the coke, and he did want some so he played it off and agreed. Still he was acting strange. She had almost had enough and said to him, "Look if this is bullshit, I have things to do. I'm just gonna go if you don't get to it." Still smiling, he sat up and said, "You're in no position to bargain. But so be it. Here's the deal. I have been in some shit, and fell out with my parents. I want you to help me get back in." She looked confused. "What can I do?" "You'll be amazed at what you can do for me Micki." he told her. She asked what he had been talking about at school. He thought about it for a minute, and then told her he had seen her smoking pot in her yard with a guy in a green Pinto. Micki seemed relieved. "That's just Cameron. He's an old friend." He was still amused. "Are you going to help me?" She was pissed deep down at the way he was going about this, but her instincts screamed at her to play along. "What do you want me to do?" He handed her the box. She opened it. Inside there was a long black dress that was split in the front and bound with black silk cords at the waist. The cords twisted upward and created the straps that attached at the low scooped out back. It looked expensive. She looked at Evan for an explanation. "I want you to have dinner with my parents, and pretend to be my new girlfriend." Micki was still looking at the dress, "do I get to keep it?" He loved her smile. "If they're happy, it's yours." She thought for a second, "When is this dinner?" He was still smiling at her. "Soon, very soon, will you do it?" "Okay," she said. He told her she should try the dress on in case it needed to be altered, and she said she would take it home and do so, but he insisted that she do it there. How could he be sure she wouldn't just keep the dress and never come back otherwise? He didn't want her to "take advantage" of him, he said. She conceded and went into the bathroom to try it on. The dress fell to the floor and she loved the way it felt. She couldn't wait for Billy to see her in it. She came out of the bathroom and modeled it for him. He was speechless for a moment. It fit her perfectly, like it was made for her. He said, "Perfect," trying to sound casual. He then told her she should come there to get ready, but be sure and fix her hair. He would tell her more when he set the time with his parents. After he paid her for the coke and they did a line together, Micki left and went back to Jenny's. Jenny again, thought it was weird, and it was. Jenny told Micki she shouldn't do it. But Micki said she felt like she should. Make him happy, he'll be cool after that, she decided. Jenny promised to help her with her hair and they did their homework.

Evan couldn't believe how well that had gone. Micki had seemed so impressed with the dress. Maybe this would be easier than he thought. He had other boxes for her, but these things take time. He took out some of the coke he had bought from Chemo on his little shopping trip, and did two lines. He thought Micki probably had the better cocaine. He was going to spend the afternoon trying to determine which was the most potent. Whatever she did now, he intended to be a part of it.

Halloween was coming, fourteen days away, the school was getting ready for the fall festival and Micki was as excited as she had ever been. Micki and Billy had spent hours on a Saturday afternoon making out on the chaise lounge in front of the big screen television at Cal's house. She was "hypnotic" he told her, like a drug, and she liked that adjective, it seemed to apply. They were alone, completely oblivious to Cal's dad when he walked in the room. Billy had his hand in Micki's unbuttoned shorts, clearly committing a sex act. They were kissing and her shirt was completely undone. Cal's dad would note to Freddie later that she seemed "pretty aggressive" to him. He'd say that Billy would be in a" ton of trouble" if that "little girl gets pregnant." He threw his keys down on the table and startled them. She sat up breathing heavily while trying to button her pants and tie her shirt back up. She'd felt like she was high and a little drunk. Billy did not jump up or try to leave quickly. He apologized to Cal's dad for being "out of line" in his house. And then asked Micki if she needed a ride, they left giggling a little and went back to Billy's house to finish what they started. She was painfully aware of the effect she'd had on Billy's life. She regretted that he had to sneak around with her. Every time she heard him make an excuse for being with her, or to be with her, she felt bad. He wasn't a liar, or he hadn't been. He had sacrificed his own principles because she couldn't leave him alone. She knew. She felt like she was destroying him, but she couldn't stop. The sex was exhaustive. She didn't understand anything she had read in romance novels at this point. She didn't like cuddling so much. She didn't want to talk afterwards, she just wanted to sleep and she liked to stretch out when she slept. She had agreed to keep the sneaking out to a maximum of three times a week, on different nights each week, so as not to create a pattern. She imagined that her mother might really like him someday. It all seemed so far-fetched. Billy had told her that Freddie suspected, actually, "knew," that he was "...Fooling around with that little girl." Billy had tried to lie but Freddie didn't believe him. Billy didn't care at this point, but he told her he could feel the axe dropping and wondered how long it would be before everybody knew. That they should "plan for that day."

Micki busied herself writing her story that week. She wrote part 13 to "Demon High" and true to her word, wrote Evan in as the unlikely super-smart, holy-water-gun wielding hero. She sought him out at school to let him read it first. He seemed really excited and grabbed her and kissed her, quickly, on the mouth. Micki was clearly startled but tried not to be offended. She figured he was just happy to be in the story. Most people didn't get that excited, but "to each his own" her mother always said. When he read it later, he thought it was an essay of Micki's inner feelings for him. What she was trying to tell him, was buried in the words, deep in her psyche. She had found him at school and put it in his hand. It was a testament to the fate that was bringing them together. She had made his character strong, a powerful senior with amazing mind power, who turned the demon's power back into itself. It was amazing he thought. She really did like him. She thought he was smart and heroic, and sexy too. He couldn't wait to tell her what he thought of her. He took the folder home with him and kept it. Their dinner was that coming weekend, just two days after she gave him the folder, and she seemed to really be looking forward to it.

Evan had talked to Boudreaux, like she suggested, in the name of consistency, and had gotten pretty good at driving his boat. He now knew the lake even better, and had seen most of the cliffs where the kids liked to dive in the summer. Except for the pot smoking, he had thought Boudreaux and Jake were pretty cool, and he had them over to his house a lot lately. They had told him more about Micki than anyone else had. Boudreaux confessed he had a thing for Micki since the seventh grade, but that he also had a thing for Juanita and Jenny as well. He laughed then and said, "What can I say, one woman just won't be enough for me. I am a man of many tastes." Jake who had been quiet up until that point said, "I heard she made a pass at her step-dad and that when he rejected her, she ran away from home in shame, but..." before Jake could finish Evan whistled and said "There it is...I knew it." Boudreaux, having heard the same story but not one to tell tales, didn't say anything, but he stopped laughing. Evan was terribly interested and said, "Are you serious?" Jake just shook his head yes and opened his mouth to say something but Evan cut him off again and blurted out without thinking, "Oh my god, she's a bigger whore than I thought." Boudreaux, who knew better and didn't like the way he said it, stood up and told him to take it back, that Micki was nice, and she was "not a whore." When Evan refused by saying with a laugh "All women are whores Boudreaux! Just because she never fucked you, doesn't mean she's not a whore." Boudreaux took a swing at him. Evan, who was far more physically fit and quite a bit taller than sixteen-year-old Boudreaux, ducked, and hit him in the face hard enough to cause blood to spew from his lip. Jake jumped between them telling Evan to "Get the fuck back." Jake, who always seemed to have his shit together, was a black belt in Kung Fu, and everybody knew it. Jake said to him, "I said I heard that you asshole, we all heard it, but we know what really happened. I heard you were a little bitch in Juvi too and maybe that's true, huh?" Evan looked surprised that Jake knew he'd been busted. "You're a real shit Evan, you don't really know any of us still you think you're better than we all are, but you're just as fucked up as anybody living here and more so than most." Evan backed off and told them to leave, and to not come back. Boudreaux said "Don't worry asshole, no one wants to hang out here with you anyway." He and Jake got into his boat and drove away. Evan wished he hadn't said it out loud, he really liked those guys. It was too late now. He just hoped they wouldn't say anything to Micki about it. Not before Saturday anyway.

That Friday night, before the Saturday dinner at Andrews, Micki slipped up to Billy's. He was waiting for her. A creepy movie was on the satellite and he had popcorn and cokes, just like the theater, but he also had tea, which she wanted instead. He didn't want her to go to that dinner, but she insisted it was not a big deal, and besides, Evan basically threatened to tell her mom she was getting stoned. She couldn't wait to show him the dress, but he didn't want to see it. He told her he wasn't jealous, he just didn't trust Evan and a five hundred-dollar dress wasn't going to change that. He asked her if expensive clothes were what she wanted out of life, and she said that she wanted more important things than clothes, but clothes were nice too. Billy was sure he would never be able to give her things like that. He was hurt, but tried not to show it. She was still too young to understand the implications of it all, and he was sure, at least on her part, it was completely innocent. He was also sure that tonight would not be the end of Evan's blackmail but he kept it to himself for now. He didn't want to seem too possessive. She promised to come to him as soon as dinner was over. He said he wanted to take her to a real movie, and a real dinner, a real date. She said she was going to cut school the following Wednesday, because she had no tests, and it was completely random, and he could do all those things with her. He reluctantly agreed because he really meant it, and he could think of no other way. He walked her home but not until they were sure Brett was home sleeping. She slipped in the back door, and he went home.

The next day Micki woke up to screaming. Jeff was there. Apparently he was still drunk from some all-night binge. Sara was trying to get him to go to bed and sleep, but he wanted to fight. Micki got up and locked her door, and sat holding a pillow while Jeff screamed and cursed at her mother. After about a half-hour, they must have gone to bed, because she didn't hear anything else. She slowly unlocked her door and went into the kitchen. Brett was there, staring out the kitchen window. He looked at Micki but didn't say anything. She said she was going to Jenny's and opened the kitchen door, he was shaking his head okay. As she was going out the door she said, "She likes you, you know. Jenny, I mean." Brett almost smiled as he went to his room thinking Micki was playing another trick on him. Micki closed the door and took off down the trail to Jenny's house. Micki felt guilty about that, as if she had thrown Jenny off a cliff but she tried to put it out of her mind.

Micki and Jenny spent the day giving each other manicures and pedicures and doing Micki's hair. Dinner was at eight, but Micki had to be there by six at Evan's request. His parents would arrive at seven, and she would need to be ready. With her mother thinking she was going to spend the night at Jenny's, Micki slipped on some tennis shoes and went to the old mansion at five-thirty. Evan answered the door and let her in. He directed her to the upstairs bathroom just outside his own room. He said he had made it female friendly and her dress and shoes were there. She put on the dress and slipped on the shoes, she detested pantyhose and refused to wear them. She took the pins out of her hair and rings of curls fell to her shoulders. She took some hairspray from the bag she had brought with her and sprayed it all over. She let it dry, and sprayed it again. Aquanet from Jenny's mom, it was like shellac. She touched up her make-up and brushed her teeth again before putting on lipstick. She knew she was beautiful. No one ever had to tell her that. She gave herself a once-over and satisfied, left the bathroom. He greeted her at the foot of the stairs. He was wearing a suit and she was aptly impressed. She told him he cleaned up nicely, and he said he had a lot of practice but could say the same for her. He told her she was stunning, and presented her with a gift box. She asked him what the catch was, and he said, "No catch, I just want to complete your outfit." She opened the box to find a bottle of Chanel #5. She smiled and took it out. He took it from her and sprayed behind her ears and the back of her neck. She sensed he was about to try to get intimate with her and she wondered in that split second, if his parents were coming at all. Had it all been a trick? They both heard the car in the driveway and Micki was relieved. She put away the perfume and got ready to meet his parents. Micki was gracious and polite and even curtsied. Rita was taken with her and Jack was obviously impressed. At dinner, Micki surprised even Evan with her knowledge of many subjects including the country club in Montgomery. After his look of surprise she confessed her dad had been a member before moving to Florida. This only convinced Evan that he was right about her, that she was right for him. Rita had brought the maid and pulled out all the stops for Evan's new friend. She hoped Micki would give Evan a new sense of direction. She certainly seemed poised. One awkward moment Evan kissed her in the great room, "Just for affect." he'd said, but it really bothered Micki. When the night was over, Jack told Evan he should take Micki home in the beamer. She gathered her things and her gifts and when they reached her house, she started to get out saying it was fun and thanks for the dress but he stopped her putting a hand on hers and holding it there for a second. "It was fun wasn't it? It could be like this Micki, we could have a lot of fun together. You should think about it, about what's important to you, to your family." He picked up her hand and kissed it, and told her to wait. He got out of the car and went around to open her door. He held out his hand to her, she seemed to be a little put off by this but she didn't say anything. He walked her to the front door and she slipped inside before he had a chance to try and kiss her. She thanked him again before closing the door. He stood there for a moment imagining her face if he kicked the door in behind her. "Patience" he reminded himself and instead went back to his dad's car believing in time and fate.

There was a big party planned at Cal's house on Halloween. Because so many people would be there, Billy, still feeling ashamed of being caught with her, wanted Micki to come to his house instead. She agreed to make an appearance (because she really needed to see Cal) and then leave the party early with him. They would slip out together, and spend the fright night watching scary movies on satellite. She would have no curfew that night, and it would be perfect. Except for the nagging thought that she was ruining the best year of his life. After she made the required apron in home economics, she spent many days working on her costume. The "grave dress" amounted to an old black string bikini she'd gotten from Kena, with several yards of sheer gray material sewn to it. She was going to be "a woman who crawled out of the grave to take revenge on her murderous lover." It was all so dramatic and Micki was very into it. When her mother commented on the material and style of the outfit, Micki had told her, "Blame yourself, you bought me the Barbie dolls," and Sara had actually laughed. Jenny and

Sophia were putting their costumes together as well. Sophia would be a French maid, and Jenny, was going as a gangster. They planned to meet at Sophia's and ride to Cal's house together.

Evan was ready to make his demand. She would come to his house on Halloween and they would have fun. He knew what she wanted now. He'd picked up that album she asked about when they had first met, the one with "Hells Bells" on it. An album, because she seemed to be a sucker for a turntable. He would play that for her. He would tell her the truth about his past, and she would understand. He would be the person she saw in him. Then she could stop acting like such a whore. First he would help her with her wardrobe. He would buy her the things classy girls wore. She would be stunning in those clothes he thought. Jasmine would never be the same. He spent a few hours in her room one day when he ditched school. He waited for her mother to leave, but her brother was still in the house sleeping. The step-dad could have been there, but he took that chance. It had paid off and Jeff was nowhere around. He went to her room and took some dresses, cut-off shorts and other things that made her look like a slut. When she was his girlfriend, he thought, she would have to do better, because although he liked the idea that she was a slut, he didn't date girls who looked like sluts and he had enough of her personal style already. Micki had to know that she was flaunting her body. How could she not know? He picked up the brown bikini he had seen her wearing all summer and smelled it. It smelled like the lake, and Micki. The top was too small. He remembered her tits bulging in it, and all the guys staring at her. He put it back, she might miss it. She had the most amazing tits. He spent many nights thinking of those tits while Sandy got him off. Her stomach was lean and her belly button was deep. He thought of it often. He found a pair of her panties on the floor and put them in his pocket. He wanted her so bad. He went to her dresser and opened a trinket box. An old string of pearls was inside, with a very old, gold, man's Bulova watch. It was the type with the tiny second hand inlaid into the base. He wondered if it had been Micki's dad's watch. She had a Van Halen poster on one wall, and a Dark Side of the Moon poster on the other. A small record player with Led Zeppelin still on it, was turned off. He knew she only hung out with stoners. That was going to have to change. He couldn't introduce some pot smoking whore dressed like a prostitute to his parents. He needed Micki to shine. She would be his ticket back. Rita would love Micki and her "I'm so sweet." routine. She could be the kind of girl you take home to your step-mother, and the kind you take to bed. She was just a little rough around the edges. She had a filthy mouth, and legs like peanut butter, he thought of the joke, "smooth, creamy and easy to spread." He could feel himself getting hard thinking about it. She had so much shit, and he didn't have time to go through it all, he would just have to set some ground rules. She just didn't understand how it all made her look. She would love what he had planned for her. He imagined her lying by his parents' pool on Bell Road, and what his ex and all her cunt friends would think. It made him smile when he thought about it. They would know that they couldn't fuck with him, that he didn't lose. Now it was just a matter of waiting for the right moment to invite her. He was looking forward to it, and couldn't wait to tell her. He knew how she felt now. Soon, she would know how he felt. He slipped out the way Micki always did, through the kitchen, carrying the bag of clothes. Brett never came out of his room.

The Monday before Halloween, the school was buzzing with excitement, the gym was being transformed into a carnival. They'd planned a cakewalk, a booth for bobbing apples and even a makeshift "haunted hospital" they would put together in the girls locker room. The Friday night festival would include the regular football game and related activities during which the students would sell tickets to the festival. Micki had been selected to run the "Fortune teller" booth. She couldn't wait to bring her crystal ball and give everyone the willies. Evan had seen them working outside the gym and stopped to ask Micki what was happening. By now, Micki was sure that Jenny was right about Evan when they met him, he was a strange one. He had been giving her the creeps lately. Feeling pretty strange herself, she didn't hold it against him. She told him about the festival, which he was already aware of and he offered to help. She was grateful to have someone help her make the cardboard booth. She didn't tell him that she would be the fortune teller, she wanted to test her costume and see how many people would recognize her, or not. Evan didn't get permission to work on the gym. He decided in all the confusion and excitement, if he told his teachers that he had been asked to work on the decorations, they would believe him. He put down his satchel and helped her measure the cardboard for the walls. "I haven't seen you around much," he lied. He was stretched out across the cardboard sheet on his hands and knees with a tape measure and a marker "where you been?" She had a box cutter and was carefully cutting along the line he had marked. "Oh, I've been getting ready for Halloween, my costume is almost finished." She looked up and smiled at him. "What are ya'll doing? Trick or treating?" he asked with a sly grin on his face. She laughed and said "Maybe, maybe more tricks than treats." and she winked at him. That wink, sent a thrill through him. He wondered how many times she winked at Billy like that before he forgot she was just sixteen. She would have to be kept on a short leash, he thought to himself. "What are you going to be doing?" she asked him. It was the first time she ever seemed to care about his plans. It seemed that she might be getting more confident about her feelings toward him. "I'm having a little party at the house." She stopped cutting for a moment, interested and asked him, "Really, I haven't heard about it," "Well, it's kind of exclusive, I didn't want word to get around because if too many people show up and trash the house, my dad will have an aneurism." She picked up the pieces to the little shack, one by one to make sure they fit together properly and then said, "Now we have to cut the windows," she laid the board back down on the concrete and he started drawing the windows so she could cut them. He almost reached out to touch her hair but stopped himself when she broke the silence again. "So who's going to the party?" She smiled at him before he said, "You, hopefully." He stopped what he was doing and looked at her seriously. At that moment she understood that he really liked her, that he maybe more than liked her. Her face turned a little red, and she told him that she didn't know if she could make it or not, that this was so last-minute, that she didn't know if she would have time. He couldn't believe his ears. She should be jumping at the chance. Maybe he had misread the moment. Maybe she was still just a little nervous. He would let it play out. She told him about the big party at Cal's and the midnight grave-walk at the Marina, where they were going to dig faux graves for prizes. She then promised him that if she had time, she would be happy to stop by. "You should make time." he told her, "You won't regret it." she smiled and said "Okay. Now let's pick this up and put it together and tomorrow, we can paint it." After it was carefully glued and taped, they pushed it to the side and she told him she was going to help work on the "haunted hospital" they were building in the locker room. She asked if he still wanted to help and he said "I am at your service, lead the way." As they crossed the gym, Ms McCain, their organizer and Home Economics teacher, called everyone's attention saying she needed some strong boys to help her move some sound and stage equipment from the drama department. Micki laughed and pointed at him to say, "That means you Evan," He smiled and said, "Yeah, I guess I'd better go." and went with the other boys and Ms McCain, thinking he would be glad when all this nonsense was out of the way and he could stop pretending to like all this stupid shit, he glanced back at her as he left the gym.

He and Micki worked on the festival for the rest of the week. When Thursday rolled around it had come together nicely. Ms McCain had them all in the gym going over the planned activities. She told them that all the students who were working the carnival should be "ready and in their booths when the football game ends, so some of you may want to leave the game accordingly dependent on your own final preparations." She noted exceptions for Danny and Boudreaux, who would be late for their appearance as monsters in the haunted hospital, as they were actually on the team. As they were leaving the school that afternoon Evan caught Micki in the parking lot and offered her a ride home. She said that Kena was picking her up and they were going to do some Halloween shopping. He said okay and said he would wait with her instead. She was going on about the festival, and how cool she thought it had turned out when he reached out and took her face in his hand and attempted to kiss her. He put his mouth on hers and felt the warmth of her tongue on his and then she was resisting. She pulled away from him and looked shocked. She said, "Evan, what are you doing?" He said, "It's all right, don't be upset. I know how you feel." Just then Kena drove up beside her. Micki glared at him and said, "Don't ever do that again." She got in the car and he watched the car disappear. Even though she was fighting it, he knew she felt the fire in that kiss. He went to his bike and headed for home with a renewed enthusiasm.

Micki could hardly sleep that night, she needed to see Billy. The stress was going to drive her crazy she was sure. She hadn't been able to see him this week because she had been working at school every afternoon. Now Evan. What the hell was he thinking? Micki had to see Billy tonight. They had agreed she wouldn't sneak out this week, but tonight was different, she reasoned. She was so anxious, she needed him to calm her nerves. When she was sure it was safe to go, she slipped out and went down to the pasture, hoping he would be awake.

Evan wasn't watching her house when she slipped out. He was angry now. She was a fucking tease. How could she lead him on like that? Maybe she wanted him to take control of it all. He had to. He decided a course of action and he was sticking to it. Tomorrow night he would tell her that she had to come to his party, and she would agree, he knew, it didn't matter what she did now, it was just a matter of time. He was home with Sandy, expressing his aggression. Sandy would be working at the Marina on Halloween. She had been a faithful surrogate sex partner in the weeks before and tonight was no exception. She had invited him to the Marina for the grave walk, and he told her he would go. She was probably in love with him at this point, he thought. He chuckled a little when he imagined the look she would have when he didn't show up.

Billy was watching late night TV when she knocked on the door. Just a little tap, he knew it was her. He got up thinking something must be wrong for her to break her own rule, and opened the door pulling her inside. She was standing there in a t-shirt and a pair of cut offs with no shoes. She immediately threw herself into his arms and kissed him more aggressively than normal. He put his hands on her waist and asked her what was wrong, "Nothing," she said breathlessly "nothing at all, I just really missed you, I wanted to see you so bad." She kissed him again, and he complied. He pushed her against the wall. She ran her fingers through his hair before she changed direction and put her hands inside his green t-shirt until she found his back, She felt the chill bumps rise on his skin and that excited her. He started taking off her faded, raveled shorts, and she was suddenly taking down his zipper and kissing his neck where she had buried her face. Billy got on his knees on the floor and pulled her down into his lap. She wrapped her legs around his back. As he entered her, the denim of his jeans created a sensation in her thighs that nearly made her squirm away but she held on and cried out throwing her head back exposing her neck for him and he buried his face in her warm flesh and when he pulled her hips in firmly, she cried out again. He lifted her up without separating to carry into the bedroom. They fell on the bed together. She was so urgently passionate, he had to hold her face still to tell her she could get pregnant if he didn't stop right then, and get a condom. She gave a disappointed groan but let him go, as she didn't want to be pregnant, ever, she thought. When he came back they made love, without keeping track of time. When it was over, she told him she hated to leave him, and exhausted, he told her to just stay. "You know I can't" she said," just one more night, and then I can stay with you all night," she kissed him again and put her hand on his stomach, feeling his arousal she asked if he had another condom. He went to get it and she asked if she could put it on him. He said "Sure," and showed her how. When it was all the way on, she leaned over and kissed it, The act seemed to startle him a little, "What are you doing?" he asked her, "you do it to me all the time. . . ." she said, ". . . and I've been thinking about it," He raised his eyebrows and said "You dirty girl." as she slowly traced his erection with the tip of her tongue as he watched. She felt him tremble and he grabbed her by the waist and pulled her on top of him pushing her down on the erection she'd created. This time, she was definitely more aggressive, he thought. She didn't want it to end, she said but it was over in just a few minutes. She cried when she climaxed and he held her unsure what else to do. They took a shower together and within the half hour, he was walking her across the pasture headed to her house. He stopped at the curve in the road and watched her cross and sneak in the backdoor. He wondered if they could possibly make it the year or so it would be before she would be eighteen, and free. At this moment, he really hoped so. He would be twenty-three by then and Micki still wouldn't be as old as he is now. His head was aching. He was walking back home when he noticed the cigarette butts. They were strewn along the ditch on the other side of the lake road within sight of Micki's house. He knew she didn't smoke that brand and wondered who would have thrown so many of them there like that. Maybe Jeff emptied his ashtray there. He would mention it to her tomorrow at the festival, when he went to get his fortune told. He went home and didn't sleep. He figured this is what shit really felt like. The weeks he had been sleeping with Micki had been great and that's why he felt so bad. He knew he was fucking her up but he couldn't help himself. He had decided to go to the festival only because, one, he would have gone, even if Micki wasn't there, and two, because it was a booth type thing, and Micki wouldn't be in class. She would be just like any other booth, made up of parents, teachers, alumni and students alike. It wouldn't be hard to get through. He tried to tell himself it would be all right, but he didn't really believe that. Micki would have to end it, he was sure of that. He was powerless to resist her now, he was afraid he might be in love with her. The absurdity of that realization made him sick to his stomach. He started thinking about maybe getting some therapy.

When Micki slid into her bed she was so tired she didn't remember going to sleep. She dreamt she was in a forest somewhere. It was strange because she was holding the hem of the green silk gown she was wearing because she was worried that it would snag and tear. She was looking for the little girl, the little girl who was lost. She followed a trail cut from years of use that passed old moss covered trees. Everything was beautiful and wet. The ground was soft dirt that was really just decades old dead, rotting leaves maybe six inches deep. It reminded her of the fairy tales she'd heard when she was a child. She wasn't sure how far she had walked when the path was suddenly cut off by a deep ditch that had a small stream at the bottom. She looked left and then right for a way across and noticed a fallen tree in the distance. The tree seemed to create a natural bridge across the stream so she headed in that direction. When she got closer she could see past the ball of tangled roots that had partially hidden the other side of the fallen tree and there's where she found her, walking gingerly across the fallen log to the other side. The girl seemed unaware of the huge velvet covered rattle snake that was about to lunge up at her from the roots. When it struck Micki reached out and grabbed it by its neck. It writhed and hissed and the girl turned to face her. Micki was staring into the eyes of the snake and said firmly "No." before she hurled it into the stream below. When she turned to face the girl there was a moment of faint recognition and then she was awake. She sat up in bed and realized it was still dark outside. She heard something move in her room and held her breath so she could hear it better. She still heard breathing. She thought of Evan and panic welled up inside her, before she said out loud, "Who's there?" But no one answered her. She was afraid to get out of bed or make any noise that might indicate she had moved at all. She carefully reached up to her head board remembering the two glow sticks her cousin Ricky had given her. He was a soldier in the Army and she was his favorite "little fighter." She'd never thought about breaking one before but now she was afraid and Evan might be about to kill her. So as quickly as she could, she shook the stick hard and when the glass broke inside an eerie green light flooded the room. Still she couldn't see much. She got out of bed and moved to the foot, there, crouched in the corner, someone was still trying to hide. "I see you." she said and went to the door to flip on the switch. There in the corner, with her open treasure box, the one her dad had given her for a birthday in another time, sat Brett, with all her money and a sack of weed in his other hand. She went over and snatched the money from him but he threw the pot across the room. She told him to "get out." of her room, but he was standing over her now and she knew it wasn't going to be that easy. He grabbed her hair pushing her down to the floor. She almost screamed but knew she would never survive it if her mother came in right now. "Give me the fucking money," he said through gritted teeth. He was having trouble holding her. She was strong for a little sister. She said "No." in the same tone but he just twisted her hair tighter around his fist and pushed her down again saying, "You give me the money right now, or we'll go tell mom how you got it you little cunt." She hesitated still but decided she could get the money back, so she said okay and gave it to him. He shoved her to the floor when he let her go and started counting the money as he walked away. At the door he turned to her and said, "Thanks, this will fix my car." and then he left the room. She knew she had to get that money back. She and Cal were friends, but if she couldn't pay for her goods, that friendship would be tested. Cal had even said that he loved dealing with Micki, she was "always on time and always with the right amount." He'd said so more than once. She couldn't let Brett fuck that up and she knew she had to figure out a way to get it back. She knew right then that she really hated Brett, and his Chevelle. After he left her room she took her wasted glow stick and went out the back door to cross the road to the trails and headed back past the quarry to the lake. She climbed down the side and onto the ledge and then jumped the sixty feet into the water with the glow stick still shining wearing only her sleep shirt and panties. The water was cold but she looked around anyway, the water was cloudy but it was beautiful. She would dive as deeply as she could and still be comfortable holding her breath. The lake was cool. Slick rocks and unidentified creatures on the bottom and fish everywhere. It was awesome. She came to the surface to float and held the stick underneath the water illuminating everything underneath her. This was easing her mind and soon enough she didn't feel angry or desperate. She stayed there floating and diving, enjoying the eerie chemical light till she could see sunlight breaking on the horizon and she dropped the fading glow stick to watch it fall to the bottom. Then she crawled out, climbed up and went home.

CHAPTER 8

"I have, indeed, no abhorrence of danger, except in its absolute effect- in terror." ~Edgar Allan Poe

Everyone was getting out of school at noon for an early pep rally and to prepare for the festival. Pumpkins, dried corn, hay and carved Jack-so'-lanterns decorated the hallways. They had all worked so hard on the gym and there was excitement in the air. The girls picked up the costumes they'd made from the Home Economics Department and went to Jenny's house to get ready for the festival. Once there, Jenny took a pack of camel cigarettes from the carton her mother always kept in the kitchen. They smoked and showered and put on make-up and redid their make-up. Jenny used all blacks and rays for her Mafia look but Micki chose deep purple and cobalt blue for her eyes. Jenny's sister Alexis was home and was having fun helping Sophia get the dead look. They hadn't had so much fun in some time, and they would all agree if asked. Alexis gave them each one more go over to make sure everything was in place and then she told them they looked great. Alexis, a freshman at college now, wasn't coming because she was dating a guy from the city, and they were going to dinner and a movie. Her boyfriend was 26, much to her mother's dismay. Micki wished she could see Billy openly. Alexis wished them well and warned Jenny about stealing her mother's cigarettes as they went out the door to Sophia's car. They pulled out of the drive and headed to the festival, Micki the Gypsy, Jenny the mad gangster and Sophia the bloody patient. Toni, who would be greeting people at the door and selling tickets to the booths, was dressed as a scarecrow. It was going to be an excellent precursor to Halloween the next day. When they arrived, they took their places and waited for the people to come in. The team had won their game, 28-0, and everyone was in hypermode. After a few minutes, the doors opened and the people came. Micki's booth required one ticket. She was busy most of the night being right next to the entrance. Telling various ridiculous fortunes, she was having a blast. Her make-up had started to run, but she didn't care. Ms McCain kept bringing her lemonade and cookies, and they kept the people moving through. She had used her own black light and her own "crystal ball." A snow globe that had been given to her by a babysitter named Haywind, before her parents were divorced. Haywind had committed suicide at a time when Micki was very attached to her by throwing herself in front of a car. The snow globe was all Micki had left of her relationship. There was tiny log cabin inside with silver and gold maple leaf shaped glitter. The base said Canada, but Micki just wrapped it in a piece of purple satin and in the black light, it looked pretty good. She was telling a man, who she knew was Jake's dad, that he would meet a "tall dark handsome stranger," he laughed and told her "that was pretty good." As he left the shack, Billy backed into the booth watching Evan uneasily. He really didn't like that kid and every time he looked up, there he was. Something about him bothered Billy, but when he was being honest with himself, it really could have just been jealousy. Evan waved over at him but Billy did not acknowledge him. The way he blackmailed Micki into that dinner with his parents was just creepy. He finally lost sight of him and closed the satin curtain on the fake window. "You came." Micki said smiling as he sat down on the stool opposite her. "I told you I was coming," She looked into his eyes and told him she could see his future. He played along and said "well, then, spit it out." She told him in her best gypsy voice "put your hands on the crystal ball touching mine," He did, and she continued, "I see a beautiful blonde girl, but you are very afraid." "Why am I afraid?" he smiled, still playing along, "Because you are watching horror movies together." His face broke into a smile, and she smiled back. He said she was corny and put his ticket in the bowl on the table. He asked her, as casually as possible, "Will I see you later?" She hesitated as if thinking about it and said "Of course." He left the booth. Evan came in right behind him and sat down in the chair. "Wow, Micki, you've out done yourself." She took it as a compliment and smiled when she asked, "Is it that obvious that it's me?" He said "Oh, I saw you arrive, and I watched you come inside the booth." Something about his demeanor, and the way he said it made her uneasy. He just kept staring at her. "I can see your future Evan." She began and he cut her off, "No, Micki, I am going to tell you your future." She looked somewhat taken aback but was still trying to have fun. "Okay," she said, "you tell me my future." He sat there staring at her thinking how stupid she must really be to not get this. She raised her blackened eyebrows at him, "You," he began, "are going to come to my house tomorrow night. You won't be going to Cal's or to the Marina . . . " She cut him off, "Evan I already told you." and he cut her off, "Right," he said angrily, "but now I'm telling you, that you will come to my house, because if you don't, I'll have to have a little talk with the authorities about your little side business and then I'll visit your mother and we'll talk about what a little slut you've been with that old pervert Billy boy." Her eyes got wide but she was frozen in place, "That's right," he said, "I thought that might get your attention." He sat back in the chair and cocked his head to one side, "What are you talking about..." she began again and his tone changed, "Oh Micki, Micki, you silly little bitch. Do you think I'm fucking playing with you? I'm tired of these games" he grabbed her hand tightly as if about to rage at her, and then seemed to calm down, "I would never do that, you can trust me not to play games with you....okay...Do we have an understanding now?" He looked out the cardboard window in Billy's direction who was now cake walking. For the first time she realized how intimidating he was, her heart was pounding loudly. His black jeans and motorcycle boots now looming like a bad omen. He looked back at Micki with raised eyes waiting for an answer. "What do you want from me Evan?" She asked. "I just want you to help me have a party, okay?" All the color had drained from her face. She shook her head in agreement, he said "good." He put his ticket in the bowl, stood up and told her, ". . . and I'll have an eight ball of that good cocaine you've been slinging before you leave tonight." She nodded her head and pulled one out of the gypsy bag she'd stashed under the table. That was one short she would be tonight and she wondered who would miss out and how upset they might be. He seemed surprised that she was bold enough to sell right here at the festival but he just chuckled and said, "Very Good." He finally exited the booth saying "Come early Micki, don't keep me waiting." She tried to shake it off and enjoy the rest of the night. Her gym teacher came in to get an eight ball from her as they had arranged the day before. Micki had thought she was in trouble the first time Ms Black called her into her office in the gym. "I know you've been selling coke." She had told Micki, as if she had told her to run laps. Micki was so nervous and ready to lie but Ms Black only wanted to buy some. She was "tired of driving all the way to Montgomery just to risk getting killed in the Ghetto." she'd said that she had to use it to keep the weight off because "Nobody wants a lard ass for a gym teacher." She didn't treat her any differently than any of the other students, but when they were making a deal, Micki was allowed to call her Joyce. She then had two more to sell and then she would pay Cal the following night and get another batch. She wondered if Evan might want money. The night seemed to drag on after that. Evan had already ruined it for her; she just hadn't realized it yet. By the time Cameron came into the booth she was tired and agitated. Things between them had been strained since she'd started sleeping with Billy but he still felt like he had rights to her company. He offered to take her home, and she told him she had a ride, and then he asked her if maybe she didn't want to grave walk with him the following night. She almost said yes. Everything else had become so complicated and he seemed a warm refuge right then. She told him that she would like nothing more than to grave walk with him, but unfortunately she'd already promised to be at three different places. He said okay and started to leave the booth but she asked him to wait. She missed him. She got up to hug him and wanted to lay her head on his chest and forget everything else but he took her wrists and said "What are you trying to do to me? What the fuck is this? If you love me and want me in your life then by all means, continue, but if you're just using me as some kind of distraction you'd be ashamed of tomorrow then don't bother. This may be nothing to you but it's something to me, it could be everything, but you know, Micki. You know you could destroy me and I'm afraid you wouldn't think twice." She looked down at her feet as he let her go. "I would never use you Cameron and I've never been ashamed of you. I do have deep genuine feelings for you and I am no longer afraid of them, things actually could be different, maybe even fucking great, I don't know. I made choices," She broke down "you fucking blew me off, I needed you, I'm sorry, I was fucked up, I know that" She tried to regain her composure having been unaware of the power in the emotions she'd been holding in. Now they were spilling over and she was trembling... "I don't know what the fuck's wrong with me..." She paused "...but I was never ashamed of you, I worshipped you. I wish I could go back but I can't...but I can't lie to you, you were the only one, ever." She looked at him and nodded her head holding back tears, "It should be you...It should be you... but, you're right... it isn't." With that said he threw his ticket in the bowl and left the booth without another word. Her heart broke and she knew she would never be the same.

Sophia had asked Billy if he could stick around and help the girls carry all that "crap" back home and he said he would. They took down all the things they had brought with them as well as the props they had made at school. They had planned to take them all to the party at Cal's house for decorations, and they packed it in Billy's car. He volunteered to take Jenny and Micki home and they agreed. The back seat was packed, so Micki got in the front, moved to the middle and Jenny got in behind her and closed the door. Billy had won a cake, and Micki had to hold it. He didn't say much on the drive and though Jenny seemed to be in a great mood, Micki was off. Jenny had decided that Micki was nervous about being so close to Billy, and said goodbye when they dropped her off, smiling with a devilish wink at Micki she said "Don't do anything I wouldn't do, but if you do, name it after me." She giggled and closed the car door. Bill turned the car around and went back the way they came but didn't stop at Micki's house. She liked that he had stopped pretending, but she wondered what would happen if Evan told everyone about them. When he pulled into the pasture driveway she said, "I might be late tomorrow night." He pulled the car into the yard and turned off the engine. "Look Micki, if you want to back out..." She abruptly interrupted him, "No! I don't want to back out, I'll be there, I just have to do something else first." he looked concerned, "Something you can't tell me?" he asked. She half smiled at him thinking of all things she hadn't told him. He was trying to be masculine she knew. "Afterwards, I'll tell you okay?" He just looked at her. She leaned over and kissed him and got out of the car and went inside his house, still holding the cake. He finally got out and followed her. After they made the kind of love two people make when they're afraid it might be the last time, they lay in bed together until Micki was sure he was asleep. Then she quietly left and locked the door behind her. She wasn't sure what Evan actually knew, but she didn't want to take any chances until she did know. She could get Billy into trouble and though he liked to walk her home, it was better tonight if he didn't. When she got home, she went in the front door. Brett and Jenny were on the couch making out. She stopped and looked at them for a minute. Jenny smiled and said, "I came to spend the night with you." Micki, looked at Brett, and then back at Jenny with a sick look on her face and said, "ew. I'll be in my room." and walked down the hall to the sound of Jenny giggling. She was so tired. She wanted to tell Jenny some truths about Brett, but the two of them together might make her life easier. She just couldn't bring herself to intervene right now. In all actuality, she hoped Brett would keep his focus on Jenny, and not on her.

CHAPTER 9

Years of love have been forgot, In the hatred of a minute. ~Edgar Allan Poe

Micki dreamed she was in a stone palace wearing the most beautiful dark emerald gown she had ever seen. She was lying on a huge canopy bed in a room just off a banquet hall. She got up and moved to a vanity sitting on top of a dresser. She opened the one drawer and found a wrist watch. It was made of gold and beautiful. She took it and went out to the hall. She sat down at the end of the table but couldn't see the other end as it seemed to go on forever. A voice at the other end of the table was telling her something she couldn't understand, and then she went to the low stone window, and crawled out, holding the hem of the gown up over her bare feet. Time is a gift from God, she thought, and looked at the watch. Once outside the window she found herself on a dirt road and she saw a little boy running, seemingly frantic, looking for a place to hide. In a moment she was with him, hiding behind a tree. A car was speeding down the dirt road and she held the boy and comforted him as the car drove by slowly. A man was hanging out the window searching the trees with a stick in one hand. He was strangely familiar to her. His hair was dark and his skin was pale, too pale. The car drove by without seeing them. She quieted the boy and told him everything was going to be all right but he was inconsolable.

"The man is after me," he cried to her. He couldn't have been more than seven or eight at best, "I know he gone catch me," he bawled. She took his face in her hands and told him, "I will never let him harm you, I will destroy him first." He hugged her then so she picked him up and carried him back to the palace. As she placed him inside the stone window, she kissed his forehead lightly and suddenly she woke up in her room, in a cold sweat, to the sound of loud knocking at the front door and the doorbell ringing in between. She was almost out of bed to go answer it when she heard Kena's voice. "Hi Sara, how are you?" and then her mother "I'm fine, how is Jim?" "He's fine," Kena replied, "Is Micki up?" Sara told her that she wasn't but should be, so it was okay to go on in. She was sitting up in bed when Kena came in closing the door behind her pretending to be quiet but smiling ear to ear. The conversation with Evan came flooding back and pushed the dream out of her head. Micki decided she would tell Kena what happened. Micki got up and looked out the window. "It's really creepy," she said, "You should have seen his face." Kena asked if Micki didn't want her to go with her, but Micki said she was afraid of what he might do if she did anything differently than what he'd asked. That if he told anyone about her dealing and Billy, it could ruin her already pathetic life, and Billy's life, and that's not what she wanted. "He's probably just lonely," she speculated. Kena said "He may be lonely, but he may also be a psychopath." Micki told Kena she wasn't afraid of him, and that she actually felt sorry for him. That he had been somewhat isolated since he arrived on the lake. Kena said, "Well hon, he needs to get over it." Micki said she could have done more for him but had been so wrapped up in her own "self-created soap-opera," that she had forgotten about him and might have even given him the wrong impression. "You know I'm famous for that," she said, without smiling. Kena pointed out that she wasn't "the official tour guide of Lake Jordan." Micki said "yeah, but he knows about the coke, the weed and Billy. If I can help him out, maybe he won't say anything. I can't let my mom find out about any of that, she already hates me and Billy doesn't know I've been dealing, I know he wouldn't understand, he's never been broke. She was crying now and told Kena what happened with Cameron and how she was afraid she "fucked up cause it felt like somebody died." She said she must really love Cameron and she just told him the worst news he's had in two years. That Cameron had been hers, only hers. He was twenty now, and she was sixteen, a place in time they used to dream about together. She looked at Kena, devastated, eyes red and puffy, wide with recognition. Tears still ran slowly down her cheeks in thin sheets that refused to cease. "If I can reason with Evan and get him to loosen up, maybe even go to Cal's party, maybe he'll forget about me and my shit. Maybe it's not too late for me and Cameron. I fucking love him. What the fuck am I going to do?" She started rocking back and forth slightly and Kena put her arm on her shoulder. "Maybe," Kena said, "or this is just the beginning, and you'll be his social slave from now on." Micki laughed at that, wiped her tears and said she had to try. Kena told her Jim had gotten some "skunk bud" and that they should go for a drive. She decided she could use the buzz. They told Sara they were going to buy candy and they did. When they returned, she got out of the car with an intense high, a grocery bag full of candy and a promise from Kena, that she and Jim would wait up for her call, no matter what, even if it took all night.

Sara had draped real moss all over the trees in the yard, and there was a "decayed" looking scarecrow by the driveway. Her brother had taken some of the large rocks that were in abundance in that area, and made a temporary graveyard in the patch of yard inside the half-circle driveway. Bats, which were out every evening this time of year, were flying around the streetlight to one side of the yard. It was appropriately spooky she thought as she went inside. She went into the kitchen and put the bag on the table and got 3 big bowls from the cabinet. She filled each one with a mixture of candy carefully making sure each bowl contained some of everything. All the small kids on the lake would soon be driven from house to house on the lake road, collecting candy, and enjoy being scared. Micki envied them right now, and wished she could go back.

Evan was getting ready. No way would she defy him now. He had all the power. He had never felt so in control before, He was high on the thought of it. He would be in control, and he would not be ignored. When this was over, he thought, she'd be grateful he saved her from her own self-destruction, and even if she wasn't she would still heel, the thought made him smile uncontrollably. He went around the house making sure everything was ready. He hid the keys to the deadbolts so they couldn't be seen and put the last one to the patio into the deadbolt. He was proud of himself for making this all come together. He did a line of the coke he'd gotten from her and sat down to wait.

Micki was taking a shower and trying to remember the details of the dream but all she could remember was time. Unable to understand what it meant she gave it up and turned off the water. She grabbed her towel and began getting ready for the night's events. She used a ton of hair spray and powder to give her hair a texture that resembled gray construction paper after she had curled it with her hot rollers and pinned it to her head. She tied the strings of her costume in double knots to prevent any accidents and determined that barefoot was the way to go. She wrote a note for Billy and told her mother she was going to meet Jenny. She brought the bowls of candy and set them on the console stereo by the front door. She told her mother that she wanted to try and spend the night at Kena's. Her mother said okay, and told her to be home before dinner the following night. She said that she would, and she gave her mother a kiss on the forehead, leaving the impression of a pair of black lips. She slipped out and closed the door behind her. She ran down to the mailbox at the end of Billy's driveway. She put the note inside and turned up the flag, hoping he would see it when he left for Cal's party. She turned and walked to Jenny's house and went to her door. Jenny's dad answered the bell, and he said hello to the "zombie queen" and invited her in. She went straight to Jenny's room and told her she wouldn't be able to go to Cal's party with her, but that she might show up late. Jenny, who had missed the last party, was disappointed but, took Micki at her word. She walked out into the night and left Jenny getting ready for the party and set off down the off-road to the mansion.

Evan was starting to wonder if she was testing him, when he heard the knock on the French doors. He smiled at his own impatience and got up to let her in. When she came inside, he turned the key in the dead bolt, took it out and put it in a bowl on a table by the door. She had walked all the way to the great room, and turned around to ask him where everyone was. "You look amazing," he said to her, and she thought it sounded slightly sarcastic, and then he said "like a dead prostitute." He wasn't smiling. "Evan, where is everyone?" She asked again. "Okay, first we're going to set some ground rules . . . I talk, you listen. I ask questions, you answer them, got it?" She shook her head and he said "No, you answer me with words," There was a tense silence as if she was trying to think of an answer. When he glared at her, she found her voice and said "yes." "Good..." Evan said, "...and to show you I'm a nice guy, I'll go ahead and let you in on something. You are the party Micki, you are everyone." She began to panic but tried to remain cool, "They didn't show up?" she asked innocently. Evan screamed at her, "Did I say you could ask a question? I see your mouth has the same loose hinge your legs have. There is no 'they' Micki." He could see the fear in her face and it aroused him. This was exciting. She was starting to cry, "Evan, I don't know what you want, but . . . " he cut her off." That's okay. . . You will." At this she bolted for the French doors and found them locked. She was about to break the glass with a decorative pot when Evan reached her. He grabbed her by the hair on the back of her head taking the pot with the other hand and slammed her down hard to the floor. "You stupid bitch, if you break that door, do you know what my dad will do to me?" he asked her, "don't fight me; I don't want to kick your ass all night. Besides, I am sure your mom would just love to hear how her whore of a daughter loves to get fucked by older men or do you think she'd rather hear the story of how you're slinging dope all over the lake, huh?," He slammed her head on the floor again when he said, "and I wonder if she would press charges, you and Billy could both go to jail.. Hmm, you tried to put her husband in jail, what would she think of William?" She tried to protest, she was saying "no, you're wrong, no, no you don't understand." He was standing up now. He had her by her hair on her knees. "I should have known you'd act like a bitch. No class Micki, that's what your problem is." He jerked her up to face level and grabbed her throat to scream at her, she was choking for air and slapping at his arm with both hands but it was useless, his arm was like steel. "Stop lying, you fucking liar." he shook her and squeezed harder and she was sure he would strangle her. "I saw you.... I saw you so many times. I saw you slip up to that assholes door. I watched you fuck him!" He moved in close to her face and said quietly, it was almost a whimper. "You liked it. I saw the whole thing. Don't fucking lie to me." She was scratching at his fingers, her eyes wide with realization, she felt like she had lost the circulation in her head when he finally let her go. "Okay, Okay," she said, "I'm sorry, Evan please," pleading with him to "just let me go." Her feet kept slipping on the hard wood floor as she tried to get her footing. He dragged her by her hair to an antique high backed formal chair he had placed by the fireplace in the great room. He pushed her down in it and duct taped her wrists to the armrests. She scratched him once across the cheek. He growled in pain and then finished taping her wrist. He got down close to her face and growled again, "If you shut the fuck up, I won't have to put tape on your mouth," he said. "Do you understand?" He was so close the sound of his voice was offensive and she closed her eyes to the noise. She was sniffling and a whine kept emitting from her throat that she couldn't get control over but she managed a "yes." He started stroking her hair, "Oh now, it's not that bad, you're going to be happy, you'll see, calm down." He took her face in one hand and made her look up at him, "I've got something planned for you that you are absolutely going to love." He could hear her heart pounding and put a hand on her chest, "I can feel your heartbeat racing. You're going to have to calm down now. I'm not going to hurt you." He lied, she knew, he already had hurt her. She had to get out of there somehow. She managed to stop whining, her mind was racing, she was tied to a chair, how could she get free now? What would be next? Sensing panic rising in her again she told herself that she had to remain calm, hide her fear and try to figure out a way to get him to trust her enough to let her go. When she finally stopped trembling so badly he said, "That's better," and walked into another room. She was looking around for something, anything, she could get to and get out of this house, but he came back quickly and she hadn't seen anything. "Why are you doing this Evan?" He stopped and looked at her, "because I love you ...and you love me." She felt like the wind had been knocked out of her. "Now, no more questions, you'll understand everything soon enough." He was carrying a laundry bag and put it down next to the fireplace. He asked her if she wanted something to drink and her throat was on fire so she said, "Yes, please." A trickle of snot was running down her lip, "Very good. That's the way I like to be addressed." He went into the kitchen and came back with a glass of wine, and a box of tissues. He took a tissue from the box and wiped her nose, holding it for her to blow as if she were a child. He said, "I know you like wine, I hope this is okay," he held the glass of wine to her lips and she took a sip, he held the glass back from her and said, "This is a party Micki, drink up," and put it back to her lips tipping it up so she was forced to drink it or wear it. She gulped it down and it was painful when she swallowed. She decided that if he offered her another glass she would pretend to choke. He would be forced to release her from the chair, and then maybe she could get away, but he didn't offer and she didn't want to infuriate him again by asking. He was building a fire in the fireplace. It was so warm she thought, and she knew one thing for certain now, he was crazy. She wished she had let Kena come with her or that Jenny was spying. Did she know deep down and inadvertently sabotage herself? What the hell am I going to do now? She thought. Her chair was so close to the fireplace that when the blaze was finally burning, she became hot very quickly and a sheet of sweat formed on her skin. In the light from the fire, she looked wet from the glitter and gloss she was covered in and she was concerned that the hair spray on her hair might catch fire. He stood in front of her now. "Look at me." he said, and she did. He told her about his criminal record, and about his ex, and how in a jealous rage, she had told on him for something completely unrelated, how he was busted for cocaine, how important loyalty is, he understood betrayal he said. He told Micki that he understood her, better than her friends did, because he knew what she wanted and how to give it to her. He said she was not to see William, as Evan called him, or Cameron again. That she would cease flirting with anyone at school, because she was a prick tease, and that was banned behavior. She could no longer wear the "dark" make up that she wore, and needed to be more conservative on the eye liner. That she would be the star in his life, and he would give her everything she ever wanted. He promised to always keep her satisfied, in every way, as long as she looked respectable and did what she was told he would pay for proper clothing because he knew her mother wouldn't, but that she shouldn't worry about it because she couldn't help that she'd been born to trash, and his dad was "loaded." He said there were more rules they would have to "go over later." He told her weed was a filthy habit, and she would cease to sell it or smoke it. He couldn't take a chance on a stoner. He told her she would stop selling coke or any drug and when she needed something, anything and everything, she would get it from him and only him. He got down on his knees and reached out and touched her breast as she squirmed in the chair. "Chicks with tits like that have to wear a bra Micki." Then he walked back to the fireplace. She was trying to control herself now and listening to him, terrified that any wrong move would be the catalyst for disaster. She watched in terror as he pulled clothes from the laundry bag, her clothes. He held up a short red dress that her cousin had brought her from Mexico, "this is a dress for a Mexican whore." he told her, and burned a hole through the skirt with his cigarette. "When you wear this dress everyone sees your ass and you look like a whore." He threw the dress into the fire and then took out a t-shirt she liked to sleep in. "You're out there, flopping your tits around in this thing, bouncing all over Williams little dick, never again Micki. You don't leave the house in t-shirts." He was so angry, and with every word he became angrier. He tore it in two pieces and threw them into the fire. He threw the clothes in, one by one. She was hanging her head now, crying softly while "Hells Bells" played on the record player. She understood. He'd been following her, he snuck into her house the same way she did.

She felt completely naked and ashamed but mostly she was afraid. He snatched her head back by her hair again and she cried out in pain, "Why are you doing this?" She cried. He grabbed her face in one hand squeezing so hard she was sure it would bruise and told her, "Pay attention Micki, if you break these rules, there will be consequences. I can't save you if you don't pay attention. You have to be perfect, so you better pay attention." He threw more of the clothes into the fire and picked up a beer he had been drinking. He finished it watching them burn and took another from a paper bag on the hearth. He asked her if she wanted a Valium. She shook her head no and he said, "Are you sure? You might regret it later." He winked at her then put two of the pills in his mouth, and opened the beer. He put the rest of the Valium back in his pocket and then took a long drink staring out the window, before putting it on the coffee table. Then he walked over to the dining table and did a line of the cocaine that was laid out there. "You should have tried this Micki, Valium and coke together is the shit." He said closing his eyes for a minute and then looked at her blankly. He seemed to snap to attention before he put down the beer and walked back to the fireplace. He opened the laundry bag again. "And this," he slowly pulled a towel from the bag that had what looked like blood on it. She recognized it from that day at Billy's, when she'd had sex for the first time. She started to shake her head side to side, closing her eyes so she didn't have to see. "...I'm going to forgive you for this, because I love you," he said, almost crying, and threw the towel into the fire. He leaned over the chair and grabbed her hair again, putting his mouth on hers and trying to force her mouth open. She bit his lip as hard as she could and he screamed out in pain, cupping his throbbing, lacerated mouth in one hand and backhanding her with the other hand that was unfortunately still holding the gun. "You fucking bitch!" he screamed at her. She could taste blood in her mouth, and she was afraid he might have cracked her jaw but he was clearly distracted from her for the time being so she kept struggling, trying to get loose from the tape with no success. He was wiping his face with a towel from the kitchen when she realized he was standing over her again. He put down the gun for a second and slapped her hard across the face. She was glad it was just his hand. She was sure her head was bleeding behind her ear from the first blow. He hit her once more open handed before he picked up the gun again. She had stopped fighting, her head was reeling and everything had become blurry. He put the gun in her face. The barrel dug deep into her cheek. "I told you Micki. Stop making me hurt you." He sat down on the hearth. "You . . . you. . . You think you're so special, and hell, maybe you are. I do have you taped to a chair in my great room, don't I? Micki? You're just like me. Don't you see it? We're soul mates. I know how it is, you just want to have fun and everyone else is a drag, you like dark things, and I am a very dark soul. I know you think you like William, but trust me, after tonight, you won't ever want him again. You just haven't been around enough to know better. But I'm going to show you things, things you want to know, things you need to know. I'm going to teach you. I'm the only one who can. I've been there. You get bored, you sneak off to Williams' house, I get bored, I make a phone call." He tilted his head to look at her and smiled a little before he finished, "Sandy has been an inspiration. I really mean it she is a girl with exceptional stamina." Micki's eyes welled with tears, what did he do to "Sandy?" She had said her name aloud and now was shaking her head from side to side saying "no" over and over again. "Don't worry, I'm not in love with Sandy, but she is a lot of fun. You will feel better Micki, You will, when this is over, you'll be a brand-new person." He walked back to the table and did another line of the coke. He said "Ahhhhh," as if he were testing a note and cleared his throat. He washed it down with beer and moved back to the chair. The look on her face was sheer terror and anger. Make-up streaming down both cheeks, her hair a wad of tangles and some sort of sick gray paste she had used to dirty her hair for costume, she really did look a fright. Amused by the coincidence, he laughed out loud. He sat in front of her with his eyes closed for a minute before he started stroking her face with his fingers. The costume turned him on, the hair, all of it, it somehow validated his intentions. He was overwhelmed by a good feeling not unlike being on a steep roller coaster and he couldn't suppress a smile. He went into the kitchen and got some towels and wet them at the faucet except for one in which he piled crushed ice from the fridge and made a pillow for his lip. He came back and started wiping the ruined make-up off her cheeks, carefully preserving what he could. He said I'm sorry about your costume, you could have forgone the make-up if Id told you not to bother with a costume, but that might have ruined the surprise." He finished cleaning her face and she said "Fuck you Evan." He wanted to hurt her; he needed to hear her cry. The sound excited him and the throbbing in his lip where she'd bitten him seemed to be adding to the exhilaration. He needed to hear her break. It was the sound of his power. Not yet, he thought, although she was making him crazy and he really wanted to teach her a lesson, he just needed to remember to go slow and use some restraint, he didn't want it to be over too quickly. He held her face up by her chin and said to her, "No Micki, it's fuck you." He walked to the kitchen and was back in just a moment. Kneeling down beside her chair again, he said, "You'll have to give up a lot, there is so much unnecessary bullshit that comes out of your mouth, but you don't have to sacrifice everything." He said softly as he stuffed a black bandanna into her mouth and covered it with duct tape. She was kicking wildly and he taped her ankles to the chair legs. When he pulled at the strings on her costume, she started slamming her head against the back of the chair. He slowly pulled the suit loose from underneath her then sat back down. Her cry was reduced to a low whine because of the bandanna. He leaned back and looked at her. "My, my, Micki, you are perfect aren't you," he said, "I knew when I was watching you with William that you had something I could appreciate. When I look at you, you make me want to die, cause that's what I would do before I ever left you alone. . . This is probably the best you will ever look in your life; I can't let you waste it on some old loser. Just look at you, It's gonna be hard to top that. One day you'll be sitting in your trailer, wondering what happened, how you got to be such a miserable slob. It will be because you are a pot smoking whore with no self-respect who wasted her only gifts on losers," her cries turned into muffled sobs, "Or," he continued, "I can save you from all that, and babe, I read part 13. I understand you. I can be that man for you, I am the fucking anti-hero." She was crying deep in her chest, she had never been so terrified. He leaned in and put his hands on her thighs, "Believe me, Micki, I have never wanted anything this bad... and I have done some really fucked up shit to get what I want. Don't fight me. Just relax and enjoy it." He leaned into her face to kiss her cheek lightly in some twisted display of affection as he grabbed her legs at the knees and pulled until her butt was on the edge of the seat. She was trying to back away but there was nowhere to go. She started sobbing and whining uncontrollably again unable to do more than react to his assault and unable to think clearly, feeling doomed. She hated him so much, all the anger she had inside her was building up against Evan. He was watching her face. He knew he was out of control, but he couldn't help it. He wanted her to succumb to him. He needed to make her do it. She treated him like he was some piece of dirt and she was beneath him. She still couldn't see it, but she would. He said, "We have no secrets now. You know everything. " She hated him for the things he was making her feel, the fear, the pain, the panic and the humiliation. She started freaking out, trying to tear her arms out of the chair saying "no" over and over again. The more she squirmed the more excited he seemed to get and he put a finger inside her as he put a hand on her neck to hold her still to watch her face and her whine became louder. It reminded him of the time Jasmine had let him pretend to be a rapist and rape her. When he had her tied to a chair, she had looked at him and said, "Evan, I would be a lot more comfortable if I was tied to a bed, and not a chair. This sucks." It had pissed him off at the time because it had been his rape fantasy and not hers. She was always such a selfish bitch. He had left her tied to the chair for an hour before finishing the game and then she just laid there pissed off and didn't even pretend to be scared. It had ruined the fantasy altogether. Jasmine was always pissed about that. He didn't want to make that mistake with Micki. He looked at her thoughtfully and said, "Me too," and her eyes got wider in confusion. He stood up and left the room and she managed to sit up straight in the chair again. She looked around again, for anything, any hope at all was better than none. She was pushing at the floor, trying to turn the chair over, thinking it might break or maybe she could crawl to the fireplace and get the knife he left lying there and cut herself free. If only there was a distraction that took him away from the room long enough for her to actually hold that knife. As it turned out that kind of thing only works in movies and fairy tales, her toes were slipping on the floor. The chair was standing firm on the edge of the Persian rug. She was sobbing harder as she realized she had no chance of getting free she screamed as loud as she could with the bandanna in her mouth and the sound made her scream again. The bandanna was soggy with her saliva now. He came back carrying what looked to Micki like a dog leash and a choke type training collar. She closed her eyes tightly and shook her head from side to side in a desperate act of defiance. Another muffled scream came from the bandanna when he said, "Don't worry, it's never been on a dog, I bought this especially for you." She was still screaming as he put it around her neck. He put the tip of the gun barrel between her legs and told her to "Shut the fuck up!" But she could not regain control of herself and the gun seemed to intensify the panic. She was near hyperventilating, eyes wide, writhing in the chair, screaming uncontrollably. Thinking she might be having some sort of fit, he hit her once, hard near her temple, with the butt of the gun, and she was out. As her body collapsed in the chair, she urinated, and it trickled onto the carpet. Evan put the back of his hands to his own temples and said "Fuck!" He ran his free hand through his hair before he put the gun down and went to start the album over. When he came back he did the last line of coke cut out on the dinner plate and took a vial from his pocket to pour more onto the plate. He got the knife from the fireplace and used it to cut out, four, neat new lines. He went to the kitchen and got towels as it dawned on him that his own place was the coolest thing his dad ever gave him. He used the knife to cut Micki out of the chair, letting her body fall twisted on the rug next to it. He used the towels to clean up the urine and put them in the fire afterwards, along with the pieces of duct tape and towels that were strewn all over the floor. He paused over her body for a moment to slowly squeeze one breast before he threw Micki's limp body over his shoulder and went upstairs.

Billy was leaving for Cal's party, hoping Micki would already be there. He was worried. She'd left without telling him goodbye the night before. He just couldn't shake the feeling that something was wrong. He knew everything about her, he even knew about Cameron, but had never been threatened by him. He sometimes wished Cameron would make the move that would get her attention, but that was before. He couldn't bring himself to push her into his arm, Cameron should have tried harder. Billy was sure she would probably end up with him anyway, he certainly didn't resent him.

This shit with Evan, this was something new. He couldn't put his finger on it but there was something so wrong about it all. He remembered the day Evan's dad Jack had stopped him in the pasture and after offering him a cigarette which he refused because he didn't smoke, asked him how most of the kids stayed busy on the lake. Billy had told him that they all loved the water, boats, had been his answer. He didn't really know Evan, but neither did she. When he slowed the car to turn onto the lake road, he noticed the flag up on his mail box. He got out of the car and looked inside. As he suspected, it was a note from Micki, it read, See you soon. M She was always so dramatic and vague. Billy crumpled the note, annoyed, and put it in his pocket and went to Cal's. When he got there, he couldn't relax. After about an hour, of dancing and listening to the wars and love stories being born there in their midst, he said "Fuck this," out loud. He found Kena outside with Jim and asked her if she knew where Micki had gone. Kena had sworn to Micki she would not get Billy involved and so she lied and said "no." Billy sensing the lie, said, "Kena, she could be in real trouble, how long will you wait before you say, don't you give a shit?" Jim immediately came to attention but Kena stood her ground and told him he didn't know the half of it, but that he should "just wait for her." Billy had no intention of waiting for her tonight and he decided to go and get her anyway. Kena hoped she was doing the right thing for Micki, she was smart, and resourceful. She seemed wise beyond her years; surely she knew what she was doing, right? Jim and Kena were getting very drunk and didn't even see Billy leave. He knew she had to be at Evan's, it was the only place they would feel the need to lie about and the only place he told her not to go. This was wasted time. She wanted to be treated like an adult and he was about to tell her she needed to act like one.

"Let me put my love into you babe...." Bon Scott was singing from somewhere far away. She was no longer taped to a chair, she was tied with nylon rope normally used to secure a boat, tied to a bed. Her hands were tied together, to one post of the headboard, and her legs were tied apart. Evan was going down on her. He was now shoving three fingers in and out of her and it felt like she was splitting apart. Her body was screaming with pain and she wondered if he had already raped her, and if she had a concussion. Her head was throbbing but she no longer had the bandana in her mouth. She tried to scream but no sound came out, just a dry cough. The corners of her eyes burned with tears and her throat was on fire. In and out, in and out and she thought she would lose her mind. He picked his head up and said, "Good, you're awake," He licked her stomach and then looked her in the eye. In and out, in and out, he had one hand on her stomach as if he was trying to touch it with his fingers inside her. "That's good isn't it, Micki," but it wasn't a question. He looked high. "I'm sorry about being so rough, but you're not quite ready for this," he used his free hand to grab his erection and show it to her. He smiled, watching her squirm and she turned her head away from him and screamed dryly in frustration, then collapsed into sobs that made her voice whine like some sort of machinery, "You have to stop this Evan...You can't do this," but he ignored her, "It's a monster isn't it?" he said as he stroked himself. His erection was aching but he wanted to drag this out. In and out, in and out, he bent his head back down and put his tongue on her again. In and out, and then he put a fourth finger inside her, and she felt another sharp pain like he was cutting her. "Nooo!" she finally managed a raspy scream, twisting involuntarily side to side trying to get away from the feeling of his hand churning inside her. He stopped what he was doing and slapped her hard with a closed fist across the face. She was still screaming so he slapped her again, "Shut the fuck up you dirty fucking whore," he said, "you should be begging me to fuck you." She had stopped screaming and crying, but he was so angry he slapped her again. "Huh, Micki, what now? Where's your hero now? This is the real world Micki, no one is coming to save you, and in the real world, the strong take what they want and the smart stay the fuck out of the way." There was blood in her mouth now and she stopped struggling. She just looked at him blankly; the only sign of life was the pain in her eyes. He loved the power he had over her right now. A man's power, he thought. He loved teaching her this, that he could do anything he wanted to her, and nothing she ever did would change one second of it. . He smiled at her and shoved his fingers back inside her roughly and said, "I bet I can make you cum," before he put his mouth back on her clitoris, moaning deep in a way that made her want to vomit, but her throat was so dry it seemed to be closed up tight.. She cried quietly, defeated, while he continued to assault her. He got so angry because she wouldn't stop crying and didn't seem to like it, that he took the gun and shoved the barrel inside her, asking her if she liked that better. He told her that he would blow her away "right now, if you don't get your shit together and try to enjoy this. Fighting me will only make it worse." Then his tone changed and he took her head in his hands so he could lean down and whisper in her ear as if he was trying to console her. "I know it seems bad right now, but you're going to learn to love it, and then things will go a lot smoother. I had to go through a lot of shit just to end up here with you tonight and I worked hard because we're made for each other." She had started to whine again, helpless to do anything else with his hot breath blasting her neck with heat every time he spoke, "You'll see it I know, because I know you, the real you, not this unappreciative cunt you feel like you have to be for the sake of social standards but you don't have to pretend with me." He kissed her hair and she was sure she would lose her mind. She tried to scream again but only a raspy sound came from her throat. He went off on her again, he lay the gun on her stomach and grabbed her hair on each side of her head and yelled at her, "Is it really so bad, Micki, You think you're too good for me? You're a fucking white trash whore," He rammed himself inside her and held her face still so she would have had to look at him if she had opened her eyes, "feel that Micki, every fucking inch," he started thrusting in and out harder each time, grunting, holding her hair at the nape of her neck still forcing her to face him and she knew if she opened her eyes she would be looking at his. The pain had ripped through her body and she was sure he was bruising her ovaries, about to burst some needed organ and wondered if it was possible that he was raping her with some hard blunt inanimate object and only pretending to have his penis inside her. It'd never occurred to her that it could've hurt so badly. She lost her breath, he didn't seem to notice as she seemed to detach. He kept pounding himself inside her, trying to make her cry out, each thrust a little harder, slamming himself against her, over and over again. Her pelvic bone felt as if it might be fractured and he said, "You feel so fucking good, you fucking slut, you're my slut now," He reached down and picked up the gun again and she was hoping he was going to shoot her right then, he kept pounding, hard and violent. He put the gun next to her head, "Tell me you love it!" He put his tongue into her unresponsive mouth moving his tongue with the same rhythm as his thrusts. She started begging him to stop and he put the gun under one breast and pushed into her skin, he had to hear her say it, "tell me you fucking love it, Micki" she told him she loved it, sobbing, He quivered, "Oh yeah, I knew you would." He kissed her forehead again, put the gun back down on the bed, and wrapped his arms around her head. "You're my whore now aren't you Micki ..." but she didn't know it was a question until he slammed into her and pulled the back of her hair till she winced with pain. "Say it." So she said, "I'm a whore." Still sobbing, she had given in and stopped struggling. He began to thrust with every word, "oh... you... are...fucking....whore." With that word, he thrust himself inside her with all his strength and his body hit hers so hard she was afraid he might have cracked her spine. He ejaculated inside her with three short thrusts. She could feel him pulsing inside her, He was shaking visibly now and told her, "You're one sweet fucking piece of ass," and sweat dripped off his nose into her eyes to make her squint again. "That's the best fucking orgasm I've had since yesterday, how about you?" He leaned down to lick the tears from her face. She was just staring at the ceiling. He laughed at her and said, "Devastated?" and kissed her mouth. She didn't try to stop him and he was pleased, "That's better now." He said before he finally got up and started untying her; she made no attempt to move. Her body was throbbing everywhere but her arms and feet now seemed to be only loosely attached to her aching limbs. Just when she thought it was over, he grabbed her by her hair, put the gun to her cheek again, and told her to get on her knees "like a dog and crawl." She wanted him to shoot her in the head, but he didn't. He told her he wanted her to crawl. "Crawl over to me and beg." She was in disbelief at his depravity, she asked him to shoot her again, but he was having too much fun. He said, "Don't worry Micki, I'm not going to shoot you, but I will beat your ass all fucking night if you don't do what I say." She got down on her hands and knees and started to crawl, her body aching with every inch she managed to move forward. He thought it was an amazing feat to have her get down on the floor and crawl to him like that. He had never felt so powerful, not even with Jasmine. He was curious about how far he would manage to take this before something ended it. What would stop him, he wondered, if anything? What would happen if nothing did? He imagined that it was almost like he owned her, the way it used to be, when women were property. This was similar to role playing. He made the connection while watching her crawl, pointing the gun toward the ceiling. When she got close enough to touch him, he stopped her so he could look at her for a minute. She was on her knees, naked. No make-up. Her big green eyes were incredible he thought. They were wide with fear and wonder. It was beautiful. She looked so vulnerable. He lifted her chin with the barrel of the gun and told her so, "You are so beautiful. You wish you'd taken that Valium now huh." He pushed the hair out of her face with the barrel of the gun, and pushed another strand behind an ear but the shit in her hair wouldn't let it stay. "Lots of girls take em, it makes the sex great. You should have one next time cause I like to fuck, there will never be a time when I don't fuck you till your eyes roll back in your head. You should try the Valium." This was the real Micki, he thought. The clueless bitch was someone else. After tonight, she would be more careful with his feelings. He snapped back into power-mode as he became aroused again and told her to, "Say please," She said "Please," "Please what?" he asked. She wasn't sure what he meant, and she thought he might be about to let her go for a second before saying "Please... let me go?" she tried. He slapped her and yanked the leash until the collar was tight around her neck. She tasted fresh blood where her inner lip had burst against her teeth. He pulled on the leash, tightening the choke collar around her neck, and told her what he wanted her to say, "Please Evan, may I suck your huge cock,...Jesus Micki, you really suck at this," he chuckled at his pun, and loosened the collar a little, "Now beg me you fucking whore." Weak and sobbing she said, "Just go ahead and kill me Evan," but he reiterated he didn't want to kill her, he just wanted to play with her for a while." He became impatient again and started to put the gun in her mouth. She knew she had no choice, "okay, okay," she mumbled. She couldn't fight him, she sniffled "Please Evan..." She sniffled again "... may I suck your huge cock," and he caressed her face with the gun, "That's better," He was in a trance now, "Yes, you can," he put the tip of the gun near her eye and leaned closer to her until his forehead was touching hers. He grabbed the collar at her throat, and caressed her with the gun in his other hand for several seconds before telling her, "You don't want to startle me Micki ...no biting." He let go of the collar and touched her lips with his erect penis. He used the hand with the gun in it to entangle his fingers into a handful of her hair on the side of her head. She opened her mouth trembling, eyes filled with terror. Micki had only read about things like this. She was scared that if she did something wrong he would kill her, no matter what he said and now suddenly, more than ever she wanted to survive. She wanted Evan to go to prison. She tried to please him, "Oh yeah," he said watching her, tangling her hair even more with his fingers. It stung at her temple but she gave no indication of it. "...you do love cock don't you Micki..." he said as she nearly gagged, "That's okay... you don't have to answer, I see you have your mouthful right now. That is one mouthful isn't it, baby. Mmm, suck it, suck it, Micki, you look so good on my dick." Tears streamed down her face and her eyes were squeezed shut. Suddenly the doorbell rang. Evan put the gun down beside him and grabbed her head with both hands and shoved himself down her throat. She tried to gag but couldn't, she couldn't breathe, her legs were flailing and she was pulling at his wrists and slapping at his arms, back and forth and then he shoved himself into her throat hard and pulled out fast, letting her fall to the floor before she nearly bit him in reflex. She was choking on his semen. He was laughing again. He pulled on his jeans as he moved to the window, where he lit a cigarette and looked down into the front yard. He noticed Billy's car, still running with the head lights on. She was on her hands and knees coughing it up into the floor. She had his pubic hair in her throat and tried to vomit with no success. She realized he had just broken her nose and blood dripped accordingly to the floor mixing with the semen and stomach acids. He watched her choke and said, "That's a big dick isn't it, babe." He laughed and then said, "Damn, Micki, who knew you could suck a big dick? I bet Billy doesn't," he laughed again. "Why don't we ask him?" He was watching Billy lean on the hood of the piece of shit he called a car. It wasn't fair he'd had to wait outside helplessly while that coon-ass pervert fucked her that night. He wished he could have made Billy watch. He decided he would do the next best thing and felt himself becoming aroused again. "This has been so much fun..." he looked at her seriously and went to help her up from the floor. She was terrified, still trying to catch her breath as she tried to get away. She had only managed to move a foot or so when he got to her. She was crying again, pleading "no, no, no." He took her by the shoulders with the cigarette in his mouth and told her it was "okay," that tonight was the worst of it. He was, "just getting a few things out of the way, so we can focus on more important things like what we'll wear to the prom." He said absurdly. "I don't want to hurt you Micki, but you have to understand how this works, and there's just one more thing you need to learn." He smashed the cigarette into her left cheek causing her to scream expectedly and then pulled her to her feet by her hair. She started swinging wildly at him pleading, "No, please, no more." She was no match for someone his size and he threw her face down on the bed, keeping one hand on her head pushing her face into the pillows. He was holding her legs firmly between his as he took himself out of his pants. He moved one leg between hers and put a knee down on the back of her thigh, licked his free hand and wiped it across her anus. He shoved his penis inside her and she screamed again just like he knew she would. He let her scream until he was sure Billy could hear it then he pushed her face deep into the pillows and half whispered to her, "How does that feel?" She was struggling but she was pinned and running out of air. He was thinking about Billy outside, he still wanted him to hear her screaming. He thrust himself in and out of her, quickly, hard, grunting again. The flesh was tearing and she could feel the warm sticky blood of fresh wounds. He had her hair and was pulling her head back now, as if he was riding a wild bull. She was screaming and sobbing "no, no, please, god, no." He shoved her face back down into the pillows and whispered into her ear again, thrusting as he spoke, "don't... ever.... fucking... lie.......to me ....Micki...ahhh," he moaned loudly hoping William could hear that too, "oh... my...god ...you've got the tightest ass" and he kissed her shoulder, "Don't ... ever...tease me...Micki,....I really love this shit...,...do you understand?" She was sobbing into the pillow. She had cried so much she could taste the iron rich blood from her ravaged throat. She was sure then that she would never get away, that he would kill her after all even if he didn't mean to. She didn't think she could survive this, that any moment he would snap her neck. He grabbed her hips and picked her up off the bed till she was nearly folded in half. She was more grunting than screaming now and clawing madly at the mattress as he was violently slamming himself into her. His fingers dug into her skin as he thrust, again and again. She could feel her flesh ripping and burning. She was screaming and kicking but couldn't get free and then he yelled, "Fuck.... yeah..." and she thought he surely broke her tail bone. After he finished ejaculating for the third time, he dropped her limp body onto the floor.

Billy could hear screaming, he knew she was coming here but no one seemed to be home now. The screaming could have been a TV. All the movie channels were showing horror flicks tonight but what if it was her. He needed to be sure and was determined. He wasn't leaving until he knew she wasn't here. He decided to break in so he started trying to work the knob on the front door. Realizing how impossible that would be, he walked around to the kitchen door and tried to raise one of the small panes that would roll out exposing the screen. He heard screaming again and a man's scream as well. What the fuck was going on? He had to get in there; he hoped it was just the TV. He kept pushing on the glass until his finger slipped sideways and he was cut on the aluminum frame. He put his finger in his mouth, thinking maybe he should just break the glass in, and then he remembered this house had a patio entrance.

He sat on the bed and told her, "It's just me now Micki, you will do exactly what I say, or I will bury you, do you understand, no more cheating, just me, you're my whore, my bitch, you do me and that's all. Now you know it. Right now, I'm going to go downstairs, and tell your ex-lover to get the fuck out of my yard. I was just so pissed, but it's okay now. You know the deal. That's all there is, that's it. " He lit a cigarette, blew out the smoke as he looked at her thoughtfully and said, "I hope I didn't get you pregnant." He put his pants on and stood there in thought for another moment. He picked her up under her arms and held her by her throat with one hand against the wall. She had nearly passed out from having her face shoved into the pillows, and hadn't quite recovered. He was just looking at her, he held the cigarette in his lips and punched her in the stomach like a boxer and her eyes flew wide open just like her mouth but no sound came out. She would have doubled over if he hadn't held her against the wall. He said, "I know . . . I know it hurts, but we had to do it," and then, he did it again and let her fall to the floor. "Just in case," He said. "I'll be right back, don't go away." He smiled as he picked up the gun from the chair before he looked back at her once more and chuckling a little he said, "Just wait till I tell you how we're going to blame all this shit on Jeff." He blew out more smoke and left her there. Micki was weak, she couldn't move. Her mind was telling her to get up and run, but she couldn't make her legs work. She could barely breathe.

He gave up on the kitchen window and was about to go find the patio when Evan opened the door. Billy just looked at him. He was standing there only in jeans. He looked fucked up. He had a scratch on his face and a deep cut on his lower lip that looked more like a bite. "I was wondering if Micki might have come here, She never showed up at Cal's and I heard you were having a party." as he tried to look past him to see what was going on inside. Evan just looked at him. Finally, he said. "Who told you I was having a party?" Billy realized Evan was high, and he needed to be clear. "Is Micki here, Evan?" He said, "No. I haven't seen her all night, it's just me." He smiled and waved his arm stepping back as if offering Billy a view of his loneliness. "I heard screaming," Billy said. "Did you?" asked Evan suppressing a laugh." I've been . . . watching horror movies. I didn't realize the sound was up loud enough for someone outside to hear..." His face became more serious, "How long did you listen?" He slowly started smiling again as if he was waiting for him to get the joke. Billy's heart was racing. "Is the movie over?" "What?" Evan asked as if he hadn't heard him correctly. "Is the movie over?" Evan chuckled and said, "No, it's just now getting to the good part." He smiled, his eyes were wild. "Why can't I hear it now?" Billy wasn't ready to give up. "What?" Evan said again, and Billy lost his patience as he lunged at the doorway saying "Why can't I hear the fucking screaming now." But it was no longer a question. He nearly knocked Evan to the floor trying to get by him to see if Micki was in trouble. Evan stepped aside and let him in. Billy burst through calling her name, and then saw her costume on the floor. He stopped, frozen. What had he walked into? Was Micki here, asking Evan to send him away? It was impossible, his face got warm. He turned to confront Evan, who now had a .45 caliber handgun pointed at him. "Sit down William." He told him sniffling back the cocaine that was still running down the back of his throat. Billy sat in the chair Micki had been trapped in earlier. From the position of the costume on the floor, he determined as much. "Where's Micki?" He asked Evan. "She's getting herself together." Evan laughed. Billy almost jumped at him but Evan raised the gun and pulled the slide back " uh uh uh, I will shoot you and I swear to god I will fuck her in the ass on your dead fucking body," Billy sat back down still trying to process the situation and Evan handed him the duct tape telling him to tape one of his arms to the chair. Then Evan stood behind him so he couldn't see him put the gun in his pants and taped the other one. He took the gun out again and walked back in front of Billy to tell him. "So you heard us, that's unfortunate. I told Micki, she shouldn't be so loud." Billy was cursing, "You mother fucker, if you did something to her you better fucking kill me now because I swear to you, I will never get tired of punishing you and making sure you spend the rest of your miserable pussy-ass life in prison,.." Evan became furious and said "Oh, I'm not the only one who could go to prison here asshole, how fucking old are you anyway, like 30? I watched you fuck her don't even try to deny it." He paused and a sober look washed across his face. "I almost killed you then and there." Even though Billy was only twenty-one he knew Evan was right, it was the difference between aggravated rape and statutory rape, but it was still rape, Billy hung his face, his mind was racing now as he pieced together what was happening, Micki was there to protect him. Evan was crazy, doing coke perhaps delirious, and god knows what else. He walked over and sat down next to Billy sitting on an end table he'd pulled over earlier. He said "I could fucking kill you right now and hide your dead rotting body under my pier, and no one would ever even question me." Evan was cool, he'd imagined many confrontations with Billy and still wasn't sure if could let him live or not. He hated him so much. He got up and walked away from him and said, "You should be ashamed of yourself William. Teenagers should have sex with teenagers." He looked back at him then, "But I gotta say, you didn't hurt it, I suppose I should thank you for that. You were so careful with that pussy it's like you were saving it for me. I wish I could say I returned the favor…" He walked back over to the chair and looked him in the eye to say "no. Fuck that, I fucked her, William, I fucked her proper, and there's not one inch of virgin left upstairs, and no place you can go that I haven't already been." And he smiled a satisfied smile and waited for him to react. Billy was biting his lip and nodding his head fighting back tears, "You're fucking insane." He said almost breathlessly then started frantically struggling in the chair, but it was of no use as Micki had learned earlier, the duct tape wouldn't budge. Evan was amused. Billy stopped struggling and looked at Evan, "What is it Evan? Did your mother abuse you? Poor little Evan is that it? Trying to get daddy's attention? Daddy's approval? What's your particular malfunction? Your empirical delusion? You think she'll love you now or something?" Evan said, "She doesn't have to love me, as long as she does what she's supposed to, I don't give a fuck if she hates me, I'm going to fuck her anyway. People survive that way every day. It's the big picture that matters. She belongs to me now." He tapped his chest with the barrel of the gun and Billy, now trying to diminish him, said "Yeah well, there's something you forgot Evan, no matter what you've done, or what you'll do now, what you'll ever do to her, she never wanted to be with you, she never will. You can't force people to stay with you." He was looking at the floor again almost crying thinking of what she must have gone through tonight. "You had to lie, blackmail,..." he had to raise his voice now because Evan was screaming at him and pointing the gun at him saying "Shut the fuck up" over and over "...and rape her like a fucking animal because she fucking detests you, she doesn't want you and she would never be here voluntarily, nobody would, not even your mother right? Because you're fucked up, Evan, you need help. You should be in a mental hospital..." He walked over and hit Billy hard with the gun, and then he hit him again on the temple. Billy was still mumbling, so Evan hit him again behind his ear. Billy's head was lolling from side to side. Evan took four of the Valium from his pocket and crushed them with the knife. He scraped it into a spoon and put it in Billy's mouth the way you would feed a baby. He held his mouth shut long enough to be sure he had swallowed any saliva he might have in his mouth. Then he backed off and watched him. His eye was swelling from where Evan had hit him with the gun. He walked closer to the chair, grabbed his hair and pulled his head back as he told him "Micki, is none of your fucking business any more you fucking pervert, If you so much as fucking breathe on her I will fucking kill you William. I will fucking kill you! Don't test me" He hit him again with the gun, rendering him unconscious, and went back upstairs.

Her body was throbbing in pain. She thought maybe she was already dead, and this is what it was like. She'd heard screaming but didn't understand what was happening. Struggling, she managed to put her hands down on the floor but she kept falling on her busted face when she tried to push herself up on them. He came back in the room and pulled her head back, so she could see his face. He had a wet towel and was wiping her face with it. Her face was sore and she cried softly as he washed it. "Micki, you do understand now, don't you? See what you've been missing. All the messy stuff is over now. This is how it's always been. Things will be a lot easier now. It's just how it is Micki. Right?" She nodded her head yes and he said "Good girl." He said "It was good right?" and she nodded her head yes too afraid to do anything else. He told her that when she went home the next day she was to say that Jeff did these things to her, and he understood why Jeff had to go, and he was happy to come up with a way to get rid of him, "killing two birds with one stone," he'd said. "The most logical end to our biblical honeymoon and a dowry for my future queen, I give you his head, figuratively speaking anyway." He said they would get married one day, and maybe even have kids eventually, "but not too soon," he tapped the tip of her nose. He kissed her neck and earlobe as he pulled her to a standing position and held her head against his chest. He leaned down over her to squeeze her ass and then laid her on the bed. He was caressing her stomach and started kissing her breasts. He said he was sorry that he was so rough with her but that she had made him crazy, fucking William, and Cameron too probably. He said that for someone so intelligent that she never even wondered why the dress he'd bought her fit her so well, that he'd been sure she would understand when he gave it to her, understand how much he cared for her, how far he would go for her, but that she hadn't even realized his interest at that point. That she was actually kind of clueless and didn't even miss the clothes he'd taken. He said he had expected it to be a lot harder but that she had made it easier just by following instructions. He liked that. He said he was relieved it was done, and it would feel better next time and eventually she would come to love it, to want it, to want to beg for it. He said the hard part was over now and he knew she wouldn't sleep with anyone else in the future, because she knew how much he loved her; she knew what he was capable of. They had an understanding. He told her she would be alright tomorrow, and that one day they would look back on this and laugh. He started biting her nipples hard as if to remind her it could never really be funny. He had to make her cry out. He secretly wished Billy could hear it. Encouraged by her cries he put two fingers deep inside her again, and told her, "I had to thank William for not fucking that pussy up, cause I know I hit virgin territory every time. It doesn't matter what happened before, it's only me now" He smiled at her and kissed her face and then her stomach. She wondered if she could hit him hard enough to stun him and knew she couldn't. She was so tired. Then he climbed on top of her holding her arms above her head without resistance, and raped her once more. He was acting as if he was making love to her. It was absurd. It seemed to last forever, and though she still wanted to cry, she didn't have any tears left, she did not fight him. Micki felt like she was bleeding internally, like he'd worn a sandpaper condom. Her throat was on fire and she could still taste the blood and semen in her mouth. She regretted fighting him now. As this realization hit her, he finally ejaculated inside her again, and she was reminded of him punching her in the stomach. She had to get away. He lay down on the bed next to her. She sensed that he was satisfied for the moment, and since she hadn't tried to get away this time, she decided to try something else. She found her voice and told him she needed to use the bathroom, "I am sure you do, sweetie, you go right ahead, take a shower, wash that shit out of your hair." he said, waving the gun at her. She dragged herself off the bed, and managed to walk a little, it was slow. She went into the hallway, listening to him talk about his mother, she'd abandoned him he said, she was a whore like Micki, he said. Running out on him "... in search of a big dick." That he would kill her if she ever did that to him. She stopped at the upstairs bathroom and opened the door for a minute. She stepped inside the bathroom to turn on the water in the shower and caught her reflection in the mirror. She almost screamed again but put her hand over her mouth and caught herself. She backed out carefully and locked the door as she came back out on the landing. Watching carefully behind her, she closed it again loudly with the water still running inside. When he didn't come out of the room and sensitive to every creaking board in the floors, she carefully made her way downstairs. The fire was still burning in the fireplace and she saw her costume lying on the floor by the chair. She walked over to pick it up and found Billy, taped to the chair and bleeding. He looked at her without really seeing her and she almost lost her bearing. She put her hand to her mouth and choked back the cry before going over to the chair to release him. His eyes were strange. He was staring blankly. One eye was full of blood. She could still hear Evan talking upstairs believing she was in the bathroom. She took the tape off the chair as quietly as she could and Billy fell into the floor. It was noisy, and she looked up the stairs. She was too weak to help him up. She had to get some help. She whispered that she'd come back for him. He didn't speak or even indicate that he understood, he just looked at her as one tear rolled out of his eye. Her lips were quivering again. She picked up her costume and looked back at the staircase, nothing. The AC/DC record had played to the end and was making a scratching sound, over and over. She was starting to feel more confident, and a familiar rush of adrenaline. She limped over to the French doors and looked on the secretary that sat near the kitchen. She picked up the phone to call the police and realized she didn't want to call them, this was one big mess, and it was her mess. She did need a phone, but if Evan caught her, she might never escape. Though she was terrified, she was afraid of what might happen if the police came. Could they even get here in time to save Billy? She needed to go. There was the key, inside the bowl where he had put it. She carefully took it out; afraid that one clink would bring him down those stairs, to punish her. God only knew what he might do to Billy now that she had loosened him from the chair. She put the phone down and slowly unlocked the door, carefully turning the knob and opened it. She looked back but couldn't see Billy on the floor from there; the sofa was in the way. She slipped out quietly and then closed the door just as carefully as she had opened it. She locked it back using the key which she put in a flower pot on her way down the steps. She was trying painfully to put her costume back on, thankful that she had used a string bikini, because her legs and buttocks were too stiff and sore to bend very much. Her whole body was on fire, she thought. She choked back the sobs she could feel taking over. She was so dirty. She needed to save Billy. She tied the strings as tightly as she could in double knots and then went to where his car was parked. It was locked. She headed to the dirt road, she was moving a little faster as she got further from the house. She needed to find a phone; she was going to call Jim and Kena. Jim would know what to do, she thought and she hoped he wasn't too fucked up right now to help.

Evan was lying there, thinking how great it had all turned out. Except for Billy showing up, it had been an awesome night. She had been in that bathroom for a long time. He got up and put his pants on. "Sweetie," he called out but got no answer. He took the vial of coke from the pocket and tapped a little in the cap. He put it to his nose, and snorted. He closed his eyes to a slit and pressed a knuckle onto the side of his nostril, closing it to snort the coke down. He put the cap back on to put it back in his pocket. He wanted to scare her again. He went out into the hall, and to the bathroom. He stood there at the door for a minute and then thinking he would startle her if he walked in unannounced, he tried the knob. It was locked. "Micki..." "You've been in there a long time babe, are you okay?" he laughed at his words. She didn't say anything. "Micki, come out of the bathroom." He said more firmly. Still she said nothing. He went to his room and opened a drawer on the dresser. He took out a small set of screwdrivers that his dad had given him for working on a model airplane he used to have, He took out a long skinny flat head, and went back to the bathroom. She wasn't screaming as he picked the lock, and as he had begun to suspect, when he opened the door and drew back the shower curtains, she wasn't in there. The cocaine was making his sinuses feel dry and his face felt tight. He sniffled, and turned on the water in the sink. He put some in his hand and sniffed it up through his nose, and let it run down the back of his throat. "Micki!" he yelled, "You shouldn't have done this." He went into his room and picked up the gun. Slowly he pulled the slide back as he walked down the stairs. He didn't see her. Billy was no longer in the chair but was passed out on the floor. Evan walked over to him and squatted beside him. The gun hung loosely in one hand. "Well damn, William, it looks like the game isn't over yet. She left us buddy, both of us"

Billy was starting to feel more in control and turned to look at him. His throat was stuck together, he thought, and he couldn't make a sound. Everything was spinning, he felt like he was down in a hole. He could taste the medicinal powder in his throat, making his tongue stick to the roof of his mouth, unsure what it was. He needed a glass of water. He couldn't make a sound, but could hear his head throbbing in his ears. He wanted to kill Evan, but he couldn't pick himself up off the floor, everything in the room seemed to have turned pink. Evan said, "We could have been friends' Billy, if you weren't so fucking selfish, you useless fucking prick. Sit tight," He pointed the gun sideways in the direction of the patio, "I'm going to go, bring her back." with a devilish grin, he winked at him before he went to the table by the French doors, and looked in the bowl. The key was gone. He tried to open it and realized she had either hidden the key, or locked it back from the outside. He knew the answer and went to the front door. He reached above it, and took a key from the door frame. He unlocked the dead bolt and went outside.

She was almost to the bend in the road when she heard him. "Micki!" he yelled. She looked back and saw him coming after her with the gun. Newly horrified, she ran to the right towards the water and then she cut the sharp left at the bottom and was on the trail. Her adrenaline was pumping again, her legs felt stronger, and she ran faster, ignoring the pain in her body. "Micki!" he kept calling out to her. The sound seemed closer and closer, but she didn't look back again. He fired the gun once and terrified, she didn't think about her injuries, she just bolted. The next thing she knew she was at the quarry. She stopped running for a split second, looking around frantically trying to decide if she should hide.

Billy heard him say he was going after her. She had to get away. He had to help her. He managed to lift one hand to his face and touched it. He remembered Evan hit him with the gun a few times. One eye was blurry and he was having trouble keeping it open, he realized the reason everything was pink was because he had blood in his eyes. He felt like he was drunk, more drunk than he had ever been. He wasn't sure what the pills had been, but he was sure they were downers. He rolled onto his side and tried to push his hand to the floor to help himself up only to fall to the floor again hitting his face. He stopped moving again thinking he would just rest another minute and then try again. Suddenly he heard the gunshot and passed out again hoping he hadn't killed her.

As a light came on inside her head, she remembered something she had forgotten. She looked around trying to orient herself. Where was the lake? She started running again. She left the trail where tree limbs and bushes were thick, slapping her in the face and scratching her legs but she never slowed down. She was afraid to cry out because he might hear her. He's coming anyway she thought. She had to keep going, unsure where she was headed until the last minute. His voice sounded closer now, "There's no use in running Micki . . . you'll only have to come back. William doesn't want you now, you can't possibly want him. Don't you understand how this works?" She ran, and she ran, and then, when she was sure he was about to catch her, she jumped into the air with all the force she could muster and disappeared into the darkness. Evan kept following her, and jumped as well. On the way down he managed to grab a tree root and slammed hard into the side of a 40-foot drop off onto a huge 60-foot rock that overlooked the lake. Dirt and small rocks fell from where the root was exposed hitting him in the face and filling his mouth and the waist of his jeans with clay dust and moist dirt. The wind was whipping his pants and his bare feet couldn't find an edge, so he was swinging against the dirt wall. He could feel new scratches on his bare back. The gun was already on the rock below. He looked out at the lake and saw her. The moonlight was shining on the water like a bed of diamonds. He had not anticipated this. His dick was sore and his lip was throbbing again and he growled as he tried to find a way up.

When Micki plunged into the water, she wasn't sure if she would make it or not. She'd never jumped from that height, or known any girl who had. She plunged all the way to the bottom of the lake and kicked it hard. She fought to reach the surface swallowing water uncontrollably; afraid she might drown but grateful, and finally, broke through to see Evan, roughly 80 feet above her. Now she, was treading quietly, breathing heavily, watching him, hoping he would fall, willing it to happen, she imagined his sweaty palms, and prayed her sore legs wouldn't cramp in the cold water "Please god" she whispered, closed her eyes briefly and sniffled again. Evan hadn't been familiar with the drop off and hadn't jumped far enough to clear the rock below. If he let go of the root he thought, he would land on the jagged ledge and bounce into the water. He began to scream, "Micki! Come and help me" but she was screaming back at him, "Fuck you Evan. Fuck! You!" She was sobbing in between expletives. "You know you're going to pay for this Micki. When I get down from here you're going to be sorry." Fear shot through her again and she was mumbling "Please god, please god help me." Evan was still screaming at her. "Help me now, Micki; I won't be so hard on you later." "No way," She yelled up at him. He started laughing, "You should have seen your face when I skull fucked you, Micki," he hurled at her laughing, "you were like a retard . . . I just want to say, that is not sexy, babe. We're going to have to practice that, a lot." He laughed again. She screamed "No! You're sick!" He was still trying to get a foothold and he had finally dug a small hole in the soft dirt patch on the side of the cliff with his foot. He managed to put one foot into the small depression and started pushing himself up, reaching for another root. Micki started mumbling, "No, no, no, no, no . . ." Evan had another foot up by then and was making slow progress up the side. He yelled down at her, "You better swim Micki; you better swim fast, because when I catch you, I'm going to break my dick off in your ass this time." Just then, as she screamed "No!" and for no particular reason except that life can sometimes be like that, a very old, common King Snake, disturbed from its hiding place on the food rich cliff side by Evan's struggling with the root, slithered out of the Kudzu and upward to escape the commotion. It seemed to pause on a rock and look back down at him and perhaps noticed

Micki in the water. When Evan saw it slithering near him, he was startled and let go of the root. Even though he tried to catch himself, the roots and damp foliage slipped right through his hands and the snake continued upward off the cliff. Micki watched him fall onto the rock. His body made a thud when it hit. It did not bounce. She heard him cry out and doubted he was dead. He didn't come to the edge of the ledge and she couldn't see him. Maybe he landed on his feet, she thought. A few minutes more and still nothing. He cried out again, he was in agony. She swam to the edge and crawled out of the water onto the trail Boudreaux had made, and went up to where she could hear him whimpering. There he was, stretched across the huge rock. He had hit face first, and then almost managed to roll over. One of his shins was broken awkwardly and blood and bone were exposed. The same seemed to be true for his left arm, although not as obviously. He wasn't moving now, but his body was jerking with sobs. The blood in his nose made a rattling sound, as if he had the flu. She saw the gun and picked it up and then sat down on her knees holding the gun in her lap. He moaned a little bit before telling her, "You can't kill me Micki. We're the same . . . admit it, deep down, where all that darkness lives inside you, you liked it." Her face was bruised, cracked and bloody. Her eyes appeared to be filled with blood. She had cried so much the skin around her eyes appeared to have a rash but the cool water of the lake had made her nose stop running. She no longer felt disgusting and knew she would get over this. She looked at him and said, "I'm nothing like you." He started to half beg, "I was just trying to make you happy, it was a Halloween present," She became angry again and said "by terrorizing me and assaulting me!? You raped me!" she screamed at him. He laughed and said "Well duh, that is what you like isn't it? I read your book Micki; it's all you ever talk about. I gave you something real to write about." He spat blood that flew up and then landed back on his face in little spots, "You wanted to be terrorized, we were role playing. No one will ever believe you didn't want it." She was crying again. "I can't wait to tell William how you took it up the ass while he listened to you scream." He laughed hysterically choking and sobbing in between. Her lip was quivering but she was beyond tears, she just sat there looking at him, trying to decide what to do. When she didn't say anything he said, "look, you stupid fucking whore, I need help, this isn't a game anymore ...I ...I can't feel my legs..." It was her turn to laugh, as she remembered how she couldn't feel her own legs on the floor of his bedroom. Her laughter made him angry, he said, "What I did to you tonight . . . is the closest you'll ever get to decent. You will always be trash like your mother ..." She spit on him and aimed the gun at his face. He laughed and said "It will always be me now, my dick will always be in you, it will always be in you, Micki. I broke you in, like those fucking horses you love to ride, I like to ride too . . ." He tried to laugh again but his mouth was full of blood and made only a gurgling noise. He turned his head and tried to spit it out. She was shaking her head slowly. She told him to "shut up!" and pulled the slide back on the gun as she kept the barrel aimed it at his head. "Do you know who my father is Micki?" he asked her calmly. She said "No, and I don't care." Evan finished, "Even if you manage to get away with it, he'll own this entire lake you stupid cunt. You'll be sucking dick at truck stops to get a happy meal with your trash mother. Do you hear me, Micki? Now put the gun down and fucking help me!" He was half crying now but then got angry again, "I'll be missed Micki, you ignorant whore." He laughed hysterically again. She winced and said "No one's going to miss you Evan," and he knew it was true. It stung. He was crying out now, "Help! Help me, somebody please help me...It hurts so fucking bad. Please Micki...I'm sorry...I did it for you . . . I love you" he pleaded with her. She could feel her face swelling again. She knew that he was right; she couldn't shoot him, not like this. She threw the gun as far as she could into the lake as she decided what to do. She told him she was going to help him. He said, "Oh thank god." She picked up a rock she had to hold with two hands and put it in her lap. She sniffled once and lifted the rock as high as she could and brought it back down again on his head. Once more and she felt his skull break under the force of it. She stood up satisfied that he was dead, and tossed the rock into the lake. It made a loud splash. She looked out over the lake, thinking how absurd it was that so much beauty had witnessed such an evil act. He didn't moan again. Blood ran from the corners of his mouth and his eyes stared blankly. He wasn't going to do anything to Micki, or anyone else, ever again. He would never tell anyone anything. She fell to her knees crying, shaking uncontrollably. She reached out and closed his eyes. She finally tried to roll his body over the rocks. He was really heavy. He was bigger than Jeff she realized. She took a deep breath and pushed again. His body slid off the ledge and she waited until it fell into the water below with a splash. Micki quickly jumped back into the water after him. She didn't have to struggle much to push his lifeless body to the edge of the rock. She pushed it down under the water and then under the ledge from memory and into the depression and slowly managed to shove it into the small hollow cave she had found that summer. It was dark. The water was cold and inky. One day that rock would fall into the lake, she thought, but not in her lifetime. She pushed his body into the roots and with her hands managed to thread a thick one through his belt loops effectively snaring his jeans thinking it might anchor his body in the hollow, at least until the jeans rot. She crawled out of the water and back up to the trail. When she got to the ledge, she still had far to go. She climbed a tangle of roots and wild Jasmine growing to the left of the rock, and made it to the top. Shivering, she fell to her knees vomiting the lake water, and then crossed the quarry to go back to Evan's house.

CHAPTER 10

"The death of a beautiful woman is unquestionably the most poetical topic in the world." ~Edgar Allan Poe

The front door was locked. She went back around to the patio and retrieved the key from the flower pot. She first went to the stereo and turned off the record player that was still spinning, the source of the scratching noise. Somehow, Billy had gotten off the floor and had passed out on the sofa again. She went to the fridge and took out a plastic container of cold tea and drank it all. She took it to the sink and filled it with water her tongue exploring a crack in her lip that screamed with pain after drinking the tea and was now throbbing. She snatched paper towels off the rack under the cabinet and wet a handful, taking the rest with her from the kitchen. She went to where Billy was lying on the couch and put the wet towels on his face. He startled awake, but was still groggy. Her voice was raspy and she had to clear her throat once to make a sound but managed to say to him as she held the container to his lips. "Here, water, drink it." He picked his head up a little and she poured the water in his mouth. He soon took the plastic container from her with both hands, and started sitting up as he gulped the water down. When it was gone he fell back on the couch, before rising to a sitting position. He had been holding his breath while he drank the water, and was now breathing rapidly. He shook his head, and said, "I'm fucked up." Micki sniffled and almost cried but half smiled when she said, "I know." relieved that he was somewhat coherent. She went and filled the container with water again. This time she put it to the ice dispenser and let some ice fall into the water. She took it back out to Billy, who was almost passing out again. She nudged him to take the water and he did. She took the paper towels from the coffee table and cleaned up the streaks and puddles of her blood, and Billy's. She threw the garbage into the fire that was still burning. The smell was terrible. When she was a small girl, she and her brother and a few cousins would play in the yard fires her grandmother made. They would put plastic bottles on the end of sticks to set them on fire. They called it the dripping torch. Her grandmother would be so angry when she caught them doing it, they would have to go inside, the girls in one room, the boys in another. That's what the fire burning now, reminded her of, burning plastic. "Where is he?" Billy asked from behind her, coming to his senses. He was standing up holding his head. She turned to look at him and said, "He's gone." Billy stammered and said, "We need to get out of here, we need to call the police." Tears were streaming down her face now and she stood up and walked over in front of him. He finally focused on her face and vaguely remembered a dream, where he had been falling to the floor, and she was above him, beaten and bleeding. He looked stricken and just continued to look at her face. She closed her eyes and turned away. "We can't call the police Billy." He was asking her "What?!... Why? . . . He's a maniac. . ." but she kept talking. "He's dead, Bill. He's fucking dead okay. I killed him. I had to. He had fallen, and was probably already paralyzed, I could have just left him there to die, but I hated him so much, my bite is imprinted on his face, and I was so afraid of what he might do to me if I let him live. He told me that he would hurt me again... He told me to 'believe it.' and I did . . . I . . . I bashed his head in with a rock, and hid his body in the lake. He's dead. I killed him. If you call the police, I will go to jail."

He was alert now; the pain in his head was unbearable and his stomach was threatening him. He slipped out the now open French doors and vomited over the rail. He let what she was saying sink in. He was stunned. He had come there to save her and hadn't changed a thing. He went back inside to get more ice water first, her eyes were wide and she was talking faster now. Adrenaline he knew. She was in shock and panicked wandering around the room picking up garbage and throwing it into the fire trying to remove any evidence of her presence there tonight. He decided he could still help her and asked, "What do you want to do Micki?"

Upstairs, she cleaned where she had choked on the floor in Evan's bedroom. She had asked Billy to straighten everything downstairs because she didn't want anyone to see this room. What he had done to her here, was painfully evident. She saw Chapter 13 on the night stand and picked it up. She glanced through the worn pages thoughtfully and threw it on the bed. She picked up the black bandanna which still had duct tape on it, and grabbed the rope that had been thrown in the chair. She threw them all on the bed and wrapped it all up in the blood speckled sheets. She went back downstairs and put it all in the fire where he had burned her clothes. She took the poker leaning on the hearth and stirred the fire with it. "This is what I think, Evan." She said aloud. Billy was just standing there now. He had seen her come down with the stained sheets. He felt like he needed to do something, but she'd told him there was nothing he could do upstairs. He just stood there silently and watched her go back up before looking at the floor again feeling ashamed for some reason he couldn't explain.

Though she was weak and broken, she flipped the mattress on Evan's bed to hide the blood stains. She then made it up with fresh sheets that were on the dresser. She found his satchel and sat in the chair to go through it. She took out an old letter, read it and then put it back. She took out a school notebook and put it beside her. There was about $2000 in cash that she removed. Keys were clanging together in the satchel and she took them out and looked at them. Two sets of keys, she held them in her hands for a moment and then laid them on the notebook with the cash. She went back down the stairs to the fireplace and threw the satchel in the fire, and then went back up for a third time.

Billy had moved the chair, and tried to spot clean the Persian rug where it had been. His head was throbbing again. He couldn't believe what had happened here. He just wanted to save her, to help her. No way could he even get near her now. She was far away from him. She was alone, and didn't want to let anyone in. She came back down the stairs carrying a notebook and some keys. She sat down at the secretary by the French doors and wrote something in the notebook, leaving it open when she was finished. She picked up the leash and the collar from where she had thrown them down when she had escaped earlier and clipped the keys to both rings in the collar to prevent it from sliding. She threw the leash into the fire and used the poker to push it and what was left of the satchel deep into the embers. She looked around to be sure she hadn't missed even one piece of duct tape. She closed the screen on the fireplace and watched it burn. She turned around and faced Billy, who had been watching her. She told him, "You need to go now. Drive slow and keep your headlights off till you pass my house." This is not what Billy had been expecting. "What? What are you going to do?" She was adamant. "Don't worry about me, I can't be seen with you tonight. If something goes wrong, you could get in a lot of trouble, this is my problem." She picked up the collar. He saw it and a vague memory of her on the stairs , naked except for the blood she was covered in and that collar, flashed through his mind and he trembled visibly as if he were cold when he said, "Oh my god, what did he do to you?" He didn't really want to hear the answer she knew. She looked down at the floor and told him he couldn't know what was going to happen next, but that she had to finish things. She told him to go. She gave him the cash and told him to hold it for her and she'd come get it later. He just stood there, but she said "Go!" more firmly. Unsure what options he might have, he did as she asked. He went to his car and found the door locked, he opened the back seat door, (that never locked) reached in and unlocked the driver's door. He got in and drove up to the lake road, just like she directed. When he got to the pasture, he realized he wanted to keep going. He turned into the drive and went to the house to wait for her one more time.

Micki went back out the front door locking it behind her. She put the collar around her neck and attached the key to the key ring as she started off toward the trail again. This time Micki knew exactly where she was going. She stepped off the trail that she was sure was about 100 yards behind Freddie's house hoping Billy had gone home without calling the police. A thin mist of fog had settled on the lake as if aiding and abetting her crime. She dove into the water and the coldness of it felt good to her, she had been looking forward to this swim. She swam down the lake toward the Marina. When she saw the lights, she swam away from them, around to the floating dock where she and Kena had watched the naked Satanists run. She crawled out of the water, and lay on her back on the dock long enough to catch her breath. Her feet felt numb. She got up shivering from the cold water or the shock she was in, she couldn't be sure, and took the collar off her neck. She walked around to the service road looking for Sandy. The grave-walk was long over as she had suspected, the clock at Evan's had shown it was after 2 a.m., and that had to be over an hour ago. She didn't have much time. To Micki's relief, most everyone was gone. Micki saw Sandy sweeping the party deck outside the Marina and started throwing small rocks onto the deck to get her attention. Sandy looked up toward the trees at the end of the dirt parking lot and Micki rattled the keys until she saw her. She put down her broom and came over to her. As Micki told her what happened she kept saying "I'm so sorry. He was an asshole, he really was." Micki told Sandy what she wanted her to do. Sandy said she knew her friend Chain would be happy to help her clean up the mess, "no problem." Micki gave her the keys and the collar. Sandy looked at it and then back at Micki who sniffled and nodded her head lifting her eyes toward the moon. They didn't say anything, but the collar in her hand, now made it too real. Sandy's eyes filled with tears, she remembered her own ordeal and felt so bad for Micki at that moment. She hated assholes. If she had thought for one minute Evan would have done this, she could have disposed of him long ago. She turned her head and got herself under control. She'd known Evan was unstable, she just didn't think he was psychotic. Sandy then offered Micki a ride, anywhere, and Micki was so sore and beaten, she accepted. They got into her grandmothers old truck, and left. She took Micki to Billy's house and Micki asked her to "please wait." Sandy said she would. Micki knocked on Billy's door and he opened it immediately, "I've been so worried" he said and she stepped inside. He was already staring at her again, in disbelief; it was too much for her. The coincidence between her costume and the night's events were not lost on her, but she kept those thoughts to herself, she didn't want to talk about it. She had used Billy. If Jeff had never touched her, it wouldn't have happened, but he did. He made her feel dirty and she'd buried that feeling under hours of passionate ecstasy with Cameron but then he had become impatient and she'd turned to Billy. Then just when she thought she'd had an epiphany, Evan had buried that passion under something else so ugly, she could not find the words to express what she was feeling. She had tears in her eyes and could hardly look at him. He tried to put his arms around her, as she was clearly traumatized and visibly shaking. She shrugged him off as if his touch burned her, and turned away from him. He looked like he had been punched in the gut as the realization of what this all really meant hit him. "Oh god . . . why did you go?" He asked falling to his knees in front of her with his hands up, as if he were worshipping at an altar. Sobbing softly, with a hoarse voice, she told him "I . . . I can't see you any more Billy. I can't . . . do this anymore," he took her hands and told her "Okay, whatever you want, just please let me help you." She opened her mouth to speak trying to find a way to tell him what Evan had really done to her, so maybe he would understand that he couldn't help her, but she couldn't say it. She just shook her head, tears streaming down her face. Instead she said, "You can't help me, nobody can." He said, "oh my god, why do you have to be so hard? It doesn't have to be this way. We can go to New Orleans, it can be alright. We can get through this together." She said "stop it, just stop it, it's too late! I am not your responsibility Billy, you can't protect me and it's not your job to protect me. You should have your own life, a normal life and I need to be on my own for a while, maybe forever." Billy wanted to say something but Micki said "No. We've said enough." He was begging her to let him take her to the hospital, but she said no, it was better if she said goodbye right now. He nearly screamed but managed to contain it, he wanted to shake her, but he knew he was just crazy right then and managed to stop himself, "Micki, Please . . . " She said, "let me use the phone?" He put his head down and said he was sorry he yelled at her, He had no right to do so. He walked outside the door and stood there, staring at the truck from the Marina in the driveway. He looked directly at Sandy and nodded his head. Closing his eyes, he turned back toward the house. She picked up the phone and called Kena, who, true to her word, was waiting by the phone.

Billy was actually crying. He hadn't cried since he was a small boy. It was alien to him to be that emotional. He went back inside and fell back on the couch, placing the frozen juice container back on his face. He didn't look at her again. He just stared, listening to her on the phone. She said she was going to Florida to stay with a great-aunt of hers who had invited her after the Jeff incident. When she hung up the phone, she told him she would always hold him in a special place in her heart, she said she was sorry, for everything. She kissed his head lightly with broken lips, and then she was gone. Billy slid off the couch and sat on the floor. Like Jeff, Evan had taken more than sex from Micki. Whatever had survived of her innocence had been brutally murdered tonight. He was so angry at himself for not stopping her, so sorry that he had ever done anything to her. It had all gone so terribly wrong. Powerless to change anything, he put his head in his hands and sobbed, ashamed, but more than anything, he felt a great sense of loss, like somebody died.

Micki asked Sandy to drop her off where the lake road meets the highway. Sandy said she could take her all the way but Micki said she needed to walk. Sandy told her she should call her later that afternoon and gave her the number to the Marina where she would be working. Micki got out of the truck and watched Sandy drive away. She was terribly sore, all over, as she started the quarter mile or so down the highway to the dirt road that led to Kena's house. It had been so dry, the dust was still settling on the lake road, and had anyone been there to see it, would have seen Micki appear from a cloud of dust. The temperature was dropping now. It had been warm when Micki came out dressed in her homemade costume. The thin, gray material of her grave dress was now whipping a little in the early morning wind as she walked along the isolated rural highway. Though her skin had been numbed by the icy water of the lake, her face was throbbing again now. Her costume lent itself to cuts and bruises, she thought. The few houses that cut the edge of the gloomy horizon were dark and silent. It was so quiet. Her own deep, steady breathing was loud and the sound reminded her of being underwater. The new stone bruises on her feet were screaming at her. Her thighs ached, every step reminded her. She had been grateful for the cool water in the lake. She felt oddly redeemed by it. Broken skin inside her lips cracked and bled as she began to hum a song she remembered from her childhood, though the words escaped her. Her throat was so sore. This time of night, closer to morning, always gave the southern sky a sickly looking glow that Micki had always liked, bluish-green, like a yellowing pair of bleached-out jeans. It made her stomach stir. Old, tattered roofing on the housetops looked like the fringe on a tablecloth her grandmother always used. It frayed over corners and around crumbling brick chimneys' that appeared to have burst through in the dim light. It started to rain softly. The rain was warm and Micki raised her head and let it fall into her mouth. By the time she got to Kena's road, she was soaked again. Kena was waiting for her. She got out of her car and rushed to help Micki get in. Kena took her to the hospital in Wetumpka, claiming to be her sister, for an emergency DNC. Micki told them she could not identify her attacker and that she had been attacked after leaving a party somewhere in Montgomery. She couldn't remember anything else except waking up on the sidewalk. She said she knocked on someone's door and they called her sister for her. The doctor told her that judging from her injuries, there had probably been more than one attacker. He spoke with her for a minute about alcohol, and how vulnerable women are when they are drunk. She nodded as if what he was saying was relevant. He put her file down and walked out, leaving the nurse to prep her for stitches. After receiving treatment, including several stitches and a shot of Demurral, Micki said she preferred to rest at home and they let her leave with a prescription of Tylenol 3 and an antibiotic ointment. That afternoon, high on codeine, Micki wrote her mother a letter.

Sandy and Chain spent most of the morning clearing out anything of value Evan might have left behind. He'd been in love with Sandy for some time and this event seemed to be bringing them closer. He'd asked her to be his old lady many times, promising to treat her like a queen. She always resisted for some reason, preferring to take her chances with some asshole like this poor dead fuck they were going to make disappear. They took the bike first, and Chain entrusted it to two comrades. Nobody even noticed an extra bike in the lot. When they went back, they went into the house with the key Micki had given her and Chain scanned the place for drugs and anything else Jack and Rita didn't need to find. As they were leaving, they put the key in the bowl by the French doors and left the doors unlocked. Sandy took her grandmothers boat back and Chain took Evan's boat in another direction. By the time he showed up at the Marina on his bike, he had collected $5000, which Micki had agreed to split with them, less the bike, for the cleanup. Sandy was really surprised at how quickly Chain had come through and she decided that day to start taking him more seriously.

Micki gave the note to Kena and then called Sandy, who said Chain had come through for her, and she'd already done what Micki asked, "No problem," Sandy said again as if she were surprised herself, "It was fun! And it's all taken care of." Micki called her aunt Maggie and told her she would be down there in two days. Maggie was thrilled and said she couldn't wait to see her. She went out to the patio where Jim and Kena were sitting, but she didn't sit down. Jim had forgone drinking this afternoon, and told Micki he was proud of her for "kickin' that fuckers ass, he needed killin', don't you ever lose one wink of sleep over it." He said, "You're charming Micki, girls aren't supposed to be charming . . . men, they . . . take it wrong, you know." Micki appreciated what he was trying to say. He put his hand on her shoulder just for a moment and she winced a little. She hadn't kicked his ass. All the fighting and violence she had lived through before did little too prepare her for the brutality that Evan had crafted for her. She didn't know why she was still alive. He apologized and said goodbye before he went inside the house.

Kena drove her to Sandy's who gave Micki three thousand dollars, saying since Chain was keeping the bike, and her future was so uncertain, they decided it was only fair. She also gave her the AC/DC album Micki had told her about and a sincere emotional hug. Micki threw the album into the lake like a Frisbee and Sandy smiled a bittersweet smile at her. Kena took Micki to the bus station where she bought a one way ticket to Palm Beach. They said their goodbyes and having gotten there just in time, Kena was left to watch Micki's bus until it was out of sight. She felt cold, and she cried a little, she was going to miss her little friend. She got into her car and went to Micki's house. She put the note Micki had written to her mother in the handle of the screen door, and then drove to Cal's house to give him the money Micki had said she owed him. Soon she was driving back home to be with Jim and that night they drank to Micki. In the days that followed, Jack and Rita came to the lake when they couldn't get Evan on the phone. The boat was gone and so was Evan's bike. Jack had found a note from Evan which said:

Dear dad,

I found mom, I wanted to tell you but I knew you'd say no, I know how much you hate her. I just can't take this isolation any more. It's not fair for you to hide me away up here like some kind of wild animal in a cage. Please try to understand. I had to sell the boat to get the money, I hope you don't mind, but I couldn't wait and I didn't want to ask you, I have to do this, and I don't want you to talk me out of it. I love you and Rita and am grateful for all you tried to do for me. I'm sorry for everything, I have been so lonely, it's driving me crazy. I wish I'd been a better son.

Love Evan

Although Jack thought it sounded too contrite to be Evan, he was certain it was his hand writing. He was suddenly racked with guilt over the feeling he had failed his only son. Rita, embarrassingly relieved, said that they should just let him go. That he would come back after he'd been on his own for a while or realized what living with his unstable mom would be like, that she and Jack should enjoy their time alone. She was tired, she said, tired of making excuses for him and that his mother should have to deal with him anyway because "She's the one who fucked him up Jack, not you, not me, not us." In the end, Rita won. They locked up the lake house and directed the local real estate office to offer it as a weekend rental. They never went back to the Lake and Evan never came back.

CHAPTER 11

"I'm still looking for a reason to save you; I don't need a reason to burn you. I know it takes a lot of nerve, but we all get what we deserve. Take some time, go over your lines, save your life. "~ Micki's notebook

Sometime in November of the following year there was a new girl in a quiet Palm Beach high school. Quiet and seemingly uninterested in making new friends, she preferred to spend her time writing music and reading at the library. She had taken up the guitar again and so she spent a lot of time in her room at Aunt Maggie's house. Maggie watched over the girl as if she were a much younger child, unsure what "Sara" had put her through, Micki had become the child she'd never had. Micki seemed to need that, and for the next two years it would be a factor in a future that made the events at Lake Jordan pale in comparison, but that's another story.

Rumors about Evan were rampant. He had run off to be a biker or he had been sacrificed by the Satanists. Sandy, Chain, Billy, Jim and Kena knew the truth, but they never told a soul. Billy told Freddie he had gotten drunk and fought with a man at the Marina. Freddie had asked him if the guy hit him with his truck.

For days Billy wrestled with calling the police afraid Evan's body might float up any day, but that never happened and he was sure there was no one to prosecute. He decided Micki deserved to have a chance at a new life. She'd earned that. A few months later, Billy went home to New Orleans to go back to school. He eventually married and the last anyone knew, he was happily raising several kids. He never saw Micki again.

A few weeks after Evan vanished; Brett went out to his car as usual to go to work. When the engine wouldn't turn over he became furious. He'd just paid two thousand for a new engine. He loved that black Chevelle but he didn't know what he was going to do now. He got out, slammed the door and kicked the tire, cursing "Piece of fucking shit!" When he opened the hood he found a note on a disconnected battery cable that said "I forgive you." He knew it was from Micki but he would be looking for her over his shoulder the rest of his life.

Kena married Jim, but was killed in a car accident a few years later. Even though they hadn't spoken in years, Micki cried like a baby when she heard the news. Jim followed her sometime later after complications stemming from a bad liver, but everyone said he died from loneliness.

Sophia married Jay (like she knew she would) just before he enlisted in the Army. They had about six kids. They never moved from the lake road and built a house right next to Sophia's mom.

Jenny lived on the Marina road for a while. She rented one of the cabins there and lived alone for several years. She ran into Cameron once when she was out shooting pool and later mentioned to Sophia that he talked about Micki constantly swearing he would visit her in Florida. Jenny wished him the best but she was tired of the Micki drama. She later married a man from Montgomery and had two wonderful kids of her own.

Cameron got a letter from Micki. In it she tried to express her regrets as honestly as she could. She told him he would always be her first real love, and that she would never forget him. He eventually married Jamie; the girl Micki and Ella had fearlessly defended at school that day in the smoking area. They actually had six kids last count. "It must be something in the water," the locals say. When Micki heard he'd married her she felt a deep loss for a split second, but she was happy he'd married someone so sweet, someone who would never hurt him.

Sandy finally got out of the Marina, and didn't look back. Sometime after Micki had left, she just put down her broom, and walked out to the big parking lot where Chain was gathered with some of his peers. After a brief conversation, she kissed him, got on the back of his bike, and they rolled away together. Her grandmother got letters from her, but she wouldn't return to the lake until it was time to bury the woman who raised her.

The father of Tammy's baby never came back, but she married an older wealthy man, who she had met at the Marina. One night while she was there drinking with a friend, he asked her to join him out on the deck. He was a lonely man who had taken to using cocaine as a lure for company. She followed him out to the deck and he offered her the vial he kept in his suit pocket. She refused, but didn't run back inside. He was in love, and married her as soon as he could get her to the altar, hoping she wouldn't change her mind. It's rumored that he treats her, and her son, like royalty.

Sara cried when she read the note Micki left, she loved her daughter and wished she could make it right, but, as Micki had acknowledged in the letter, she was powerless to leave Jeff. As much as Micki needed her, Sara was unable to prioritize in a healthy way. She decided that her aunt would be a good home for her daughter. Micki would never live with Sara again.

The next year, Jane became pregnant. Jeff made all sorts of excuses, but it was his baby. Jane was finally gifted with the raven-haired daughter she had always wanted. Despite the circumstances, Sara loved the baby, and at Jeff's request, would take care of her sometimes when Jane was at work.

When Micki was 21, Sara finally left Jeff. That same year she married a man from Montgomery, 12 years her junior. Micki attended the wedding as her maid of honor and even played a song for them. She left as soon as the wedding was over and didn't even try the cake.

Evan's credit cards were leaving a paper trail from Washington to Atlanta to Daytona, but after about a year the money was gone and Jack closed the accounts.

THE END

www.ingramcontent.com/pod-product-compliance
Lightning Source LLC
Chambersburg PA
CBHW051146030726
47504CB00004B/1066